THE DUKE AND THE LASS

JESSIE CLEVER

SOMEDAY LADY PUBLISHING, LLC.

THE DUKE AND THE LASS

Published by Someday Lady Publishing, LLC

Copyright © 2021 by Jessica McQuaid

All rights reserved.

No part of this book may be reproduced in any form or by any electronic or mechanical means, including information storage and retrieval systems, without written permission from the author, except for the use of brief quotations in a book review.

This book is a work of fiction. Any references to historical events, real people, or real places are used fictitiously. Other names, characters, places and events are products of the author's imagination, and any resemblances to actual events or places or persons, living or dead, is entirely coincidental.

ISBN-13: 978-1-7372120-1-0

Cover Design by The Killion Group

Edited by Judy Roth

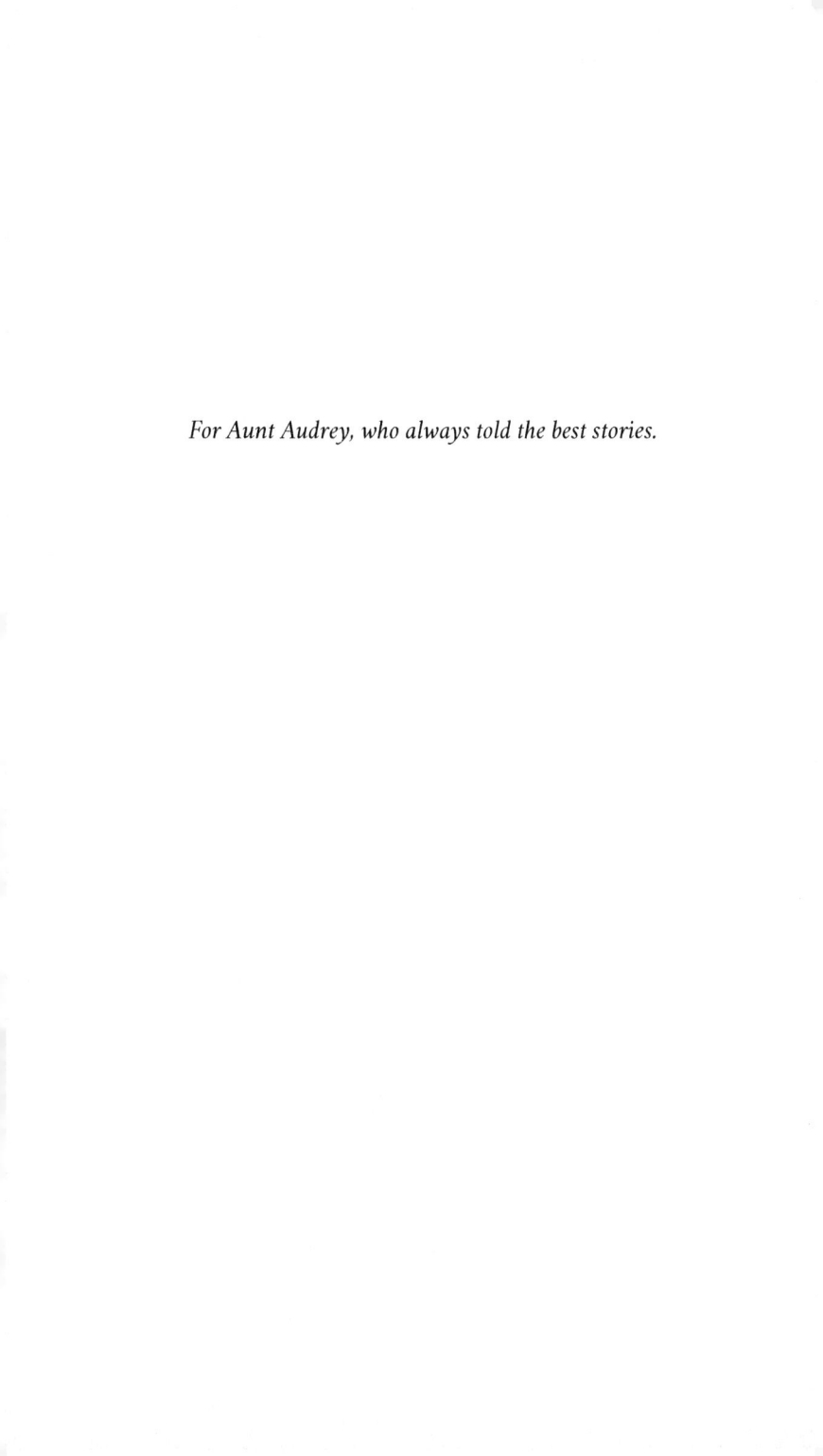

For Aunt Audrey, who always told the best stories.

CHAPTER 1

She was not surprised when the gentleman appeared in her bedchamber in the middle of the night. She was, however, surprised by what he said.

"I'm not here to seduce you. You have nothing to fear from me." He held up his hands as if this were supposed to reassure her.

She stuffed a length of shortbread in her mouth and chewed vigorously as she took him in.

Her recollection of the previous hours was blurred with exhaustion from her sudden voyage to Kettleholm, and now that she was safely in her rooms, she was attempting to reconstruct them. That was, until the gentleman arrived.

If she remembered correctly, he was a duke. An English duke. As her grandmother always said, Della's father shed friends like a dog shed hair, so it wasn't worth the effort it might take to recall their names, and so she hadn't done so with his. Once a gentleman discovered her father's duplicitous nature, he often became scarce when social invitations were extended. Things must have reached desperate levels if her father was inviting the English to his castle now.

She had arrived at MacKenzie Keep earlier that evening with a stomach twisted in knots, one thought racing back and forth until peace was nothing more than a figment of her imagination.

She'd reached her majority, and her father would now seek an advantageous match for his only offspring. That could be the only possible reason he had sent for her so abruptly after years of neglect.

It had been her mother's dying request that he not marry her off too young, and for some odd reason, the MacKenzie had honored the request. Della thought it more likely he had simply forgotten about her until the time had come when he needed critical connections in either land dealings, business, or Parliament.

Since receiving her father's letter, she had eaten nearly an entire tin of shortbread in the time it had taken to pack her trunk, and with each bite, she had contemplated whom her father may have selected for her future husband. She knew he would need to be someone of power and influence, and the very thought sent her back to her shortbread tin.

After all, she had no experience in society, had no idea how a lady was expected to behave. Grandmother had not thought her worth a season, and so Della had never been introduced. Not that there was much to be introduced to in Cumbria.

These thoughts had plagued her for the length of her journey so much so even the latest Melanie Merkett novel couldn't distract her. She'd arrived well into the dark and had mounted the stone stairs to the hulking front doors of MacKenzie Keep with stalwart resolve, knowing she would find her future husband on the other side of those doors.

Except that wasn't what had happened.

She'd been shown into the great hall where a raucous drunken spectacle was already unfolding. It had all the characteristics of a stalking party, the bawdy ones she'd remembered from the few times she had been at the keep to see her father, but that was before her mother had died and years had passed since then.

Maids dodged the exploring fingers of slimy old men while they tried to refill tankards and replace platters of roasted meat. Two men had their arms slung across each other's shoulders as they danced and sang in front of the roaring hearth. The stone monstrosity was like an angry mouth behind them, yawning as if at any moment it would swipe them inside.

Della's nervous stomach had threatened to empty itself at the sight of it, for the first time truly feeling the lack of her mother's protection.

There was one man who hadn't been drunk, however. This man. The Englishman who had found his way to her rooms.

She selected another finger of shortbread as she studied him.

"Why exactly should I believe you?"

His features suggested kindness, his eyes soft and reassuring. Of all her father's guests, this Englishman seemed the least harmful, but he was still a man, and they were very much alone.

"Because if I did anything to harm you, my sisters would have my head."

She raised an eyebrow at this. "Sisters?"

As an only child—no, more than that—as an *unwanted*, only child, she had had fantasies of having siblings, and she'd developed a rather unusual obsession about them. What was it like to share a history with someone from the beginning of one's life? What was it like to share stories and memories?

Della didn't have anyone with whom to share memories. Not even when her mother was alive.

"Four of them," he said with a grave nod. "And I can attest to their fierceness when it comes to such matters."

"Such matters as what?"

His expression turned quizzical. "Those that involve protecting a lady's honor."

She laughed until she realized he was serious. She pressed a hand to her chest. "Do you mean *my* honor?"

The fact that anyone should see to protecting her honor was rather ridiculous. Her mother had tried, but even now Della found herself in the devil's den as it were.

He gave a nod. "Yes, I do."

She made to laugh again but stopped at the serious expression on his face.

"Oh, you actually mean that." She nibbled at her shortbread while she considered this. Her father wasn't typically one to consort with honorable men. After swallowing, she used the remainder of the shortbread to point at the English duke. "You were in the great hall earlier this evening, were you not?"

His eyes darkened then, and while he took on a menacing air, she wasn't frightened. His expression was more of a self-loathing nature, which intrigued her.

"I was, and I must say I was lured here under false pretenses."

She raised an eyebrow again. "Oh? What were they?"

He crossed his arms, drawing her attention to his broad shoulders. He was a big man, probably taller than she, which was rather a nice change.

"I was told this was to be a stalking trip, that much was true. But I was not told some of the *ton*'s worst wastrels would be in attendance."

She frowned. "That's rather unfortunate." She reached for another shortbread. "I was not informed my father had guests at all when I received my summons."

"Summons?" His eyes narrowed, and she realized he took in the tin of shortbread beside her on her dressing table next to the Melanie Merkett novel she'd been unable to read on her journey.

"I'm terribly sorry. Where are my manners?" She picked up the tin and held it out to him. "Would you like one?"

He shook his head, but his lips parted as if to say something. He must have changed his mind because he shook his head again and closed his lips.

She withdrew the tin but said, "Is there something amiss?"

He scratched at the back of his neck. "I don't mean to imply anything. It's only…that's rather a lot of shortbread. I worry you may make yourself ill."

She studied the piece of shortbread still in her hand before looking back at the gentleman in her bedchamber.

"I eat when I'm nervous." She held out her arms to indicate her person. "As you can see, I'm rather nervous a lot." She popped the rest of the shortbread into her mouth and turned to set down the tin.

"Why are you so nervous?"

She glanced sharply at him. "I was raised by my English grandmother, you know, and I don't have the same reservations about Englishmen as my father, but you're giving me reason to doubt." She pointed to the floor below her as if to indicate the spectacle that had been the evening thus far. "My father did request my attendance at his stalking party, as you put it. And he has never been one to protect my reputation."

Della could recall all too clearly the first time her mother had fled MacKenzie Keep and the accusations she had flung at Della's father. Even at such a young age, Della understood that her father saw a girl child as nothing more than a nuisance. Nuisances were not cause for concern.

The English duke dropped his arms. "That's the very matter I'm here about. I suppose then if you weren't aware of your father's guests, you weren't aware of the necessity of bringing a chaperone with you. I would hope had you been aware of the need to protect your reputation, you wouldn't have come here just now and most certainly not alone."

She wanted another shortbread, but his previous comment stopped her, and she folded her hands in front of her to keep them occupied.

"I was not aware of any of this, but I'm not surprised by it."

His lips parted as his eyes widened. "Not surprised by it? What kind of father would have his unattached daughter come to his home in—" He pointed to the floor again, but he seemed suddenly unable to form words.

She twisted the sash of her dressing gown between her hands. Surely one more piece of shortbread couldn't hurt. But the English duke was right. Another piece could very well make her ill, and her stomach was already somersaulting because of the gentleman in her room.

"My father has always said the only thing I'm good for is marrying. I'm not surprised he hasn't given thought to anything else about me."

The Englishman shook his finger at the floor. "But all of the men your father has assembled here are lecherous, old—" He closed his eyes against the word he'd been about to say, and she found herself keening forward in hopes he would finish his sentence, but he didn't. Instead, when he opened his eyes, he drew a full breath before continuing.

He had the nicest eyes. Deep, chocolatey brown like the smooth top of caramel shortbread.

"The men your father invited here are not of the highest regard. They're not of any regard really, and he should have thought of that before risking your reputation."

"My father cares not for my reputation, Your Grace. I'm sorry if you've been misled to believe so."

His eyebrow went up at that. "Why would your father not care for your reputation?"

She spread her hands in front of her as if to suggest the entirety of the situation.

"It's a tale much like many others. I was the only child born of my father and mother, and sadly, I was not a boy, so I was useless. I went to live with my mother and her parents almost immediately when it was determined my mother would never carry another child. Why would my father begin to care of my existence now?"

The Englishman's expression was stricken.

"I'm sorry. Have I done something to upset you?" She took a small step forward as if to reassure him but stopped and picked up the tin of shortbread again. "Are you sure you don't want one?"

He closed his eyes slowly and opened them again, shaking his head. "Yes, I'm quite sure."

He moved then, and it was several seconds before she realized he was removing his coat.

A lightning bolt of pure pleasure shot through her at the sight of his white sleeves, the simple silk at the back of his waistcoat. She had never in her life imagined watching a man undress, and she certainly had never believed she'd see a man as gorgeous as this one disrobe in front of her, and for a moment, she was rendered completely speechless.

Until he folded the jacket into a neat square and tossed it on the floor in front of the fire.

"What are you doing?" The words came out far more strained than she'd meant them to.

He glanced at her over his shoulder before—

Oh God, he was on the floor. His incredibly long limbs, his muscled shoulders rippling beneath the linen of his shirt, his buttocks.

Dear heavens, it was so firm and defined. She didn't know a buttocks could be like that.

For a moment, she was tempted to reach behind her and squeeze her own buttocks for comparison, but she knew hers would never attain such prowess.

"I told you. I'm here to protect you. Not seduce you."

She blinked. "And that requires you to recline on the floor?"

He pulled the folded square of his jacket closer and relaxed with one arm behind his head.

She wanted to sink to her knees beside him and curl into his warmth.

She reached for another finger of shortbread and shoved the entire thing in her mouth.

"I plan to spend the night here." He gestured to the door. "That flimsy lock will not keep those bastards—" He closed his eyes again. "I beg your pardon. Those men your father invited will not be stopped by the lock on that door. I made my presence here known, and I can only hope that is enough to keep them out. I have no desire to resort to fisticuffs."

She swallowed the last of the shortbread. "Do you really think fisticuffs will be called for?"

She'd never been one to elicit such attention, and the idea that men would fight over her was ridiculous.

Unless they were vying for a connection to the great MacKenzie of Kettleholm.

Once more she wondered why her father had truly summoned her.

She placed the lid on the tin of shortbread for even they were not enough now.

She turned to the Englishman. "You really mustn't sleep on the floor. There's no reason you cannot use the bed."

She indicated the Jacobean behemoth on the other side of

the room. It was large enough that they could both be in it and never find the other until Candlemas.

But it was then that the Englishman stretched out his long, muscled legs, and she very much wanted to try to find him in that bed.

She worried her lower lip. Where were these thoughts coming from? Perhaps she really did read too much as her grandmother feared.

"The floor will do just fine. Thank you, Lady MacKenzie."

"Della." She spoke the name automatically. She had never been called anything other than Della in the whole of her life, and it felt odd to have the Englishman call her by her title.

He'd shut his eyes as if intending to go to sleep, but he opened them at this.

"Della? I thought your given name was Catriona?"

She shook her head. "It is. I mean, Catriona is one of my given names. It's only—" She could see the story laid out before her as if it were a carpet unfurling for the entrance of a king, and she found the entire matter exhausting. She drew a deep breath and pressed on anyway. "My name is Lady Catriona Cordelia MacKenzie. My father chose the name Catriona, and my mother refused to use it. My mother chose Cordelia after her paternal grandmother. My grandmother—that is, my mother's mother—hated the woman with a great ferocity and refused to call me Cordelia, so it was determined I would simply be known as Della."

The Englishman blinked at her. "You're a woman without a name."

She opened her mouth to refute the accusation, but then she realized he was right. She shrugged. "I suppose that's accurate."

"And you don't have an accent. A Scottish one that is."

"My mother was English, and I went to live with her as a child if you remember."

He shook his head. "Without country as well," he muttered.

She tightened the sash of her dressing gown. "And I suppose you have both."

He gained his feet with a gracefulness she couldn't have fathomed, and she found herself staring up into his delicious warm eyes and wondering what it would be like to stand in the shelter of his arms.

And then he bowed and said, "Andrew Darby, the Duke of Ravenwood. It is an honor to make your acquaintance, my lady."

Oh bollocks. She was going to fall in love with this man.

* * *

HE HAD NOT HESITATED to act the knight gallant, but that was before he realized the danger of the situation.

Lady Catriona MacKenzie was beautiful.

Having grown up under the constant pressure of protecting the reputations of four sisters, Andrew had developed an immunity to beautiful women, his only protection against finding a wife before his sisters were wed, and he had believed such a defense to be insurmountable.

Standing in Lady MacKenzie's bedchamber in the middle of the night proved him wrong.

He could sense the tightening in his body as if it were physically preparing to defend itself from the ever-growing attraction. When he had first seen her hours before in the castle's great hall, the dim light had required his imagination to fill in what he couldn't see, and he had formulated a rendering of her that did not do the reality justice.

She was tall, magnificently so, and terribly, he wondered what it would be like to kiss her without having to bend halfway over to reach her lips. She was curvy and thick, not the willowy waifs society believed acceptable, and he found his fingers tingling as if anticipating what it would be like to caress her curves, feel the strength of her.

For the first time, he understood the true meaning of the word voluptuous, and he found himself utterly attracted to this woman's strength and power.

He wasn't sure why it hit him the way it did, but he thought it likely due to those same sisters that had inadvertently prevented his marrying. The Darby sisters were rather infamous for their stubbornness and bravado, and when he had contemplated finding a wife, he'd worried the insipid debutantes of the *ton* would not be a match for them.

This would not at all be the case with Lady MacKenzie.

Not that he was thinking of her as a potential wife. He had only just recently crawled from beneath the responsibility of seeing his sisters safely wed. He wasn't yet ready to take on the care of another female. He was only there that night to stop her from being raped.

The thought had him swallowing the bile that rose in his throat at the notion. Her father, the drunkard and bastard who had lured him here to MacKenzie Keep, had not veiled his intentions with any sort of decency.

The man had given no warning to his cronies to keep their hands off his daughter and her goods.

The carnal goods.

It took all of Andrew's strength to resist toppling the man right on his drunken arse in the middle of the hall.

He'd chosen a less violent route to protecting the woman, and so here he was. Standing in front of her in the middle of the night and wondering how he was going to keep his hands off her.

He was no better than the rest of them, except he was.

Because he *knew* he wouldn't touch her.

His honor and the weight of having to protect his four

sisters' reputations prevented him from doing so, yes, but it was more than that. He was tired, weary, and he didn't want the complications such a move entailed.

His plan had seemed so easy at first. He would simply spend the night in the lady's rooms, and by fact of his sheer presence, he could keep her safe.

Everything had been going swimmingly well until that very moment when he'd introduced himself.

Because it was at that moment he saw the heat flare in her eyes.

The same heat that boiled low in his stomach, and which he resolutely was attempting to ignore.

She blinked, and it was as though she slid a shield in front of her feelings. It was so graceful and complete he wondered if he'd imagined the entire thing.

"Lady Della MacKenzie," she said with a curtsy. "You must call me Della, Your Grace," she added as she straightened. "I think titles in a situation like this would be rather cumbersome."

He looked about the drafty bedroom of stone and tapestries and could readily agree with her.

"Then I insist you call me Andrew."

She gave a perfunctory nod. "Andrew. Yes, of course."

He watched her eyes dart momentarily to the tin of shortbread beside her, noticing for the first time the novel that lay beside it, and he took a step back, hoping not to worsen her nervous state by his proximity.

He went back to the floor before the fire, but she stopped him.

"Please, Your—Andrew. Please. You mustn't sleep on the floor. It's literally stone, and it's freezing, and I will not allow you to perish there this night even if you are an Englishman."

He grinned. "Didn't you just say you were raised by your English grandparents?"

Her smile was mocking. "Yes, but you're in the Lowlands now. Anything is possible."

He crossed his arms over his chest. "And I suppose you are granted immunity because half of your roots are Scottish."

She wrinkled her nose. "Yes, even if those roots are rather rotten."

Her gaze traveled to the floor as if she were remembering the uncomfortable scene earlier that evening in the great hall.

Andrew cleared his throat and pointed to the cloak she had discarded on the chair in front of the fire. "Did you only arrive tonight?"

When she had appeared in the great hall, he couldn't have been sure if she had already been in residence or not as he'd only arrived that morning himself.

Her eyes followed his gesture, and it was as though she saw the cloak for the first time, her gaze widening.

"Yes, I just arrived from Bewcastle this evening."

He had recalled the vaguely rumpled appearance she had presented, and he wondered if she could have understood what awaited her at her father's home.

"I can imagine it's rather disappointing to encounter such a cold reception upon your arrival. I only arrived this morning, and I must say I'm glad I had planned to keep my trip short."

She laughed, the sound soft and surprised. "You're assuming I didn't leave an equally cold situation in Bewcastle."

He stilled. "Equally cold?"

She wrinkled her nose again. "A great deal more…moldy, actually."

He followed her gaze about the room, taking in the dark and damp corners where the light didn't quite reach.

"I cannot believe you came from a situation worse than this. Surely your grandparents cared for you."

She blinked as if trying to see her grandparents. "They were kind enough. It was only they, like many of the peerage, don't possess a great deal of money but rather a lot of moldering estate if you take my meaning." She shrugged again, something he was beginning to realize she did with alarming frequency. "And it wasn't as though I needed much. I didn't wish for them to spend what little funds they had on me." She spread her hands. "I was quite fine just as I was."

He took in the faded pattern of her dressing gown, the frayed edge of her traveling cloak, the scuffed and unraveling toes of her slippers.

"Your grandparents are of the peerage?"

"Yes, the Earl and Countess of Bewcastle."

He let his teeth grind together to keep from speaking. He had seen the Earl of Bewcastle drop a year's income in the betting books at Covington's in London without hesitation. He did not believe the man lacked the funds to purchase his granddaughter a new pair of slippers.

Much as with everything else about Lady MacKenzie, he was beginning to piece together a picture of sorry neglect about her.

"I haven't the pleasure of an introduction, but I know of your grandfather from the clubs in London," he said, keeping his thoughts to himself.

While he could sense the general state of neglect Lady MacKenzie seemed to exist in, she did not appear to wield it for sympathy or wallow in it for pity. She was either oblivious to it or she was predisposed to observe a sunnier perspective.

Either of these ideas did not help his stance to remain objective when it came to her person.

He was not only attracted to her; he was beginning to *like* her.

He went back to the spot on the floor in front of the fire and dropped down before he could think any more on the subject.

"You should get some rest, Lady—Della. Tomorrow should prove interesting."

The MacKenzie had claimed to have invited the gentlemen for a stalking party, but Andrew was beginning to suspect the man had other motives. He was glad he'd be leaving soon. Only now his gaze slid to Della and the complications she represented.

Andrew had thought when he'd married off his last sister not months before he would be free of the responsibility of protecting the women in his life. And here another one had not only walked into it, she'd barged in with her tin of shortbread and her unfailing smile.

He laid his head back against his folded coat and shut his eyes.

"Good night, Della," he said into the room and wished for sleep.

The cold against his back was incredibly more punctuated than he had anticipated, and he knew soon he would ache from the unrelenting hardness of the stone.

He was exhausted, and he should have slept instantly, but he found himself inordinately tuned in to the sounds of Della presumably preparing for bed.

There was a rustling somewhere in the distance, and he thought her pulling back the bedclothes to get into bed. Only the sounds grew more agitated as though she struggled with the quilts. There was a thud followed by a dragging noise, and before he could get his eyes open, the first quilt hit him.

His eyes were open then, and he nearly sat up except

another quilt, this one rather heavy, landed on his chest at that moment.

He blinked up at Della, hovering over him, her arms full of bedding.

"If you insist on sleeping on the floor, you should at least have a proper quilt," she said.

He tugged at the one that had landed haphazardly across his chest. "I assure you I am quite all right without it. It's only a few hours until sunup and the fire is—"

"You are sleeping on a stone floor. Surely even an Englishman can understand how quickly you will become chilled." She cocked an eyebrow as if to emphasize her point.

He pulled the quilt more fully around him.

"I appreciate your astuteness."

He expected her to return to the bed then, but she did something entirely unexpected, which, he was becoming to realize, was just like her.

She dropped the rest of the bedding on the floor directly beside him and proceeded to make a nest of it.

"What are you doing?" It was as though alarms were shouting in his head.

"Making my bed."

"But it's on the floor."

"Yes. That's where you've chosen to sleep, isn't it?" Her stare was unblinking, daring him to contradict her.

"But this isn't my bedchamber."

"It isn't mine either if you recall. I'm merely a guest here." She flopped a pillow over at one end of the quilts, and worst of all, she sat down in the middle of the nest of bed things.

He sat up.

"Lady MacKenzie, I cannot allow—"

He didn't finish the sentence. Couldn't finish it. She sat there, nestled into the cocoon she'd created from the purloined bedclothes and blinked at him. Much like the rest

THE DUKE AND THE LASS

of her, her eyes were big and wide, and they were a blue so rich he thought he could slip into them and disappear as if diving through a wave of the purest sea. Her hair had come loose from its braid, and silky, blonde tendrils framed her face, accentuating her cheeks and the rosiness of her lips.

She was stunning.

"Are you all right?" Her brow wrinkled.

He swallowed and looked away, tried again to find words.

"I cannot allow you to sleep on the floor. It isn't done."

She gestured around them. "What of this evening is done, Your Grace? I would surely like to know." She dropped her hands in her lap as if defeated.

She was right. There was nothing ordinary about their situation, but he was damn sure he would not endanger her innocence with his physical reaction to her.

He pulled the quilt tighter around himself as if it were a shield.

"If I agree to sleep in the bed, will you sleep in the bed?"

She nodded immediately, her teeth worrying her lower lip in such a way as to have his stomach clenching.

This was a very bad idea.

He stood before he could think further, pulling the quilts up with him. As a gentleman, he should have offered Della a hand up, but as a man, he knew he didn't have the resolve to stop touching her once he started.

He marched over to the bed and flung the quilts across it. By the time he had arranged them in some semblance of normalcy, Della appeared on the opposite side with her own mountain of quilts.

She tossed them on the bed and climbed directly atop them. At least, she left her dressing gown on. Had she taken it off, he knew it would all be over.

He swallowed and climbed onto the bed, being particularly careful to keep as much distance between them as possible. In fact, had he gone any farther away from her, he would have fallen from the bed. Satisfied this would do, he turned his head to take her in.

Another mistake.

God, she was striking.

"I hope this is adequate."

A line had appeared between her brows as she studied him.

"If you were any farther away, you'd be in England." She canted her head. "Are you afraid I'll ravish you?"

He resolutely moved his gaze to the ceiling.

"The only person in danger of being ravished is you, Lady MacKenzie. Otherwise, we wouldn't be in this position."

She flopped back on the bed, pulling a quilt over her.

"I do hope we mustn't do this every night during my stay. Did my father say when the stalking party should end?"

"I'm not sure. I only planned to stay a couple of days."

He heard rustling beside him as though she looked at him. "You traveled to Scotland only to stay a couple of days?"

"I have responsibilities that require my attention in London."

More rustling. "Those sisters you were speaking of?"

"Something like that," he muttered, shutting his eyes.

There was a brief pause before she said, "I understand you are trying to do the noble thing, Andrew, but I must warn you of something."

At this, he turned his head to look at her beside him.

Her expression turned serious before she said, "I snore."

Then she closed her eyes and went to sleep.

CHAPTER 2

She woke up in his arms.

She froze instantly, her brain scrambling to understand where she was and who she was with. The events of the night before came to her in pieces like a picturesque landscape revealed by a lifting fog.

Andrew Darby, the Duke of Ravenwood.

She remembered the warmth of his eyes when he'd bowed to her, the way her stomach had rolled in a delicious and curious way she'd never felt before. It wasn't the usual twisting of nerves. This had been something liquid and soft and compelling.

He had come to protect her from her father's guests, but it was more than that. She just knew, she didn't know how, but she knew, Andrew Darby was kind.

Kindness was rare in her life, and when she saw it, it was more tantalizing than shortbread.

Heavens, he was strong. And heavy. He had one leg wrapped over hers, his arm tight along her torso as if he were afraid she'd float away.

For the first time in her life, Della felt *small*.

It was an extraordinary feeling, and she let it wash over her like sunlight after a long rain.

She fit so neatly against him, his body curved entirely around hers. The sensation of being held, of being touched, it was heady and drugging, and she didn't want to move for fear it would be over.

But it would be over.

At some point, he would wake up, and the dream would vanish, and she would be all alone again.

Catriona Cordelia MacKenzie, the woman without a name or a country. That's what he had called her.

She closed her eyes and wished.

She wished for this. For this to be real and true and lasting. She didn't know anything about Andrew Darby. He could have warts on his feet. He could have an unusual fetish for liverwurst. Perhaps those sisters he'd mentioned were formidable and judging and cruel.

Maybe none of that were true, and he would still wake up and leave her. After all, he said he hadn't planned to stay long.

But what if her father intended for her to marry the Duke of Ravenwood?

Her eyes flew open at the thought. Suddenly the idea that her father had summoned her to marry her off took on a glowing light of anticipation. It wouldn't be so bad if she were to marry Andrew.

But as soon as the thought came, she dismissed it. Good things like that just didn't happen to her.

He stirred then, and she held her breath, wishing with all she had that he wouldn't wake up. Not yet. Just a little bit longer. She wanted to remember what this was like.

He stretched, and she swore she could feel every one of his muscles—and there were many of them—move against her, and his hand tightened its grip on her rounded belly, and then—

He pulled her more tightly against him, his nose nuzzling the back of her neck.

Her heart thudded in her ears, and her lungs burned for air, but she couldn't bring herself to draw breath.

The nuzzling continued, along the back of her neck, up to the spot behind her ear.

Oh God, he was kissing her. Right there. Behind her ear. His lips were soft, his touch so gentle.

It was heaven and it was torture because it was too much.

If he woke up now, he would be embarrassed, and he would regret what he'd done when it was the most glorious thing to ever happen to her, and it would crush her.

He moved again, burying his nose in her hair as he drew a breath.

"Della." Her name, sleepy on his lips, and her heart clenched at the sound of it.

Tears smarted her eyes, and she knew this was it. She had to end it because if he awoke, if he realized what he'd done and apologized for it, it would shatter her.

Slipping away was far easier than she had imagined it would be. He was a heavy sleeper, it would seem, and she eased her way out from under his arm and leg. The loss of heat was the first thing she noticed, but she was too busy scrubbing the unshed tears from her eyes as she made her way over to the dressing room.

It wasn't until the door was shut securely behind her that she sucked in a full breath. Her heart still pounded, and the sound was loud in her ears in the small confines of the room.

She let a multitude of feelings wash over her, and a chill passed over her skin as if those same feelings were tangible.

So, this was what it was like to be loved.

She shook her head almost immediately. It wasn't love. It

was only proximity. He had been asleep in the same bed with her. He could have mistaken her for anyone.

Except he'd said her name.

She straightened away from the door and saw to her needs before beginning her morning toilette. She hadn't a maid, but she'd never had a competent one, so it mattered little. She could see to the simple gowns she had brought with her, and a chignon wouldn't be much bother.

She tried to occupy her thoughts with the necessity of getting ready for the day, but it was no match for the novelty of the feelings that coursed through her.

To feel the weight of his body beside her, against her, atop her. To have him hold her so tightly. The touch of his lips against her skin.

The sound of his voice soft against her ear.

It hadn't meant anything. That was the crushing reality of it, and yet it was likely to be the most affection she would ever receive from a man.

It was only fitting that it was all an illusion.

By the time she emerged from the dressing room, he was gone.

She didn't want to examine why it pained her to see the bed empty, his coat gone from where he'd left it on the floor.

It wasn't until she was in the corridor that the first lick of fear crept up her neck.

When she had walked into the debauchery in the great hall the night before, she hadn't thought to be scared. She had had the absurd thought that she would be safe in her father's house. In the light of day, she realized how ludicrous the idea was.

She peered about her, wondering what other guest rooms the stalking party members had been given. Were they nearby? Would they try to accost her now? In the daylight?

She supposed evil gave no heed to the clock.

THE DUKE AND THE LASS

She rubbed her neck and shook the tension from her shoulders. This was ridiculous. She was bigger than half of those men, and her lungs powerful enough. Surely Andrew would hear her scream should any of her father's guests try something untoward.

Andrew.

It was a funny twist of fate that the most incredible thing to happen to her should happen now, while she was surrounded by wolves. And he said he would leave shortly. But when?

She descended the worn stone, circular steps to the great hall with care and noted the lack of voices echoing up from the cavernous space below. When she stepped down into the room, she was surprised to find some of her father's guests milling around the high table at the opposite end of the hall set up on the dais.

She eyed them and the distance she would be forced to travel to reach the high table. She let her gaze wander about the room now that daylight poured through the tall windows along the wall opposite the massive fireplace. The ceiling trusses were blackened from hundreds of years of smoke from the great fires in the hearth, and the chandelier looked more like a curiosity from a traveling circus with its many antlers and rams' horns.

She dropped her gaze to the floor and kept walking.

Finally, she drew near enough to take in the gentlemen scattered about the table. She didn't recognize any of them, but they all carried a different shade of green, likely from the antics of the previous night.

She nodded her head in greeting. "Good morning, gentlemen."

She had spoken softly but in the cavernous stone space of the hall, her words echoed with alarming ferocity, and the gentlemen groaned, keening forward in their seats.

"Do shut that wench up," one of them muttered, a Lord Mitchum, she thought.

He was old, very old, with a permanent hunch and gnarled hands. He was also missing several teeth.

"I trust you had a fine night, lassie," another said with a scalding Scottish accent. He made a vulgar gesture with his hands.

She tilted her head. "Are you having a stroke, sir? There appears to be something wrong with your hands."

His hands froze, and his expression turned sour, but the gentlemen around him broke into weak laughter, as much as their current poor conditions allowed, she assumed.

"She got you there, Ronnie." Another gentleman cackled. This one she believed was some sort of viscount.

The man called Ronnie lowered his hands into his lap, but he continued to glare.

Footsteps on the stones behind her had her turning slightly.

Andrew.

She worked hard to keep her features neutral and simply nodded her head in greeting as she had done for the rest of them.

"Your Grace," she said.

"Lady MacKenzie." He bowed and stepped up to hold out a chair for her.

"Ain't the niceties unnecessary now, boy?" The viscount's laugh dissolved into a coughing fit, and he pressed a dirty handkerchief to his spittle-covered lips.

"Niceties are never unnecessary," Andrew replied before taking the seat next to her.

The table had been laid with platters of eggs, beans, and kippers, but it was rather untouched, the other gentlemen having only partaken of coffee and tea and toast.

"That's what I like about you, Ravenwood." Her father

appeared behind Andrew and grabbed the younger man's shoulders in a hearty display of masculinity. "You never give a wit for other's opinions." He shook Andrew a few more times before letting go and clapping his hands together, much to the dismay of the other gentlemen at the table.

Lord Hamish MacKenzie, the Earl of Kettleholm, had years of practice being drunk, and her mother had always said its ill effects never seemed to touch him. He was not an attractive man. He was short and barrel chested, and his bulbous, blue-veined nose hooked over scraggly red whiskers.

Remnants of his previous meal still lurked in those whiskers, and she looked away, eyeing the kippers and toast. It was probably too much to assume the cook of MacKenzie Keep knew how to prepare a proper English breakfast with tomatoes and mushrooms.

"Gentlemen, I trust you found the accommodations to yer liking," her father went on.

He stopped at the viscount's chair and shook the man heartily on the shoulder as he'd done to Andrew, only the viscount turned green and looked as though he may tip over into his toast.

Finally, her father made his way to his seat, an ornate Jacobean construction with a plush green velvet pad and a lion man carved into the back.

But instead of sitting, her father merely leaned one elbow on the chair and addressed them all.

"I'm verra pleased to see ye all here, gentlemen. I ken I asked ye here for some stalking, but as ye might have guessed, my intentions were not at all pure." He laughed at this as did those gentlemen who could stomach such a gesture. But soon her father's laughter faded, and his gaze landed on her.

Della straightened her shoulders, her hands twisting in

the skirts of her gown hidden beneath the table. She did not, however, relinquish her father's gaze.

"Ye see my bonny daughter here," he said, extending a hand in her direction.

The gentlemen about the table sent leers in her direction, but she ignored them all.

Suddenly a hand found hers under the table. It took all her strength not to react as she felt the now familiar curve of Andrew's fingers, the pressure of his grip as he slipped his hand into hers and held fast.

She curled her fingers around his, but she hadn't the time to think of it because just then her father said, "Gentlemen, I've asked ye here to vie for my daughter's hand in marriage."

* * *

THE CAUSE of her sudden invitation to MacKenzie Keep had lingered around her like a ghost, but to hear it spoken aloud was something else entirely.

She was going to be sick.

Likely for the first time in her life when her nerves had frayed to an insurmountable level, food did not appeal to her.

She dropped her gaze to her lap, to the hand that covertly held hers so tenderly. She returned her attention to her father, who appeared to be enjoying the collective intake of breath and general mumblings around the table.

It was several seconds before Della thought to look at the other men scattered about the table and when she did, she wished she hadn't.

They were all looking at her.

No, not merely looking.

Assessing.

Cataloging.

Leering.

She swallowed, forcing her gaze to hold steady, when suddenly Andrew squeezed her hand beneath the table. It took all her fortitude not to look down. Not to see the thing that was happening at that very moment.

Someone was reassuring her.

Andrew was reassuring her.

The notion was so foreign to her she wanted nothing more than to observe it in reality, but she daren't lower her eyes. She daren't let anyone suspect something was happening between them.

Because she didn't want Andrew to become a target.

It was odd this. Della had always been alone. Had never had someone over whom to worry. She wasn't sure if it were refreshing or merely added to her already heightened nerves.

Her father seemed pleased with the reaction around the table because he finally sat and helped himself to eggs and toast and a hearty helping of sausages.

The viscount stirred first. "You're saying you've chosen us as potential suitors for your daughter? I hardly see why we should be pleased with the notion."

Her father's eyes flashed as he speared a sausage. "Ah, but I haven't gotten to the juicy bit, now have I, Strickland?"

Strickland toyed with his napkin, sending a scornful glance at Della. "Is there a juicy bit?"

She did not have a great deal of experience interacting with the opposite sex. Her grandmother did not think it necessary to expand Della's social circle, and so it left her rather unschooled in that moment. Was the viscount suggesting she was somehow lacking or was he making a rude innuendo? She couldn't be sure.

"No matter the result, I think it would be in your best interest not to insult the intended before the game has begun, don't you think, Strickland?" Andrew said calmly from beside her.

She couldn't help but look at him. His voice was like steel while at the same time it sounded like he was speaking of nothing more than the weather.

Was he defending her? Once more she couldn't be sure. To her, these men were speaking in riddles. Books were far easier to understand.

Strickland set down his napkin and returned his attention to her father.

"I say, Ravenwood, I took a gamble on inviting ye here. Rumors always suggested ye were like a nun in a cloister, but yer turning into a right fine bloke." Her father's laugh was grating.

Andrew's attention never wavered from his plate. "I think it's rather too early to make such judgments."

More laughter from her father.

"Well, be that as it may, I think ye find yerself rather inclined to participate, Ravenwood. There is, after all, a great deal of money at stake."

The table went silent at this, and every foggy head around the table suddenly perked up, their attention turning to her father.

"Money?" said the lecher Mitchum who had first told her to hush up when she'd arrived at the table that morning.

Her father leaned back in his chair and spread his arms. "Of course there is money. I wouldn't plan to marry me only daughter without a dowry to match her—" The gleam in his eye turned malicious. "Magnificence." His laugh now bordered on vulgar.

Della found herself pulling her stomach taut as if this would reduce her somehow, as if by holding her breath she could make herself smaller. It was something she had started doing at such a young age, she couldn't recall a time when she hadn't done it. Anything to make herself take up less space as if by doing so it would help ease the burden she had placed on the people around her.

That she should do it now spoke to how engrained it was in her.

She had not seen her father more than a handful of times since her birth, and now he summoned her to auction her off, and she still felt as though *she* were the burden. It was horrible and silly and nonsensical, and she felt every inch the fool for believing it.

But that was just it. She did believe it. She did believe she was the burden because she'd been the burden for so long. It was hard to believe anything else.

But it seemed her father wasn't finished.

"Of course, I wouldn't be giving away such a fine specimen without expectin' something in return." He ripped off a piece of toast with more brute force than was necessary, crumbs scattering across the table. "The gentleman who wins my daughter will swear his fealty to me."

The men assembled about the table seemed to absorb this, their gaze focused on the MacKenzie.

"Whoever takes me daughter's hand will swear his allegiance to the MacKenzie in the marriage contracts. I shall expect his favor in all political dealings. Do I make myself clear?"

Della didn't know entirely what this meant. She had assumed it was enough that he should get rid of her through marriage, but no, he had something far more sinister in mind.

She would be his pawn in a political power scheme.

Oddly, the assembled men laughed, the sound grating at her taut nerves.

Andrew let go of her hand and stood, the laughter about them fading as the MacKenzie took in the man standing next to her.

"I beg your pardon, MacKenzie, but I am not in want of a wife as it were. I have familial matters to attend in London. Do pardon my sudden departure, but I find I can no longer stay." He bowed and with the scrape of his chair, he left.

He left *her*.

Coldness swept over her, swift and complete, and she tried so very hard to keep from watching him leave the great hall. Leave *her*. It shouldn't matter. She was left so frequently. What was once more?

Except now if she closed her eyes, she could feel his lips against her skin, hear the way he whispered her name in his sleep.

Involuntarily her eyes drifted to each man around the table and found those same assessing gazes staring back at her. Her skin crawled, and her stomach churned.

"You don't care to make an alliance, Ravenwood?" MacKenzie called after the Englishman.

Andrew stopped several feet away and only half turned to face her father.

"I'm sorry if you were led to believe differently, MacKenzie, but I only form alliances based on merit. Not on bribery." With that, Andrew left, and she was entirely alone.

The MacKenzie grew quiet then, and she feared the silence even more than the leering glares sent in her direction.

Finally the MacKenzie settled back in his seat and crossed his arms over his barrel chest.

"I hope the lot of ye dinnae prove as virtuous," he said, eyeing each of the men in turn.

There was a beat of silence, and then the rest of the table broke into the same raucous laughter that was beginning to grate her ears.

She stood, having eaten nothing.

"If you will excuse me," she said with a nod.

"Where da ye think yer going, lassie?" her father called after her. "Looking for a final tup from yer beau?"

More of the same laughter.

She dropped her napkin to the table and held up her chin.

"No," she said calmly. "I just find myself rather...bored." She spoke the last word with a shrug and turned to retrace her steps back across the great hall and up the circular stairs to her rooms, silence ringing behind her.

She held herself together long enough to make the stairs, and only after she'd spiraled upward did she allow the tremors to come. But once released, the shaking overtook her, and she was forced to sit down on the top step, the worn stone cold beneath her. She laid her head against the wall beside her, allowing the icy smoothness of the rock to soothe her.

Until someone placed his hand over her mouth.

She started, the scream sticking in her throat as she registered whose hand it was.

Andrew.

Her heart thudded instantly, and she tried to stand up, but between the slippery rock and her clinging skirts, she struggled. Andrew slipped his arms around her and hauled her up to the corridor above, holding her tightly against him without moving. Her cheek was pressed to his chest, and a thrill shot through her, remembering what it was like to wake in his arms.

But the embrace was awkward, and she knew this was not a moment of tenderness.

He was listening. Listening to see if someone had followed her.

When silence was the only thing to surround them, he eased her back, his hand slipping down her arm to capture her hand.

Her silly heart sang with the casualness of his touch, of the way he so perfectly knew what to do.

On soft feet they made their way down the corridor to her rooms. Once inside, he locked the door behind them, and then, seemingly unsatisfied, pulled her heavy traveling trunk over to block the door.

"Andrew—"

He held up a finger to his lips, and she shut her mouth immediately. He touched his ear, and she looked about them, wondering who could possibly hear them through the stone walls.

But it wasn't that which concerned him. Because just then, he dropped to his knees, peering beneath the bed. Next, he poked behind the tapestries and the drapes, behind the bed curtains and finally, scoured the dressing room.

Having found no stowaways it would seem, he returned to the main bedchamber and approached her with such directness, his face hard with determination, she almost wanted to step back.

Almost.

She raised her chin. "Andrew, you mustn't—"

"We need to get you out of here."

The words stopped all the thoughts in her head.

"Get me out of here?"

He looked about the room as if surveying it for escape or perhaps something else.

"Pack your things." He shook his head. "No, you can't pack. We can't let him know your intentions. Only pack what will fit in a satchel, something easy for you to maneuver."

He picked up the cloak she'd discarded over a chair the previous night as if looking for some kind of bag beneath it.

"Andrew, I think you must know—"

"We can use my carriage. It will be slow, but we must only

THE DUKE AND THE LASS

get you to Bewcastle. Return you to your grandparents, and then—"

"Andrew." She spoke loud enough now that he stopped in his hasty search of her belongings for a satchel that would do for his intentions.

His eyes were so dark when he looked at her, and she felt a heat curling in her stomach.

She didn't want this to end.

Whatever this odd encounter was between them, no matter how illogical, she just wanted to be with this man forever. It made no sense, and yet it made perfect sense.

She had never felt more like herself than she had with him.

She swallowed. "Andrew, I can't leave. Don't you understand?"

He came toward her, his hands flexing into fists at his side. "But you must leave. You cannot allow that man to marry you off to—"

She shook her head. "I have no say in the matter, Andrew. My father is allowed to do with me as he wishes."

He stalked away at this, pushing his hands through his dark hair. She memorized the way it curled over his collar, and she wondered if he wore it that long or if he were in need of a trim.

"No one is allowed to treat a human being as not more than—" He stopped entirely as he appeared to struggle with his words. "We must only return you to your grandparents. They can help. They'll see to your wellbeing."

She shook her head, hating to put into words what she knew to be true. Either he didn't see her, or he refused to understand, because Andrew continued.

"We can make Bewcastle by nightfall if we hurry. Where is a satchel? You must start packing at once. Just take what is irreplaceable." He gestured to the frayed cloak he had left on the chair. "Surely your clothes are in sore need of replacing so leave those."

Finally she stepped forward and placed a hand on his arm, and he stopped, arrested at the moment of her touch.

He looked at her; he really looked at her, and for the first time, she felt as though someone truly saw her. It was beautiful and heart-wrenching, and she licked her suddenly dry lips.

"Andrew, my grandparents don't want me."

CHAPTER 3

Her words rang with the clarity of truth, and he saw in them no hint of pity or self-loathing. She was stating a simple fact.

The woman without name or country was without family too. Without support and allies.

She was entirely alone.

And she was ready to submit herself to her fate with dignity.

His heart squeezed at the sight of her just then, her eyes quiet and knowing, her mouth relaxed and accepting. She would walk into the cage her father had manufactured, and she would do it with her head held high because that was how Lady Della MacKenzie did everything.

Something inside of him slipped, like stone falling to gravel it made a noise that rang through the stillness deep within him. He pushed it aside, walked away from Della to pace to the other side of her bedchamber.

"There must be someone else. A cousin. An aunt." He turned and held out a hand. "Your mother. Della, where is your mother?"

He knew the answer even before she spoke.

"She's dead." Her voice was quiet in the room, and it was as though the temperature around them dropped several degrees. "She died when I was nine."

He wasn't sure why, but he said, "My mother died when I was ten."

He didn't need to tell her that, and really, it hardly had relevance in their current situation. But for some strange reason, he had wanted to comfort her through a shared experience. Now was most certainly not the time, and yet he felt a small measure of relief as her eyes widened at his revelation.

"I'm so very sorry," she said softly.

All he could do was nod, his throat suddenly tight. He paced away, hoping if he didn't look at her, he could regain his ability to speak.

"You must have distant cousins. An old aunt or some such." He glanced at her. "Everyone has a doddering old aunt somewhere."

She gave a now familiar shrug. "If I have one, I have no knowledge of her. I wasn't…" She looked up at the ceiling as if gathering her thoughts. "I wasn't exactly brought round to the family things. My mother's marriage to the MacKenzie was a black mark on the family, and my grandmother did her best to hide the evidence of it."

He stopped, arrested by her words. "Black mark?" He took a step toward her. "Evidence?" He rubbed at the back of his neck, the urge to flee springing up inside of him.

He'd known this trip was a bad idea. He had told his sisters he deserved a moment of peace, but he knew it was only a farce to keep them from knowing the truth of the matter. They had husbands to care for them now, and surely a few days away couldn't hurt. But with every word Della spoke, he found himself caring more and more, which would never do. He made it two steps toward the door before stopping and swinging about.

When he reached her, he took her by the shoulders. "You are not a black mark, Della. You are not evidence." He spit the word as though it were poison, and he had to rid his mouth of it. "Don't ever let anyone tell you otherwise."

Her lips were right there. Her soft, pink lips. So full. So tantalizing. He was right. He wouldn't need to bend in half to kiss her. He had only to dip his head, and he could taste her like he'd wanted to since the previous night.

Not now. Why now?

He didn't want a wife yet. He didn't want another woman to protect. Another woman for whom he was responsible. Not yet.

He would look for a wife at the start of the new season in London next year. Not a moment sooner.

He would leave Della MacKenzie to her fate. She wasn't his responsibility. She was prepared to accept her future; he knew that.

So then why did he dip his head? Why did he capture her lips? Why did he wrap his arms around her?

Oh God, this was heaven.

She fit.

It was the first time he'd ever had such an innocuous thought when kissing a woman, and yet it was the most incredible thing when he realized it. She slipped perfectly into his arms. The perfect height. The perfect shape. The perfect everything.

She was hesitant and shy, and he realized this was likely her first kiss. He shouldn't be kissing her at all. He should stop immediately, but he knew he couldn't. He just couldn't.

Strangely, it felt as though he'd been waiting for her kiss his whole life, and now that he'd started, he couldn't give it up.

But he must.

He eased away, breaking the kiss at the last possible moment. He kept his eyes closed as he gathered himself, steeled himself for the reality of when he opened his eyes again.

Finally he let his lids open, and he studied her face. Her eyes were still closed, and her lips were slightly parted.

She was utterly still.

In the short time he had known her, he had not seen her so settled. She moved with the nervousness he was beginning to understand consumed her, and when she wasn't moving, she was trying very hard not to, to remain unseen and thus, undetected like a hare in the hedgerow.

She spent so very much on so very little that it startled him to see her at peace in that moment.

He wanted to kiss her again. He wanted to keep kissing her. He wanted to see her relaxed and satiated, limp with contentment.

He took a full step back, a foggy memory resurfacing in his brain.

He couldn't be sure, but he thought at some point in the night she had ended up in his arms. The memory of her body curving against his was like a ghost that haunted him. Her scent, lilac and fresh air, lingered, and he knew he had buried his nose in it. He knew it even as he couldn't remember it.

Had his body betrayed him in its sleep? Had he done more than was proper when he'd innocently shared a bed with her?

He couldn't quite remember, and yet, now that he'd felt her in his arms, now that he'd traced the curves of her body —God, her curves had the power to end him—he couldn't help but wonder if he'd held her before.

He took another step back and now her eyes fluttered open.

"Della." Her name came out hoarse, and he stopped, cleared his throat. "Della, I should—"

He stopped, completely this time, and drank in the sight of her.

It was as though she were transformed. In that small space where just the two of them existed, it was as though he were seeing the real Della MacKenzie for the first time. The girl shrouded in nervousness and fear was suddenly revealed for what she was.

A beautiful, strong woman.

He blinked, the realization rocking him.

He swallowed. "Della, propriety would dictate that I shouldn't have done that. I shouldn't have kissed you. It was ungentlemanly of me, and I should beg for your forgiveness for taking such liberties."

Her eyes darkened, and the corners of her mouth tightened. It was subtle and had he not grown so familiar with her expressions, he would have missed it. It was the nervousness and fear returning, stealing over her like darkness across the land at sundown.

"But I won't ask for your forgiveness."

Her expression froze.

He reached up and took her shoulders in his hands to ensure he held her attention. "I won't ask forgiveness for something so exquisite as your kiss." He squeezed her shoulders. "I won't ask for forgiveness for taking liberties with you, Della. No matter what happens now I'll be forever grateful you allowed me the pleasure of your kiss."

He released her before she spoke a word and paced away, putting much needed space between them.

He turned back to her when he was safely on the other side of the room. Her features remained relaxed, her eyes slightly wider with his pronouncement, but otherwise, she remained still, her hands loose at her sides.

"You're certain there's no one else who can protect you?" he asked after several beats.

She merely shook her head, the motion heartbreakingly brave.

He felt his decision like a physical thing, the winch of a drawbridge releasing its last measure to bring the two sides together.

He squared his shoulders.

"I have no claims on you, Della MacKenzie." He shook his head. "I will be forever sorry I could not help you."

Something skated over her eyes then, and he watched it like a shadow racing across a stone wall.

She wanted him to help her. She wanted him to change his mind. She wanted him *to do* something.

But she didn't say that.

Instead, she raised her chin and brought her hands together in front of her. "I know, Your Grace." Her words were clear and firm. "I shall remember our time together fondly."

Her smile wobbled only the slightest of degrees, but she seemed to swiftly collect herself, her chin going up another notch.

He watched her for several seconds, this woman so crippled by those who were supposed to love her and yet rising above it with strength and grace.

The resolve in him tightened to a painful degree, and he sucked in a breath.

He gave a bow. "I suppose one day I might see you in London, Lady MacKenzie. Perhaps as the wife of a viscount or an earl. Depending on who should win this ridiculous match your father has concocted."

Her smile did falter now as a nervous laugh escaped her lips. "Perhaps, Your Grace." She gave a shrug, smaller than her usual ones. "It should be lovely to see you again someday."

Her words struck him squarely in the chest.

He gave another bow. "If only time should be so kind to us. Farewell, Lady MacKenzie."

Pushing her trunk aside, he ducked out the door before she could speak another word. If she said anything further, it would render him entirely useless, and that would do her no good at all.

Not if she wanted him to save her.

* * *

She watched him leave.

His carriage rolled through the gates of MacKenzie Keep not an hour later. The family quarters were housed on the second floor in the estate house that had been built in later years to attach perpendicularly to the great hall and the original stone keep. Because of this she was able to watch him leave from where she sat on the window bench in her bedchamber.

It was as though he couldn't leave fast enough.

The thought twisted in her chest, but she shoved it aside, her fingers straying to her lips as they would so often that day.

He had kissed her.

She never thought she'd ever be kissed.

Not like that. Not out of desire.

Once more she had the sense of feeling small and fragile, a sensation she would never grow tired of. Her whole life she had felt like nothing more than a burden, too large when circumstances dictated she take up less space.

But not with him.

Not with Andrew.

She felt like herself with Andrew, whoever that might be. She still wasn't sure. But it was different and light and fresh, and she knew she wanted to discover more of it.

Except he'd left.

He'd left her there with those men and her father.

She wanted to feel angry, sad, hurt, but she felt none of those things because he was right. He had no claim on her, and he could do nothing more to protect her from her father's machinations.

Not unless he married her, and she knew someone as wonderful as the Duke of Ravenwood would never marry someone like her.

It just wasn't done.

Andrew would return to London and marry some society debutante. She had never seen one, but she had ideas. Her mother had been detailed and persistent in all the ways Della was not a lady, and from these reprimands, she had crafted an idea of what a true lady looked like, sounded like, and acted like. It was all the things Della wasn't.

She hid in her room as long as she was able to. She spent most of that time on the bench under the window that faced the gates, her mind playing tricks on her that Andrew would return, that he would change his mind and come back for her.

Eventually she got up and went through her trunk, trying to see things the way Andrew had. He had said to pack a single bag, only taking what was irreplaceable. She sorted through her gowns and underthings, her slippers and boots.

An hour later she concluded he was right.

Her gowns were worn, her shoes in need of attention. She had never noticed before how much neglect showed in her clothing, and she suddenly felt…guilty. Guilty of what though? It was as though she had let the neglect she suffered show on her clothes when she should have kept it a secret.

THE DUKE AND THE LASS

She didn't want others to know. She didn't want their pity or concern.

She wanted to be loved.

Wasn't that what she'd always wanted?

It wasn't her fault though that such neglect reflected on her clothing. Her grandmother was not inclined to order her new gowns, telling her she'd order more when Della lost some weight. Della had never pushed the matter and had only ever asked for books. She preferred novels, the more adventurous the better. It seemed she'd given herself away with her devotion to reading.

She threw her gowns and shoes back into her trunk, returning to the window bench with her Melanie Merkett novel and her tin of shortbread. Then she curled up on the bench, a quilt spread over her lap and opened the novel, letting herself get lost in the private inquisitor's endeavors.

Except her mind kept wandering and the shortbread remained untouched.

She couldn't pry her eyes from the main gates, hoping Andrew would return.

He didn't, and eventually she was forced to dress for dinner.

It was much the same as breakfast. She was largely ignored except for the occasional vulgar insult from one of the men who was supposed to be vying for her hand. Her father rather enjoyed such insults as displayed by his boisterous laughter at any jab directed at her, and she knew the man had earned a mark in his favor.

Her future husband would be determined by his prowess at insulting her.

The food remained untouched on her plate, and she willed the clock to move forward so she may excuse herself.

At some point, the men became lost in a heated discussion over a stag they'd been stalking that day and whether the animal had crossed the stream onto the neighboring parcel or if it had climbed farther into the hills on MacKenzie land.

When her father requested a fourth bottle of the estate's exclusive whiskey label be brought up from the cellars, she took the opportunity to excuse herself.

It was the first time she had spoken during the length of the meal, and suddenly, the men focused their attention on her.

Their lecherous, drooling attention.

In that moment, the coming hours of darkness flashed before her.

Why hadn't she thought of this?

The previous night Andrew had been there to keep her safe. Tonight, she was alone. She stood in her spot at the end of the table, her untouched meal in front of her, as these vile men surveyed her like nothing more than a rack of succulent pork.

Her father would do nothing to protect her. In fact, she was sure he would encourage the men to sample the goods, so to speak.

Bile rose in her throat, and she pushed her chin higher.

"Good evening, gentlemen," she said without meeting anyone's eyes.

She waited until she'd turned the corner into the circular stairs before picking up her skirts to hurry. She didn't want them to see her fear. Somehow, she knew they would enjoy it.

She gained her rooms moments later and slammed the door shut, shoving the lock home.

She stared at it. The flimsy block of wood that wedged in an elbow of rusted metal secured to the door frame with a couple of bent nails. In the old estate house it was the height of security, and yet Andrew was right.

It would keep no one out. Not someone determined to enter her rooms.

She backed away from the door, her hands fisted in her skirts. Her heart pounded in her chest so loudly she feared it would erupt directly from her breast.

She remained fully dressed, her gown, chemise, and crinolines serving as illusory armor. They would no more stop an intruder than that terrible lock, but they made her feel better.

She retreated to her window bench, once more curling up on it, her hand automatically going to the comforting weight of the Melanie Merkett novel.

Time seemed to drift around her. She knew it still ticked by much as it always did, but it was also different. She waited, knowing that at any moment someone would come to break in her door. He would come to—

She couldn't think of the word. She couldn't think of the violation that was to come.

She didn't know how long she sat there, but the stone of the window casing was icy against her back, and she grew stiff from the cold. Still, she did not move. She kept her hands wrapped around her novel and watched the door.

She didn't know how much time passed before she heard the first footsteps on the stairs. They were unsteady and scraping as though the man were deep in his cups.

She swallowed and for the first time in what seemed hours she let her eyes close.

One of her father's selected bastards had finally come for her.

Oddly, her heart stopped pounding, and her muscles relaxed. It was as if faced with the inevitable, her body's response dissipated.

She opened her eyes and raised her chin.

The knock came seconds later.

"Oh, Lady MacKenzie." He spoke in a singsong voice, the words slurred and followed by a tittering laugh. "Oh, Lady MacKenzie," the man tried again but failed when another laugh broke through his words. "Lady MacKenzie, be a darling and open this door so I mustn't exert myself."

She stayed where she was, her lips pressed firmly together.

There was more laughter now, and she realized it was more than one man standing outside her door in the corridor. Her skin rippled with apprehension. Would more than one of them attempt to rape her?

She reached for her shortbread tin, holding it and her novel against her chest like a shield. She pressed herself farther into the window alcove, her back nearly pressed against the glass.

The men at her door began to argue now, their voices no longer watery and slurred.

"I say, I was here first. I should get the first run at her."

"That's hardly relevant if you haven't the equipment to see the deed done."

There was shuffling as though one of the men had taken hold of another.

"Now see here—"

"Ah, lay off him, Roger. He's only a child. He wouldn't know a pussy from a panhandle."

This was met with uproarious laughter.

She backed up farther and farther, her feet digging into the cushion beneath her as if to propel her backward.

Only the window opened behind her just as she reached it, and she tumbled backward.

A scream erupted into her mouth at the moment the pull of gravity hit her, but it was stopped by the hand clamped over her lips. Her back hit a solid wall of chest, and arms came about her. Familiar arms. Exquisite arms.

Realization hit at the moment lips pressed against her ear, whispering, "Don't scream or we'll never get you away from here."

Andrew.

Relief. Euphoric, all-encompassing relief flooded her, and her legs went watery with it. She still clutched her novel and tin to her chest, her eyes blinking at the worn stones of the exterior of the keep, her mind scrambling to make sense even as she attempted to regain her feet.

She looked down, not understanding where she was.

She stood on the roof of the cloistered walk that ran along this side of the estate house where the family's quarters were housed. It was a more modern addition to the keep after the addition of the manor house.

It was a good six-foot drop from the window above, and for the first time, she was grateful for her height. She finally peered up through the darkness to find Andrew watching her.

She shook her head, and he bent, pressing his lips once more to her ear.

"I'll explain later. We need to get out of here."

He turned and hustled her to the edge of the roof where a scraggly pine jutted up along the side of the cloistered walkway. The ground was more than ten feet below, and she realized Andrew must have used the pine to gain the roof.

She would need to climb down then. She stopped at the edge of the structure and pulled her hands from her chest, eyeing first the novel and then the tin of shortbread. She would need her hands to descend, and yet, the thought of losing either pained her.

Andrew watched her from the darkness, and something clicked inside of her. She tossed the tin of shortbread and shoved the novel into the bodice of her gown. She reached the tree first and swung out onto the nearest branch.

The sticky limbs clung to the fragile fabric of her gown, and several times she was forced to stop and yank her skirts free. More than once her machinations were met with a terrible ripping sound, but her need to get away overshadowed any concern she might have had for the only gown now in her possession.

When her feet touched the ground, she felt another surge of relief, but she knew they were not out of danger yet.

Andrew dropped to the ground beside her, and without hesitation, he took her hand, pulling her in the direction of the gates. Once the gates would have been closed at night, but these were far quieter times, and her father was rather too drunk by nightfall to order them shut. They rounded the front of the keep as an explosion of noise erupted from the front door.

Andrew tugged her into the shadows along the remains of the original bailey, blocking them from sight of anyone coming. He pulled her into the cocoon of his body, tucking her carefully against his chest. It was perhaps the first time in her life she had felt safe, and yet the very thing that could end her freedom forever lurked not yards from her.

The commotion at the front door appeared to be a drunken scuffle. She wondered if the fight she'd heard outside her bedchamber door had spilled onto the front park when the cramped quarters of the stone corridor could no longer contain the melee. Her father stepped into the doorway then, backlit by the many candles in the great hall's chandelier. He glowed with an evil hue as he laughed at the gentlemen fighting just outside his keep.

She wanted to hate him, but instead she only felt frustration. Those stupid men were blocking her escape.

The book she'd shoved into her bodice dug into her chest, and she knew what she must do. Reaching in, she tugged the book free and laid a gentle hand on Andrew's arm, so he released her. She held a finger to her lips as she eased out of his arms.

She kept to the shadows along the bailey, ducking behind one skeleton arch after another. When she was a good distance from the front gate, she stood in the shadow, eyeing this side of the keep. She raised her hand with the book in it, keeping her eyes on the windows that flashed in the moonlight. She took aim, pulling her arm back as far as possible, and then let the book fly.

Again, she was both grateful for her height and her strength as the book soared through the darkness and found its target.

The sound of breaking glass shattered the near-quiet of the night, and she ducked into the shadows as the attention of the men turned in her direction.

No, not in her direction. In the direction of the breaking glass.

"It's the stag! He's come for us!" came a shout from the front lawn.

She watched from the darkness as the drunken lot of them scrambled over one another to be the first to get to the door, but her father was already there, bewilderment plastered over his features as they collided with him. They all went down in a heap of curses and flailing appendages.

She didn't wait. She retraced her steps through the dark, finding Andrew where she'd left him.

He smiled, his white teeth bright in the darkness. A flash of pride spiked through her, so foreign and new she couldn't quite believe it for what it was. She would enjoy it later though. For now, she only wished to be free.

This time she took his hand and pulled him in the direction of the gates. They slipped free just as the cursing behind them turned to cries of outrage and pain as the men tried to right themselves.

Once outside the gates, she headed for the road, but Andrew tugged on her arm. She turned, and he motioned to the trees that bordered the road leading down into the village. She followed without hesitation as he pulled her into the darker space beneath the trees.

She wasn't surprised when they came upon a horse, tied to one of the trees. She canted her head in question. Surely they could have reached the village on foot in time to secure a carriage before her father realized she was gone.

He pulled her close enough to whisper in her ear.

"My carriage is waiting for us in Brydekirk."

Brydekirk? Well, that was several villages over. She shook her head.

He leaned down again. "It was the first village I found with a blacksmith willing to marry us."

CHAPTER 4

He shouldn't be doing this.

Not because marrying a woman he had known for less than forty-eight hours was unwise, but rather any number of highwaymen could be waiting for them along the road to Brydekirk. He could almost feel them lurking in the trees, waiting to ambush them.

He carried the pistol his coachmen normally kept up on the box with him, but it was still only two shots. By the time he reloaded, the highwaymen would have the better of the situation.

It didn't matter.

Nothing mattered except getting Della to safety, and for her, safety could only mean marriage.

Marriage to him, an English duke.

He had had time to work it out in the hours he'd spent scouring the Scottish countryside for a blacksmith willing to see the deed done. He wasn't sure if it were the general Scottish mistrust of an Englishman or if it were the prevalent fear of the MacKenzie that seemed to linger in these parts, but he had gone nearly to the English border before finding someone willing to see the deed done.

And it wasn't as if he'd found any other eligible gentlemen along the way that could take his place.

It would have to be him, and it would have to be now.

Della was unusually quiet after his pronouncement. The furtive nature of their endeavor suggested as much, but even her constant small movements had ceased. She hadn't said anything when he'd told her of his plan and merely gone along when he helped her up on the horse.

He tried not to think about her stillness as he held her against him, the horse clip-clopping its way south. Even its hoofbeats were muted in the darkness as if the animal sensed the need for stealth in their midnight journey.

Brydekirk was nearly ten miles to the south of Kettleholm, and with their slow and grinding pace, it would take them the better part of the night to reach it. It would be faster to take the road, but prudence and his selfish desire to stay alive had him skirting it, picking his way through the forest that bordered it. He'd rather it take them all night than to meet his fate at the end of a highwayman's pistol.

He wondered if she dozed when sometimes she would grow impossibly still, but then the horse would falter on an unseen rock, and her grip on the arm he had wrapped around her would reflexively tighten.

He didn't want to admit to the eager sensation that surged through him when she did that. He was not doing this to impress her. There was no need to impress someone as brave and strong as Della. Her ploy with the book had only demonstrated her cunning and courage, and he wouldn't be so bold as to suggest she wouldn't have survived the night without him.

He only didn't wish to think about what might have happened had he not come to retrieve her.

His mind was troubled with the memory of their kiss for the better part of the day, and still, here in the quiet of the night, he couldn't say why he had kissed her. He usually had better control of his feelings, but he was coming to find his attraction to Della didn't heed to any rules he might set. The thought left him apprehensive.

If he could so easily abandon his own standards of propriety and respect, what else might his attraction to her cause him to do?

Steal her away in the middle of the night to marry her?

It possibly couldn't get worse than that, and this notion gave him some peace.

The stark glow of moonlight-dappled darkness was broken by a string of soft, orange lights in the distance. They had been traveling for more than three hours by then, and he knew they must be approaching Brydekirk.

In the daylight, the hamlet had been quaint and charming, but in the darkness, it took on the slightly foreboding look of an abandoned town as its inhabitants slumbered. He slowed the horse, navigating it carefully onto the main road, peering about them into the darkness.

His coachman and valet were to meet them at the outskirts of the village to provide protection for the remainder of the ride into town. He hadn't wanted to risk the increased possibility of exposure with a larger traveling party or else he would have had the men travel with him to Kettleholm and back.

Della straightened against him, her back going rigid as they approached the town. He tightened his arm around her but didn't dare speak to her yet.

When they were nearly upon the village, a shadow separated itself from the muted outlines of structures. Andrew slid his hand to the pocket that concealed his pistol, but soon moonlight fell over his coachman's face.

Andrew quickly scanned the area around them, but no other shadow materialized, and the skin along the back of his neck prickled.

The coachman, St. John, raised a hand in greeting as they approached, his other hand clutched his riding crop like a weapon.

Andrew stopped at the sight of tension radiating from his coachman.

"There seems to be a problem, Your Grace," St. John whispered. "It appears there was a bit of a to-do this evening in the village. Something to do with the harvest being what it was."

Andrew nodded to keep the man going.

"Well, it's like this, Your Grace. The blacksmith's gone off the drink and is slumbering the night away in a pig trough at the other end of town." St. John pointed over his shoulder in the direction where the blacksmith likely was. "There's no one to perform the ceremony is what I'm trying to say."

The poor man appeared crestfallen, a deep furrow between his concerned eyes.

Andrew scrubbed a hand over his face before slipping from the saddle. He reached up to give Della a hand, and she quietly went into his arms as he helped her down. She stepped quickly away from him as soon as her feet touched the ground, and when he tried to read her expression, she bent her head, avoiding his gaze.

He would wonder at that later. He turned back to St. John.

"Surely there must be someone else who can perform the ceremony."

St. John pointed over his shoulder again. "Aldrich is currently in negotiations with another party, but I'm afraid it's going to cost you a great deal more coin, Your Grace."

There was a small sound of surprise behind him, and

THE DUKE AND THE LASS

Andrew turned sharply to find Della covering her mouth with one hand. He tilted his head as he studied her. It was the only sound she'd made in more than three hours, and it had been one of surprise. He rubbed the back of his neck as he turned back to the coachman.

"Well, I think we'd better find him." He gestured to the road that led through the village proper. "Shall we?"

Andrew took the horse's reigns as St. John led the way down the main thoroughfare. He turned back to find Della still standing with her hand over her mouth.

He leaned in to whisper, "Are you all right? You weren't hurt, were you? When we came down from the—"

"I'm fine," she whispered, but her eyes were wide when she said it. At least, she'd dropped her hand.

He took her arm to help her navigate the road in the moonlight. Once again, she moved without resistance, as though she were merely going along with whatever he dictated. He didn't like it, and suddenly he wondered if he were doing the right thing.

He had assumed she wouldn't wish to be wed to one of those men her father had selected. More, he thought it disgusting that her father should auction her off like cattle in exchange for a man's fealty. Such a notion was archaic. But things were different for women, and he knew that. Della was not afforded the same securities he was, and he began to question his own intent.

They reached the heart of the village, and Andrew could see clues as to the to-do St. John had mentioned. Empty tankards were strewn along the door of the public house, and several gentlemen slept under the windows of the inn, slumped with their backs against the rough boards as though the drink they had consumed precluded them from feeling much.

There was more of this along the way. People sleeping in odd places. Empty tankards and discarded clothing.

They'd nearly reached the other end of the village when St. John finally stopped and turned to a shop to the left of the road. The storefronts were dark except for a single light that glowed through a dusty windowpane.

"A modiste?" Andrew whispered.

St. John lifted an eyebrow. "She's really not more than a seamstress, and I use that term without much confidence, Your Grace. But she's willing to do the deed and keep mum about it."

Andrew indicated for St. John to lead on, but before the coachman could rap on the door it opened, and Andrew's valet, Aldrich, stood in the doorway, his crumpled attire suggestive of the arduous task he had undertaken in the small hours of the near morning.

"Your Grace." He nodded. "Madame Liliberte is ready."

Andrew raised an eyebrow at the address. "Madame?"

Aldrich slid his gaze to the right and pressed a tight smile. "Yes, Your Grace. Madame," he said with greater force as though someone might overhear him.

Andrew cleared his throat. "Then I am only too happy Madame has made time for us." He tried for a more genuine smile, but he was too tired, and the strain of the day was catching up to him. If he had to stroke the confidence of an apparent charlatan, he would do so if only to see Della safe and beyond the reach of her vile father.

He ducked his head to make it through the low doorway of the modiste shop, tugging Della in behind him. The shop was small, and the front part was dominated by worn settees and overstuffed vases. The air was cloying with both the scent of decaying flowers and the lingering odor of some kind of tobacco smoke.

Della pressed against his side, and he turned, pulling her tightly under his arm.

Madame Liliberte emerged from the back of the shop. It was hard to make out her features in the dim light, but she exuded an air of tarnished quality, and he pulled Della more tightly against him.

"Madame Liliberte, I thank you for your time and attention to this matter. Your sacrifice is greatly appreciated."

Her smile was riddled with black marks he thought were either rotten teeth, likely caused by tobacco, the evidence of which lingered in the air, or missing teeth entirely.

"No sacrifice is too great for an English duke." She extended a hand, palm up.

He eyed the vulgar gesture. "After the ceremony is completed."

She shook her head. "Half now, Englishman. Half later." She curled her fingers as if to beckon the coin.

He extracted a single coin from his pocket and dropped it into the open palm.

Her fingers snapped shut around it, and she pulled her fisted hand against her mouth, her eyebrows winging up with excitement.

She dropped her hand to say. "This way, my lord."

He didn't correct her and only moved to follow.

But Della didn't move. His arm caught around her immobile body, and he turned, peering down at her in the weak light.

"Della? Are you sure you're well?"

She shook her head, her teeth digging into her lower lip.

He turned fully, placing his hands on her shoulders as he had done earlier that day.

So much had changed since that morning. What he had believed would be a temporary respite from his familial obligations had turned into a quagmire that would only serve to increase his responsibilities.

And likely make him the target of an infuriated, detestable Scottish earl.

"Della, you must tell me what it is." He looked behind him where the modiste had disappeared. "The madame will perform the ceremony, and you'll be safe from—"

But Della was already shaking her head.

"No," she whispered, and she closed her eyes, shaking her head with greater force. "No, Andrew, I can't do it." Her eyes flew open. "I can't marry you."

* * *

It had never been harder to speak in her life.

But once the words were out, she felt the tension that had been crawling along her shoulders ease, and her stomach settled with a thud.

That was when her heart broke.

When Andrew had first confessed his plan, her initial reaction was so unlike herself she'd fallen into an utter state of inaction. Never in her life had she felt such calm wash over her. Never before had she felt such rightness.

She wanted to marry Andrew. More than anything, she wanted to marry him.

That was exactly why she couldn't.

"I'm so sorry. You've gone through so much trouble." She slid a foot back, which was ridiculous.

Where was she going to go? She had no one else to care for her. She couldn't go back to her grandparents. She supposed they might take her in, but her grandmother wouldn't hesitate to manipulate Della's guilt like a torture screw, tightening it at whim. Della knew she couldn't survive that. There had to be another way.

She couldn't let Andrew sacrifice himself for her.

He shook his head. "Della, I don't understand. This is the only way to get you out from under the control of your father."

She slid a glance to the gentlemen standing in the shadows by the door. She thought they were likely Andrew's servants, judging from their neat, plain clothing and ardent dedication to the duke.

Andrew followed her gaze and taking her by the shoulders steered her to the side of the room in a suggestion of privacy.

"Della, what is it?"

She would remember this the most about him. The care that so easily came to his eyes when he looked at her. It was so very nice to meet someone's gaze without having to look down, and it was even more wonderful to see such attention in it. For the first time in her life, she felt as though someone honestly cared.

That's what made this so much harder.

She swallowed. "Andrew, I can't let you marry me."

He nodded. "Can't let me?" He shook his head. "You're right. I'm terribly sorry." When he shook his head this time, he closed his eyes, his lips tightening. "Della, I realized I should have asked for permission. It wasn't right for me to assume you would wish to marry me. I only thought—"

"Permission?" The word was the last she would think of. "You want permission to marry me."

His eyes flashed open, and even in the dim light, she saw the earnestness there. "Of course I would seek your permission. I wouldn't force you into a situation that would unerringly change your life without seeking your consent."

She didn't know how to respond to that. "It isn't my permission that I would like to give, Andrew. It's rather…" She searched for the right words, but no matter how she said this, it would sound pitiful. So, she simply said it. "Andrew, I don't wish to be a burden on anyone else. I've been a burden my whole life, and it's wearing and terrible and just awful, and I don't want to be it any longer." She squared her shoulders and met his gaze directly.

He didn't blink. His gaze remained locked on hers.

"You don't wish to be a burden." His lips parted softly when he finished speaking, and it was almost as if he were shocked by her words.

That should hardly have been the case. She was certain it was quite obvious to all. Hadn't he been the one to point out her worn clothing, the very evidence of such a burden?

"I'm the only child of a Scottish lord and a girl, no less. I've been a burden since I was born. I'm tired of it, and I will not allow you to be my next victim."

He laughed.

It was only a snort of a sound, and he stopped it as soon as he'd begun, but it was still a laugh.

Her eyes went wide. "Your Grace, this is not a laughing matter. I—"

He let go of her long enough to hold up both hands. "You're right, Della. You're absolutely right. I should not have laughed." He settled his hands once more on her shoulders and squeezed as if to reassure her. "Be that as it may, your choice of words was rather dramatic. I don't think it's as bad as you claim."

She wished very much she hadn't thrown away her tin of shortbread.

"It is very much as I say, only you cannot fathom it because you are not a woman. You're a bloody English duke, for heaven's sake."

She did not know from whence such outrage came, and it had Andrew stepping back, his eyebrows going up.

"I apologize," she said, casting her gaze to the floor,

suddenly unable to look at him. "I'm not sure why I said that. You *are* an English duke, but that's likely not your fault." She raised her chin. "But you still can't understand what it's like to be a woman in this world. It's deuced difficult."

He shook his head. "Della, I can only understand too well how difficult it is. Have you forgotten I have four sisters?"

Those sisters he had alluded to the night before. She had forgotten about them in the course of events.

She twisted her hands together. "Sisters are rather different than wives."

"But that's just it," he went on. "I've married off my sisters, and I had planned to acquire a wife this season. If you married me now, it would save me a great deal of trouble." His smile was kind and humorous, and she knew he was attempting to make her feel better about the situation.

It didn't work.

"Acquire a wife? You make it sound like you're purchasing a parcel."

His smile dimmed. "Unfortunately, as your father demonstrated, the two are not all that different."

He was right in that regard.

She eyed him, his words niggling something deep within her. "You were going to find a wife this season? When you returned to London, you mean?"

He gave a sharp nod. "Precisely. It's past time I wed and saw to producing an heir for the title. It would be an honor to be married to you, Della."

Well, he really didn't need to go that far, and it wasn't as if she believed him anyway. He was only being kind.

But regardless of how she felt, she *was* of good breeding. Her father might be a wastrel, but he was of the peerage, and her mother was the daughter of an earl. That made her a lady no matter the rest.

"Is what you speak the truth?"

"Yes, Della. It is the truth." His tone gave no suggestion he grew short with her as her grandmother always seemed to whenever they conversed.

Della tucked this away and held out her hand. "Then I agree to the marriage. I promise to be an excellent duchess."

He stared at her hand. "Are we to shake on it like gentlemen?"

She studied her hand now, hanging so oddly between them. "Isn't that how agreements like this are made?"

"I think these types of agreements are usually sealed with a kiss."

Her eyes shot up to his face at that. She hadn't forgotten what it was like to be kissed by him, and she wouldn't mind experiencing it again.

But they were interrupted by a raspy call from the back of the shop.

"I haven't all the time in the world, my lord. Some of us are not privileged enough to while away our daylight hours in bed."

Della wrinkled her nose in the direction of the shout. "She doesn't even try to affect a French accent," she muttered.

Andrew laughed softly beside her. "I suppose it's enough that she doesn't drop her *h*'s."

Della turned back to him. "Are you certain this is legal? The marriage will be binding?"

"According to the marriage laws in Scotland, anyone over the legal age can be married by anyone else." He shrugged. "I had hoped the blacksmith would do it as he is the most senior craftsmen in the village, but we are not in a position to be selective."

"I suppose we aren't," she muttered and nodded toward the back of the shop. "Shall we...*my lord*?" She exaggerated the incorrect address Madame Liliberte had used earlier.

He gave her his arm and led her to the back of the shop.

The quarters were cramped with a tatty chair and a cot, the bedclothes a swirled mess atop it. A lantern had been lit and rested on a chipped bureau to the side, and its shuttered light cast shadows over the modiste's face.

The woman held a piece of paper in her hand. "Are you of marriageable age?"

It was a moment before Della realized Madame Liliberte spoke to her.

Della gave a quick nod. "Yes, I am."

The modiste turned to Andrew. "And you, my lord? Are you of marriageable age?"

"Yes, I am." He spoke with such clarity Della felt a flutter in her stomach at the suggested strength.

She sneaked a glance at her soon-to-be husband, doubt and fear and nerves swamping her. She couldn't be doing this. She couldn't be marrying this man, and yet somehow, she was.

He had said he needed a wife, and she had made him swear to the truth of it. She couldn't be such a burden if she helped to fulfill his own obligations. She turned her attention back to the modiste, resolved to be the best damn duchess she could.

"And do you wish to be wed?"

This was directed to her.

Della nodded. "Yes, I wish to be wed."

Back to Andrew.

"And you, my lord?"

"I do," he said.

"Then you're married."

The woman set the piece of paper on the bureau top and scribbled with a pen, the nub slightly broken so black ink sprayed in untidy splotches.

Della blinked. "That's it?"

The modiste lifted her lip in a near snarl. "If you wanted something fancier, you should have kept your legs together, darling."

Della did not so much as flinch at the woman's nastiness. Instead, she said, "I suppose the same could be said for yourself."

The modiste's eyes flashed with sudden anger, and Andrew reached between them, snatching the paper from the woman's hands. Della caught sight of some of the writing on it as it passed by her face and realized it was a testament to the events of that night.

Seeing it in splotchy ink had her suddenly realizing she'd done it. She had married the Duke of Ravenwood.

He took her elbow now, tossing a coin to the modiste.

"Thank you for your time, Madame Liliberte."

She snatched the coin and tucked in into the torn and loose folds of her bodice.

She gave a funny salute. "Always, my lord."

Her smile was not more than a baring of teeth, and Della's stomach heaved at the sight of the rotten stumps.

Andrew pulled her away, and when they made it outside, she sucked in a gulp of fresh air.

They stopped in the street like a traveling theatre troop that found themselves lost in the middle of the night.

Andrew let go of her hand, and she felt suddenly adrift there in the middle of the road in Brydekirk. Her heart rabbited in her chest, and her stomach growled with nerves. She pressed a hand to it, willing it to calm.

"Della."

She turned her attention to Andrew to find him extending a hand to her. Reflexively she reached for him, and he slipped a gold ring on the third finger of her left hand.

"It will have to do for now," he said. "I don't wish for

anyone to question our marriage until we can safely return to English soil."

It was a signet ring. She could hardly make out the details of it in the fading moonlight, but she made a mental note to study it in the daylight.

Before she could respond, he had taken her elbow, marching her in the direction they had come from when they'd first entered the village.

His servants followed several paces behind them, one of them, the one with the riding crop, holding the reins of Andrew's horse, and she thought he was likely a coachman.

"Are we to continue on tonight?" She was so very tired, the kind of tired that made her bones ache, but she would not complain should Andrew wish to go on.

He shook his head, and she glanced at him only to find his face stern, all hard angles and firm lips.

Was he already regretting what he'd done? She had tried to warn him. Nervousness gripped her throat, but then Andrew slowed, his face softening before he looked at her.

"No, we're going to the inn." He licked his lips as though he were the one who was nervous. "We must consummate our marriage."

CHAPTER 5

He had felt a modicum of guilt for lying to her, but the urgency to have them well and truly wed outweighed any sense of remorse.

He had meant to seek a wife. Only with the responsibility of looking after his sisters weighing on him, the idea had remained murky in his thoughts even if he said otherwise. Though his sisters were now all wed, he was still their brother, and after the debacle that was the start to his eldest sister's marriage, he knew he could never let his guard down. It was only the responsible thing to do.

Marrying now complicated matters, but it did not prevent him from returning to London to see to his family. It only, rather, added to his familial obligations.

Responsibilities.

He glanced at Della as if she might have heard his thoughts. She thought herself a burden, which was not unexpected based on the evidence he'd gathered so far of her life. He didn't want to give her any more fodder to add to that falsehood.

It wasn't as though any of this were her fault anyway. She was simply the victim of circumstance as was he.

They returned to the inn they had passed earlier, only the gentlemen who had slept beneath its windows were no longer there. A lit lantern still hung by the door, and he could see movement through the front windows.

He had procured a room earlier in the day, but he feared the repercussions that might have assailed the inn after the evening's celebration.

The innkeeper he remembered from earlier opened the door swiftly, and Andrew was not surprised to find the man still dressed.

He nodded in greeting. "I understand there was a bit of a to-do this evening, Stuart."

The older man's whiskers twitched when he smiled. "It was a magnificent harvest, Your Grace. You can't fault the men for wanting a wee drink and dance." His eyes shifted to Della. "And is this the wife you mentioned earlier?" The innkeeper's words were soft and round with his Scottish accent, almost beckoning an answer.

Della, however, remained frozen beside him.

"Yes, it is," Andrew said. "Stuart, please allow me to introduce my wife, Della Darby, the Duchess of Ravenwood."

He wondered at the way his chest squeezed when he spoke her married name.

Stuart gave a nod. "It is a true pleasure having you, Your Grace." He indicated the stairs behind him. "I've saved the best room for ye."

He stepped away to allow them entrance to the inn, and Andrew took Della's arm to lead her inside. He glanced back and raised a hand to St. John and Aldrich as they made their way to the stables where the horses and carriage were being kept. They'd overnight there to ensure everything's safety.

Andrew felt a pang of guilt at thinking of the men being forced to see the night through in a carriage instead of a proper bed, but seeing the weary bent of their shoulders, he thought they'd likely be happy with any warm and dry place to sleep.

He would see to giving them a raise when they returned to Ravenwood Park.

"Thank you, Stuart," Andrew said to the innkeeper as he drew Della to the stairs. "Is there somewhere we might procure a meal in the morning?"

Stuart gave a short nod. "I shall see to it myself."

"I'd like to get an early start if possible. I regret that will not leave you much time for your bed."

The innkeeper waved off his concern. "It's all the same to me. I prefer to see my guests properly cared for. Good night to the both of ye." He raised a hand as he drifted toward the back of the inn and likely his bed.

They climbed the stairs in silence then, and Andrew became all too aware of Della's stillness. He wondered now if it were the weariness from their journey or the enormity of what they had just done that plagued her.

They gained the upper floor and found their room. A crackling fire greeted them, and Andrew was grateful for the warmth it gave off. Although the room was small, it was clean, and the bed looked generous.

He swallowed at the sight of it, but not for what he was about to do. Unfortunately, it was simply because he was utterly exhausted. He wanted nothing more than to climb atop it and go straight to sleep but matters dictated otherwise.

He turned to Della. "Do you require…" He didn't know how to finish the sentence.

He was suddenly struck by the realization that he had a wife, and she was there, and they were here at this inn, and

THE DUKE AND THE LASS

he must consummate his marriage to prevent her father from attempting to discredit the union.

Della's eyes darted to the side and back as if she were chancing a glimpse of the bed. He didn't miss the way her features softened as though longing for the bed the way he did.

"I can give you a few moments," he said and backed to the door.

"No." Her voice was soft, and he almost missed it.

"No?"

Her chin went up, and she faced him directly. "No, please don't leave. It's been a rather unusual night, and I should not like to be left alone."

He stopped on the threshold, his hand on the doorknob. He let his fingers slide off the brass.

"Very well. I'll stay."

The innkeeper had brought up a tray at some point and it sat on the small table in front of the fire. There was an open bottle of wine, a couple of glasses, and a plate of hard biscuits. It was hardly a meal, but then he hadn't found himself very hungry in the last twenty-four hours.

He indicated the table. "Do you require refreshment?"

His voice sounded odd. Somehow wooden and hollow, and he hated how his insides twisted with what he must do.

Was it only the previous night he had slept in this woman's bed to protect her honor and now he planned to take it from her?

He gave himself a mental shake. It wouldn't be taking her honor now that she was his wife. He had every right to be in this room with her, and he had every right to take what he wished. It did not make what he had to do right or even make him feel better about it. He cursed her father for putting her into this position, for taking away her choice.

He turned sharply, and she jumped.

"Della, I'm sorry for this. I want you to know that." Her eyes went wide, and her lips parted, and he rushed on to reassure her. "Not the marriage. I'm not sorry for that. I told you the truth when I said I needed a wife, and I am grateful that you've agreed to the match. Rather I'm sorry your father would take away your freedom like this. That he would force your hand to avoid a worse fate."

She blinked, but her lips softly came together.

"Thank you, Andrew, but it's not your fault. I shouldn't wish for you to spend another moment of regret over my father's actions. The man isn't worth the time."

He realized then she clutched the folds of her skirts in her hands. She hadn't even had time to fetch her tattered traveling cloak.

"Are you cold?" He stepped forward as if he might help, but she took a quick step in retreat.

He paused, and she stared.

"I'm not cold. Thank you," she said, her tone rather wooden as well. "It's just this is…"

"Awkward." He spoke the word like a judge doling out punishment.

Della's shoulders deflated. "Precisely." The stark look in her eyes dissipated, and she took in the room about them with a softer glance. "It is rather warm in here, isn't it?"

"You understand why we must do this, why we must consummate the marriage. I understand you might be nervous…"

Her gaze flashed back to him. "I mean the temperature, Your Grace." She hardly got the last word out when a large yawn consumed her. Her hand moved to her mouth as if to cover it, but it was too late.

He yawned in response, his body yearning toward the bed.

She gave herself a small shake as if she could rid herself of the sleepiness that clearly was overtaking her. "I shouldn't wish to give my father anything with which to deny this marriage."

He thought a shiver passed through her then, but it could have been a trick of the firelight.

"Would you mind terribly if we just got it over with?" Her hands moved from her skirts to press against her stomach, and he recalled what she had told him about her nerves. "I should very much like to try for sleep if we are to leave in a few hours." Her eyelids fluttered, and he wondered if she weren't asleep on her feet.

"Yes, of course," he responded automatically.

He had never pictured his wedding night to be like this, but then there wasn't much in his life that had gone as he'd pictured. Since his mother's death, he'd taken on a role he hadn't planned for, that of caretaker to his sisters when his father proved loving but inept for the task. Then upon his father's death, Andrew's responsibility had increased tenfold when it came time to find suitable matches for them.

Now it seemed he faced a new responsibility, one which like the others had been thrust upon him.

But as he studied his wife in the dancing glow of the firelight, he didn't feel the burden that so often came with responsibility. Instead, he felt desire. He wanted to ignore it. He didn't want to believe that he could feel such base emotions when his wife's life had so recently been turned upside down. He should be comforting her now, reassuring her that all would be well.

Instead, he only thought about how she would look in the firelight, her beautiful, curvy body touched by the soft glow.

He swallowed as he felt himself harden. It was probably best that they get this over with quickly.

But before he could do anything, she wandered over to the bed, still fully clothed, and collapsed upon it.

"I do beg your pardon, but did you…well, that is…" she licked her lips as she muttered from her reclined position atop the bed. "Do you wish for me to undress, or should you like to merely lift my skirts?" She flapped her hands in the general direction of her legs as her eyes slid shut.

His chest tightened, and he felt every inch a rake for wanting her when she was so clearly exhausted, but right then he was overcome with an intense desire to join her in bed, to pull her into his arms, and fall asleep with her pressed against him.

It was too much even for him to resist, and he turned away, shucking his boots and coat. He kept his back to her as he went to the small table and filled one of the glasses with wine. He took a long drink. He willed the alcohol to stop the riot of thoughts that barged through his mind, the self-recriminations that plagued him.

It almost worked until a snore ripped through the warm quiet of the small room. He swung about to find Della completely asleep, her mouth slightly open as another snore erupted from her. He hadn't recalled her snoring the previous night, but then, he was a heavy sleeper. He wondered if he'd simply missed it.

He set down the wine goblet and made his way over to the bed, finally allowing himself to collapse atop it. He didn't feel right falling asleep before the marriage was well and truly consummated, but he wasn't so much of a bastard to wake her when she was clearly exhausted from the events of the day.

There was always the morning to see to the thing.

He closed his eyes and buried his head in the pillow only to realize the bed was a great deal smaller than it had looked. Della snored softly now beside him, her head nearly on his pillow. Without another thought, he turned and scooped her against him, turning her just enough that the snoring ceased almost immediately.

He kept his arm around her, slipping one leg between hers before falling promptly to sleep.

*   *   *

SHE WOKE for the second time in his arms. It was an occurrence she was beginning to enjoy, and unlike the previous, she was not immediately assailed with remorse.

For now, this could happen every time she woke because Andrew was her husband.

The thought reverberated deep within her, and something warm and pleasant spread through her. Was this happiness? Was this hope? She couldn't be sure.

Her life had been so narrow until Andrew arrived. There were a whole host of things she was experiencing that she had only ever read about. She didn't even know if she could trust her own feelings. Was this truly happiness or was she simply blinded by the newness of it all?

Honestly, she didn't even know much about Andrew.

For instance, what of these four sisters? Four sisters seemed like a lot. Would they like her? Her stomach twisted at the thought. What was there to like about Della? She knew more about books than people. Surely she would make a ninny of herself the first moment she stepped into society.

Her eyes shot open, her gaze focusing on the wall beside the bed.

Oh, dear Heavenly Father.

She was a duchess now.

A *duchess*.

Her stomach rolled over and played dead, the upset causing a gurgling noise to erupt from her middle regions.

She squeezed her eyes shut, praying it did not wake her husband.

The quaint room contained only a single window, and it had been shrouded in curtains when they arrived. She eyed it now and could just make out the telltale lightening of the darkness around its edges. Morning was near, but she doubted she could have been asleep that long.

She wondered what had woken her, but then her stomach growled again. She closed her eyes, willed the noise to stop, so she could get a few more hours of sleep, if that. But her stomach was persistent, and her thoughts took the opportunity to remind her that there were plenty of new things in her life over which to worry.

Reluctantly she slipped from Andrew's arms and made her way to the fire, which had died down in the night. She reached for a log from the pile beside the hearth and added it to the embers. It sparked and flared, sending a wave of much-needed heat into the room.

She rubbed her hands, realizing the chill that had settled over her after leaving the cocoon of Andrew's arms. She slid a chair from the table and turned it toward the flames as she settled on it. She plucked a biscuit from the tray, and regret washed over her instantly.

She tapped the biscuit against the small table only to have it ring hollowly back to her. She might lose a tooth in the attempt, but if she didn't, her stomach would eat her backbone. She tried a small bite and found the morsel broke more easily than she'd expected. It was still a rather tough go, and the biscuit held no flavor at all, but it was food and soon her stomach settled into an acquiesced daze.

As she sat there, she pulled the few remaining pins from her hair and set to work on untangling it. There wasn't much she could do without a hairbrush, but she tried nonetheless.

THE DUKE AND THE LASS

She was distracted though when she realized the state of her dress.

Carefully she pulled the folds of her skirts apart to see the damage the pine tree had wrought on the delicate fabric. Puncture marks decorated the area about her knees, and the hem had come undone along one side.

But in her inspection of the dress, the firelight glinted off the signet ring Andrew had placed on her finger. She'd almost forgotten about it. She turned it to the light and wasn't at all surprised to find a dragon head sitting in the center of the heraldic shield. A dragon, the protector of treasure and valor. She glanced toward the bed and her husband's sleeping figure, wondering not for the first time what his act of valor would cost him.

She poured a small measure of wine in the empty goblet and took a sip, the heat of alcohol burning her throat. She coughed lightly, unused to such a burn, but once gaining control of herself, she drank the rest of it down. It did little to parch her thirst, but it was something.

She stood and went to the window, brushing aside the curtain to see down to the yard below. Their room faced the alley between the inn and what was likely the stables, but there was no movement in the gray light of dawn.

She let the curtain fall back as she turned to the bed and stopped.

Andrew watched her from his reclined position.

"Good morning, wife." His voice was thick with sleep, and it sent a shiver straight through her at its suggested intimacy.

"Good morning," she returned, a tightness suddenly coming to her throat.

He ran a hand through his hair as he sat up. "What time is it?" he asked even as he drew a watch from his waistcoat. "It hasn't even gone five yet. We can sleep for a couple more hours." He tucked the watch away and collapsed back against the pillows, throwing one arm over his eyes. "Come back to bed."

He meant the invitation casually, but she couldn't help the way her toes curled against the wooden floorboards.

She did as he suggested and crept over to her side. She shed her slippers this time and slipped beneath the covers, surprised to find the linens smelling freshly laundered. She settled her head back on the pillow, and her eyes fluttered shut. Her whole body relaxed into the softness that surrounded, and she welcomed sleep.

"Della, there's something I should tell you."

Her eyes opened with a flash. She turned her head ever so slightly to find Andrew had leaned over so he could see her face.

"Yes?" The word was tremulous, and she willed herself to be strong.

"You have an incredible snore." He spoke with such seriousness at first she didn't understand his meaning.

When comprehension dawned, she couldn't help the snort that escaped her. "I did try to warn you, Your Grace."

"You didn't try very hard."

"Well, I mentioned it."

He raised an eyebrow in reply.

She rolled so she was facing him. "If we are going to play this game, then might I add you didn't tell me you were going to kidnap me."

He fell back on the pillows with an exaggerated gasp. "Kidnap? I think the words you're searching for are *daring rescue*." His trembling lips hinted at the smile he was trying to hide.

"I fell out a window. A little more notice next time would be welcomed."

He frowned with such intensity a deep furrow appeared

between his brows. "Please tell me I shan't be needing to rescue you again. I daresay once was enough."

"I've never required rescuing before, so I do hope I can keep it to just the one time."

She was smiling.

She wasn't sure when it happened, but the tension of the past several hours had melted, and the muscles along her back and shoulders were loose, her stomach settled like a slumbering beast. It was odd to feel this kind of peace, especially there in the inn in Brydekirk after her clandestine wedding.

Recollection of the wedding shadowed her sudden happiness.

"Do you think my father has discovered me gone?"

Andrew shook his head, his hair rustling against the pillows.

"I wouldn't think so. We left him rather deep in his cups along with the rest of them. If the spirit-induced haze doesn't prevent him from searching you out, I'm sure his fear of the stag come to seek its revenge will keep him locked in his room for some time."

Her face heated at the memory of what she'd done with her book. "I didn't know they would think it was the stag coming back to get them. I had only wished to draw them away from the front door." She plucked at the quilt between them. "And now I've lost my book to boot. I'll never find out what happens."

His eyebrows lowered in concern. "What book was it? Not some novel, I hope."

Her eyes flashed on his. "Are you opposed to novel reading, Your Grace?"

His reply was a snort. "Hardly. I think novel reading is a splendid way for one to widen one's mind. However, I am married to you now, and I shouldn't very much like the idea of being victim to any grand ideas you may get from your books."

"Grand ideas? What do you have in mind?"

He leaned up, drawing his face so close to hers. The intimacy of the moment struck her, and she thought she should be rather more overcome than this. But she wasn't. It just felt right to be lying there with Andrew.

"My sister, Louisa, read a novel once on natural camouflaging. After that, she wanted to try out fashioning clothes that matched one's environment. She chose our drawing room because it offered the most differing aesthetic, and then she determined I was the only one tall enough to make the exercise worthwhile." He shook his head, but he was smiling at the memory. Her heart squeezed wondering what that could be like. To have a sibling over which to have fond memories. "She dogged me for ages after that."

"You mean you wouldn't let her try it?"

His features hardened in playful objection. "I most certainly did not. She wanted to dress me up like the wallpaper."

"There are worse things, I suppose." She laughed but his eyes dimmed at her words, and she wondered what misstep she'd taken.

Her apprehension at realizing she was now a duchess swam once more to the surface, and she lay back on the bed, letting her eyes drift to the calm plainness of the ceiling.

But the quiet space above was soon invaded as Andrew leaned over her, his beautiful face filling her vision.

Except concern knitted his brow. She had the audacious urge to reach up and smooth the wrinkled lines there, but instead, she curled her fingers into the quilt beneath her.

Within moments Andrew's expression began to soften, and it turned into something curious rather than concerned.

THE DUKE AND THE LASS

"Della, I think we should be honest with each other. Don't you agree?"

"Yes." The word hardly came out. She was mesmerized by the way he studied her. It was almost as if he were memorizing the shape of her face. She'd never been so observed in her life, and she thought it would be uncomfortable, but it wasn't. It was almost…wonderful.

But immediately upon that thought came another. Was he going to tell her what he expected in return for rescuing her from her father? Did he plan to keep her in his London townhome and never let her out? Was he so ashamed to marry someone like her? She hadn't even been properly introduced to society, and now she was a duchess.

Or did he have a country home somewhere? It was easier to hide unwanted wives in country homes she supposed.

But he said none of those things.

Instead, he said, "I'd very much like to make love to you."

His declaration was so unexpected it startled her, choking her at the throat until she coughed and laughed a noise of disbelief.

"You would?" she managed.

A frown touched his features. "Yes, I would. Is that so hard to believe?"

She met his gaze, more perplexed by this line of conversation than afraid of it. "Well, it is rather. Until I met you, I didn't have many acquaintances, and now I have a husband. It's an extraordinary step if you think of it."

He didn't say anything right away, and his eyes continued to travel over her face.

"Has anyone told you how beautiful you are, Della?"

She wasn't sure if it was the focus of his gaze or the intensity of his words, but suddenly there was a tightness she'd never felt before in her chest, a tingling along her arms. She wanted to reach out and touch him and reassure herself that he was real.

But then he reached up and ran a knuckle along the curve of her cheek. The touch was brief, the gesture small, but she felt it all clear down to her toes.

"No," she heard herself answer him, but it was as though she were at a distance from herself, watching this incredible thing that was happening to her.

This handsome man had come into her life and stolen her away from everything only to give her so much more back. She didn't know how she knew that yet, but she did. She could feel it. Her whole world was suddenly filled with anticipation when there had been nothing but static quiet.

"Well, I'll need to tell you every day then, shan't I?" he whispered as he leaned down and kissed her.

CHAPTER 6

She had been surprised by his last kiss because it had been her first, and the newness of what was happening outstripped the physical aspect. But now she was aware of every bit of him. The softness of his lips, the tantalizing scent of sandalwood that seemed to ebb and drift around her as he drew nearer, towering over her as he pulled her into his arms.

She was surrounded by strength and steel, her arms pinned against the wall of his chest, so she felt his heartbeat beneath her palm. He deepened the kiss ever so slightly before pulling back to outline her lips with small, fiery kisses.

His hand traced the line of her cheek again before plunging into her hair, his fingers threading the strands so delicately. Those same hands had lifted her onto a horse in the dead of night, and she marveled at how gentle they could be now when she had witnessed their strength.

With a single thumb under her chin, he tilted her head back, changing the angle of his kiss the smallest of degrees, and yet it was as though he'd changed everything. New sensations flooded her, and she became aware of a pulse growing deep in her belly. For a moment, she feared her nerves would get the better of her, but this wasn't a nervous ripple. This was something else entirely, and it wasn't unpleasant. It was just different.

She leaned into it, into him, into their kiss, welcoming more unexplored sensations. He seemed to sense the change because he pried his lips from hers with a groan and trailed kisses along her cheeks to her jaw and down.

The deep pulsing within her suddenly flared to life and heat coiled low in her belly as he moved lower, pushing the bedclothes down and away, his hands sweeping each side of her torso, and she suddenly wanted to be very naked, to have the feel of his rough hands against her soft skin.

"Andrew." The word came out as not more than a breath, but even she could hear the pleading note in it. She didn't know what she begged for or how it might come about, but she knew suddenly there was more to this than she had expected.

She had read of love, of course, but the flowery prose found in the pages of a novel were no match for this. This wasn't flowery at all. This was carnal, full of heat and tension. She didn't know what it was, but she wanted more of it.

His lips reached the collar of her bodice, and he leaned up, replacing his lips with his fingertips. He skimmed the pale skin there, and she wanted nothing more than to see his hand on her, but she couldn't lift her head.

"I've ruined your gown," he said, his eyes traveling down the length of it.

"I think it was a joint effort really," she managed.

Why wasn't he still kissing her? Why was he wasting precious time on words?

His smile was devilish as he dipped his head and resumed

his pleasant torture. His hands cupped her now as he made his way down her body, stroking every curve so she had never felt more precious.

His lips meanwhile moved along the line of her bodice, and her head sank back in the pillows as she lost what little strength she had left.

He shifted, and she lifted her head just enough to watch him make short work of the buttons that marched down the front of her dress. She was grateful for the simple gowns she favored, but she could admit she had never truly understood all of their benefits until just then.

He parted the sides of her bodice, his hands dipping beneath the fabric, and for the tiniest of moments, she froze. She knew what she looked like. She knew she was bigger than what society deemed acceptable. Her stomach didn't lie flat, and her breasts were not perky. She rather feared she looked not unlike a sow, inert in her sty.

But as soon as the fear gripped her, it released, vanquished by the focused expression on Andrew's face.

He was enjoying this.

The thought had the breath catching in her throat, and her heart thundered in her chest. He was enjoying making love to her. He hadn't said that out of pity. He'd meant it. And suddenly, she didn't feel too big. She felt perfect. She *was* perfect.

But even though she knew it, it didn't stop her from sucking in a breath and tightening her stomach when he splayed his hands across it.

"Don't do that." His words were a harsh whisper as he looked up, met her gaze. "I want to feel all of you, Della. Just the way you are." His features softened when he looked at her, and she wondered what he saw on her face.

He ran his hands along the sides of her belly and up, tracing the lines of her corset.

"This is rather a pity though," he said, the glint in his eye turning sinful. "Your corset appears to be in my way, Your Grace."

She had often been accused of being in someone's way but never like that. She warmed at the attention.

"I can take it off." Her voice didn't carry the same sultry tone his did, and she wondered if she would ever grow more skilled at lovemaking.

Would she ever master such a decadent tone? Such a playful mien? She doubted it very much, and with the thought, her confidence slipped. But perhaps for now the newness of her would hold his attentions. She could only hope.

The euphoric bubble that had surrounded her since he first touched her shattered at the thought, and doubt flooded her senses. She hadn't thought of what was to come next when they were well and truly married. She had only thought of her escape.

Did Andrew keep a lover? Was he only using her now to satiate his needs until he returned to his paramour?

Would he still plan to dispose of her at a country home and return to his life in London unfettered?

She remembered how clear he had been that his trip to Scotland would be short. He had obligations in London. That was what he had said, wasn't it? Obligations. Was that how gentlemen referred to their mistresses?

She swallowed as Andrew leaned over her, coming up on his elbows on either side of her.

"Della, did you know I can tell when you're worrying?"

She blinked. "You can?"

He placed a single finger between her brows. "You get the most extraordinary divot right here." He traced a line down her nose. "Pray tell, Your Grace. What has you so confounded? If you are worrying of anything at all, I am not doing my job properly."

"What job is that?" She was hypnotized by the lovely brown of his eyes, by the way his smile beckoned her, by the way his hair was rumpled about his face from sleep.

"To thoroughly distract you with my masculine prowess."

She couldn't help the laugh that bubbled to her lips, and he growled before capturing her mouth in a hot, ardent kiss.

His hands were everywhere, and the fire that simmered inside of her flared to new life at just his touch. She wondered if he knew only too well what he did to her, knew exactly how to stoke the flames burning low in her belly.

His lips found the sensitive spot behind her ear just as his hands went to work on lifting her skirts, one aching inch at a time.

"Do you know what I want, Della?"

She shook her head, unable to speak.

"You," he said. Her skirts moved up another inch. "Every piece of you. Every one of your curves. Every single one of your valleys. I want to see all of you. In my bed, your body touched by the glow of firelight." Her skirts were above her knees. "That's what I want, Della. Only you. And that is everything."

She didn't know if it were his words or the sudden cool air that touched the bare skin at the top of her stockings, but suddenly the tension grew too great and instinctively she raised her hips off the bed and pressed into him.

He groaned, burying his face in the side of her neck even as he grasped her hips in his hands.

"Oh God, Della, do you have any idea what you do to me?"

She stilled. "Did I do it wrong?"

"No." The word came quickly as he moved to hover above

her. He cupped her face in his hands. "No, darling. You didn't do anything wrong. You only did it too right."

She blinked. "Too right?"

He nodded as he pressed his hips into her. Her eyes widened as she felt the bulge pressed against her lower belly. She'd spent enough time in her grandfather's stables to know what that was, and the idea that she had caused it left her startled.

"Oh," she whispered.

His smile was soft as he bent to kiss her. "Oh, indeed."

His hands went back to work on her skirts, and reflexively, her thighs parted for him. He traced the line of her stocking over her knee to where the soft lace lay across the middle of her thigh.

His fingers toyed with the edge of it, dancing between soft flesh and lace. She arched into him again, the pulsing growing urgent within her.

She could feel him smile against her neck where he plied hot kisses, and finally, she let go of the quilt to touch him. She hadn't dared before as she was too afraid of getting it wrong, of giving him reason to stop. But now she could feel the evidence of his desire, and it made her bold.

She traced the line of biceps up to his shoulders and neck. He was still fully clothed, and she pitied being denied the feel of his skin. She suddenly understood what he meant. The need to see his skin, the desire for such intimacy and closeness was everything just then.

Later, she promised herself. Later she would see and touch and feel all of him. Heavens, she only hoped there was a later. She hoped this wasn't it. That it wouldn't be over when he returned to his real life.

His fingers had left the lace of her stocking, trailing heat up the inside of her thigh. He grew dangerously close to the place that ached, and she tilted her hips, beckoning him to touch her.

"So impatient," he whispered against her neck, and she dug her fingers into the muscles of his shoulders, drawing a strangled moan from him. "Minx," he whispered now, his fingers climbing higher.

They traced the top of her thigh where it melted into her hip before dipping lower, lower still. He parted her folds with ease, and all at once, she felt the enormity of what was happening. He was touching her in her most intimate place and yet nothing had ever felt so right.

"Andrew, please," she whispered, her voice dripping with need.

"Do you want me to touch you?"

She didn't understand the question. He was already touching her, and she didn't know how that could help the coiling building inside of her when it was serving to make it worse as it was.

"Do you want me to touch you, Della?" he said again and slid one finger between her folds.

Her knees tried to come together, although she didn't know why.

"Della?" He withdrew the finger.

"Yes," she all but shouted.

He slipped the finger back into the wet heat of her core, and she shuddered at the intrusion, at the intense wave of desire that rippled through her. His finger moved in and out of her, and although she thought it wasn't possible, the tension grew, heat building until she thought she couldn't bear it.

She raised her hips and pressed herself into his hand.

"Andrew, please," she whimpered now. The pleasure was too intense. Something must be done.

He withdrew his finger and circled the sensitive nub, and

the building tension turned to something else, something sharper and refined, and she could feel her body drawing itself together for something. Something she didn't know what and feared would be too great.

It happened all at once, catching her breath in her throat so she couldn't even scream. She arched, her back coming off the mattress, and her arms tightened around his shoulders.

"Andrew," she breathed when she could finally draw air.

Her arms shook, and her legs trembled, and deep within her a spectacular warmth pulsed with waning echoes.

Andrew pulled himself from her arms so hastily, doubt gripped her. She'd done something wrong again.

But no. He was opening the front of his trousers, pushing them down his legs.

He leaned back over her. "Della, I promise you next time will be better. I promise. This might hurt a little, darling."

Before she could understand his words, there was a new pressure against her core, and then she realized what was to happen. He pressed inside of her in a single fluid motion, and her body expanded for him. It was tight and uncomfortable, but there wasn't much pain.

Although she rather liked the bit when he touched her better, she wouldn't tell him so. Perhaps this was the same kind of pleasure for him, and she didn't want to ruin it for him.

He began to move, sliding deeper as he let out a soft groan.

"Christ, Della, you're going to be the death of me."

She'd never held such power over someone, and she doubted how she could now, but his face was a contorted display of concentration. She moved her hips, hoping to help, but when she did that, he ground into her, pinning her to the bed with his hips.

"Jesus, Della, don't."

THE DUKE AND THE LASS

She bit her lower lip, certain now that she'd ruined everything. She wasn't cut out to be a wife, let alone a duchess, and soon Andrew would realize it. She'd just be another burden in someone's life.

He pressed his forehead to hers then, his breath ragged. "Della, darling, you feel far too good. I can't help it."

Again, his words were cryptic, but she gathered the sense that it wasn't something she'd done. That it was instead a positive thing. She lifted her hips again.

"God, you minx," he said, the scolding tone of his voice riddled with desire.

She ran her hands down his back, once more regretting that he still wore his clothing, and grasping his hips, she lifted hers into him.

He didn't form words that time. He moaned, his head going back as he pumped into her. Unexpectedly the tension returned, growing with a frenzy it hadn't had before, and she stilled, her legs locking around his as he pounded into her.

Oh God, she was going to—it was going to happen —again.

He reached between them and touched her, and she exploded just as he did and together, they fell through bliss.

* * *

He had just enough strength left to move before he crushed her. He rolled to the side, drawing her with him so she nestled in the circle of his arms. Only then did he allow himself to succumb to the exhaustion that still plagued him and the overwhelming sense of rightness that swept over him with Della in his embrace.

He couldn't have been asleep for more than several minutes when the banging sounded on the door. He blinked, his senses suddenly alert. Della stirred in his arms, and he pressed a hand to her mouth before she could give them away with a sleepy sound. He shook his head and sprang from the bed at the second round of pounding. He fixed his trousers and ran his hands through his hair before he gained the door.

He retrieved a single boot and slipped it on before setting the same foot just inside the door to keep whoever was on the other side from barging immediately in when he undid the latch. It wouldn't stop anyone completely, but it would slow him down, and that was all Andrew needed.

He heard Della scramble beneath the bedclothes just as he opened the door.

Aldrich was on the other side, his dress much in the same state of dishabille as if he, too, had been unexpectedly roused from his bed.

"The mail coach has just arrived from Kettleholm, and the driver is going on to anyone who will listen how the MacKenzie's daughter is missing. We must leave at once."

A gasp shot through the air behind him, and he turned to take in Della's wide eyes from just over the edge of the quilt. His chest tightened with some strange feeling, sadness and guilt perhaps, and he returned his attention to Aldrich.

"Have the carriage brought round immediately. There must be a back door somewhere. Find it. I don't wish to risk someone seeing us leave."

"St. John is already seeing to it, Your Grace," Aldrich said with a final nod before he turned to the rear of the inn and vanished down the corridor.

Andrew shut the door and bolted it, drawing one of the chairs to it to wedge it under the doorknob.

Della had already flung back the bedclothes and was setting to work on the buttons of her bodice.

"I'm very sorry for—"

"Don't." She held up a single hand as if she were going to

slice the air with it. The look she turned on him was one he'd never seen before from her. It was one of impossible strength and unfailing grit. "Do not apologize for him. Just get us out of here."

He found his coat and shrugged into it, swallowing the last of the wine in his goblet before wrapping the hard biscuits in a napkin and tucking them into his pocket.

"We're perhaps ten miles from the English border." He found his other boot. "I'll feel better once we're on the other side of it."

"My father is still a member of the peerage." She stood and brushed out her skirts, and he became aware of the tattered state of them for the first time. Should anyone see them in the daylight they would know something was afoot. "He'll have some influence even in England."

"That might be, but I have powerful allies in England that can provide us protection."

She cut him a swift glance. "Protection from what?"

"Should your father try to challenge the marriage."

She sucked in a breath. "Do you think he would do that? I mean, now that…" Her voice faded away as she cast a glance at the bed.

Her meaning was clear, and he felt a wave of remorse that her first time had been so hasty and tinged with ulterior motives.

"Especially now that we've consummated it. You forget that I stole his one chance to make a powerful political alliance by marrying you without a negotiated marriage contract," he said and took her arm to move her to the door. He stopped just inside of it and placed his hands on her shoulders. "Della, I promise you I will do everything I can to protect you. Your father will never have the power to harm you again, do you understand?"

Her eyes widened, and her lips parted, but she only gave a single nod that she'd heard him.

Had he realized how blue her eyes were? They were nearly the color of a Yorkshire sky in spring, and all at once he was homesick.

No, that wasn't quite right. He wasn't sick for the thought of home, but he was rather overcome by the sudden sense that he wanted to bring her there. He wanted her to see the rolling green fields of Ravenwood Park, the neat line of oak trees his grandfather had planted that now marched to the front door of the estate, and the way the sun lit the early morning fog over the forest.

He couldn't wait for her to see all of it. But first, he had to get her out of here.

"I promise I will always protect you." He brushed his knuckles over her cheek, wanting nothing more than to linger at the softness there, but the urgency of the situation pressed him to pull away and open the door.

The corridor beyond was quiet, and he stepped out into it, pulling Della along behind him. He retreated down the hallway in the direction Aldrich had disappeared and soon found the servants' stairs at the back of the inn. He made quick work of them and wasn't surprised when Della never hesitated behind him. Her step was quick and sure, even in the muted light across the worn and warped boards of the staircase.

They were dumped out into the kitchens, which at this time of day were bustling with early morning activity. He stepped in front of Della, attempting to shield her from the servants that lingered there, waiting for trays to take up to guests. He identified an older woman as a cook and three younger women who must serve as maids. Footmen danced in and out carrying shined boots and pails of split wood.

He kept Della behind him as he eased out of the kitchens

in what he hoped was the direction of the rear door. A servant living on the meager wages a country inn might provide would be all too quick to offer up information in exchange for a coin. But they reached the back hallway without incident, and he could see a door at the end of the corridor, a small window set high in the edifice flooded with light.

He pushed Della in front of him, keeping one eye over his shoulder to see if anyone followed them. They'd nearly made it to the door when a man stepped into view at the end of the corridor.

"Your Grace!" Stuart called softly, holding a basket in the air. The older gentleman scurried down the hall, his round stomach bouncing against the basket he held between both hands. "Your Grace, I couldn't see you leave without some kind of sustenance."

Andrew peered into the basket to find a loaf of bread, a jar of jam, various cheeses, apples, and another bottle of wine. Della's stomach rumbled so loudly behind him both men turned to eye her. She pressed a hand to said stomach and gave a soft smile and a shrug. He found himself returning her smile before taking the basket from the innkeeper.

"I owe you a great deal, Stuart."

The innkeeper waved him off. "It's no such thing." He leaned in conspiratorially. "My mother didn't want me to marry me missus either." He pumped his eyebrows as though he knew what Andrew were about. "Should anyone ask, I promise you no one from this inn will ever let on you've been here."

Andrew reached in his pocket and flipped a guinea to the innkeeper.

"Thank you, my good man," he said and hustled Della out the rear door.

St. John was waiting with the carriage for them, and Aldrich stood at the door, the step already in place. Andrew handed Della inside before jumping in after her. Aldrich snapped the door shut and the carriage rocked as he gained the box with St. John. They were underway within seconds.

Andrew held Della back from the windows and peered out the one closest to him as the carriage made its way around the inn to the main road. The small hamlet was coming to life with the start of a new day, and tradespeople streamed down the road as shops began to open. The sun had risen enough now to light the storefronts opposite, and the rays reflected back into the carriage enough to have him leaning back.

Della poked the arm he was using to hold her back.

"Kind, sir," she said, her tone thick with humor. "I know you are acting the knight valiant, but this damsel in distress is rather hungry." She eyed the basket he had placed on the opposite bench. "Would you mind so terribly much?"

He released his arm immediately. "Sorry," he muttered, rubbing his hands together. "I apologize. I can sometimes get carried away."

She raised an eyebrow. "Carried away? With saving people?"

"Yes." He returned his gaze to the window.

"Are you in a position to save people on a regular basis?"

He glanced at her. "When one has four sisters, opportunities abound."

She wrinkled her nose but didn't speak as she pulled the basket over to her lap. She rummaged inside of it, the questioning look still on her face even as she didn't speak.

He crossed his arms over his chest. "What is it?"

She looked up, the loaf of bread between her hands. She split it neatly apart, steam rising from the gooey center. His mouth instantly watered as his stomach rumbled.

THE DUKE AND THE LASS

She tilted her head but only handed him half of the bread without comment about his body's treachery.

Instead, she said, "I only wonder how it is that someone would manage to get into so much trouble." She shrugged. "In the whole of my twenty-one years, this is the first I've required rescuing." She had found a knife buried in the basket and pointed it at him, the jar of jam in the opposite hand. "And if we are being fair, this wasn't even my fault."

He extended a hand to open the jam jar for her, but instead she placed the knife in his open palm.

"I haven't done anything to require the aid of another in all of that time. How is it that your sisters could be so careless?" As she spoke, she pried the wire from the jam jar and broke the lid free of the sealing wax as if it took no effort at all. She extended the jar to him in invitation.

He took the knife still in his hand to pluck a dollop of the sweet-smelling, dark jam and spread it on the hunk of bread she'd handed him.

"You might be surprised at how easily my sisters can find trouble."

He finished spreading the jam and handed her back the knife. She took it without comment, but there was a deep furrow between her brows.

"What?" he asked plainly.

She shrugged, smearing jam on her own hunk of bread. "It's only I wonder if you aren't prone to manufacturing concern where there is none."

He nearly choked on the bite of bread he swallowed. "Manufacturing concern?"

She finished spreading jam on her bread. "You mentioned your mother passed away when you were young, yes?"

He nodded.

"It only stands to reason that you might be overly protective of your sisters. There wasn't, after all, a mother figure to look out for them, was there?"

He shook his head.

She nodded as if this supported her conclusion. "I didn't have my mother for long either, if you recall, and yet I somehow managed." She placed the jam jar back in the basket before meeting his gaze. "Don't you think it's possible that you took the role of older brother rather more seriously than the situation might have called for?"

He chewed for several seconds on his bite of bread before swallowing. "I suppose you can find out for yourself from my youngest sister when you meet her."

He glanced out the window to find they had left the village proper. A few crofts dotted the hillside that spread out on either side of the road now, and cultivated fields and pasture surrounded them.

"Your sister?" Della's voice was suddenly not so vibrant.

He studied her. "Yes, Johanna. The Duchess of Raeford. She's my youngest sister and is in residence at a neighboring estate. You'll meet her when we arrive at Ravenwood Park."

She took an unusually large bite of bread and chewed furiously. He watched her as she did it, and he realized he had made her nervous, only this time she didn't have a tin of shortbread at hand.

"And when will that be?" she asked when she swallowed.

He shrugged. "It's another two days at best to Yorkshire."

Della took another enormous bite of bread.

CHAPTER 7

She hadn't realized she would be meeting one of the sisters so soon. She thought they would all be in London when in fact, there was one happily married and living at a neighboring estate to Ravenwood Park, Andrew's home.

Great bloody bollocks.

What would she think of Della?

They hadn't made many stops on their journey south. Andrew and his men had thought it better that they make as much distance as possible, and they were turning onto the drive of Ravenwood Park just as the sun was setting on the second day.

They'd stopped only to change horses and take care of necessities. Aldrich and St. John, Andrew's servants as she'd learned that first day of travel, had taken turns driving while the other slept on the box. She couldn't imagine it had been very comfortable, but it was evident the men were loyal to Ravenwood, and this made her feel less nervous about her future.

After all, she'd married a man who had kidnapped her

from her father's home after knowing her for not much more than twenty-four hours. It was the rashest thing she'd ever done, and really, she should have obeyed her father. It was what would be expected of her as his daughter, but when faced with the reality of it, she hadn't been able to do so.

She could still hear those men's voices as they scraped at her door and argued over who would have her first. She may have been a burden her whole life, but she was still a person, and she deserved at least some respect.

She did not deserve the Duke of Ravenwood, but she wasn't going to argue when the universe seemed to think this was meant to be. She eyed him now as the carriage bounced its way up the drive, her fingers unconsciously toying with the signet ring he'd given her. He leaned forward, his gaze locked out the window as if he were seeing the place for the first time.

She wondered at it. To love a place so much as to have such a physical reaction to it. She worried if they did not hurry, he would fall out the door in anticipation of seeing home.

Home.

She'd never really had one, and a hollowness clawed at her stomach. She remembered very little of her younger years when she and her mother had still lived at MacKenzie Keep, and then it was mostly the feeling of being constantly cold and having to be very quiet so as not to draw attention to herself. Now that she thought of it, her grandparents' home wasn't much different. Her grandmother had always instructed her to make as little noise as possible to avoid being even more of a nuisance.

For a moment, she wondered what it would be like to be loud. To speak when she simply wished to and not when it was asked of her. To frolic and play and laugh like children did. For she'd heard other children making noise whenever

THE DUKE AND THE LASS

her mother had taken her to tea with friends. Della had never been invited to play with the other children. It was so long ago now, she had trouble remembering why it was she had been excluded, but she wouldn't doubt if it had something to do with the fact that she always carried a book with her to those tea outings.

She pressed her hands together in her lap now, her stomach churning as the house came into view through the trees.

It was enormous.

She pressed her lips together and willed her stomach to settle. She was now the mistress of this grand home, and yet she wished her eyes deceived her.

Ravenwood Park was a massive, neoclassical stone structure with a sweeping front stair that led to a robust colonnade over which an entablature supported a frieze of sculptures she couldn't make out from this distance. Flanking the front colonnade were wings that stretched far on either side, and she knew she couldn't possibly remember all the rooms each wing must encompass.

The carriage rounded the circular drive in front of the house and came to a stop at the bottom of the sweeping stone staircase. Andrew didn't wait for the step and instead opened the door and hopped out.

She heard the crunch of gravel and leaned forward to peer out the door. She had thought it was custom for servants to be readied and presented when the lord of the estate returned home, but the stairs were entirely empty. Andrew's back was to her as he seemed to study those same stairs, and all at once, doubt swamped her.

In the two days since they'd left the inn, Andrew had not touched her. Not that she had expected him to. He wouldn't have reason to after all. It was only that…well…

She wanted him to touch her.

What she had experienced in his arms was unlike anything she had ever felt before. It was physical, yes, but it was more than that.

She finally knew what it was like to feel close to someone.

In that moment, in that room at the inn, it was as though her life had finally intersected with someone else's. It wasn't that she was a burden. It wasn't that she was a problem to be dealt with. It was that she was a woman, and he was a man, and they came together in the most basic way possible.

She had felt seen, but no. It was so much more. She had been felt and heard and coveted.

It was so many things at one time and then…nothing.

She tried to think the best of the situation. It was odd what had happened between them, and arguably, neither of them could be expected to know what to do in such a situation. It wasn't as though she were being stolen away in the middle of the night on a regular basis, and she most certainly was not marrying men she hardly knew.

Still the seeming indifference to her presence in the carriage had hurt.

Again, she tried to understand. They were both exhausted. She still wore the same tattered dress she'd worn to escape her father's keep. Andrew wore the same clothes as well, now rumpled and soiled from the long drive, but at least his trousers didn't have holes in them.

She drew a deep breath and willed her stomach to settle. This was all new and different for both of them. Things would work out. She just knew it.

She raised her chin and moved to the door. She would simply do her absolute best to be the perfect duchess. She wouldn't give Andrew any cause to think her a burden, and perhaps if she performed well enough, he might learn to love her one day.

The thought seized her, and she wondered from where it

had come. It was ridiculous, of course. Who was she to hope to be loved one day?

He must have heard her because he turned as she alighted. Too late he offered her a hand as if he'd forgotten she was there, and she pretended not to notice the aborted gesture even as her chest twisted at the sight of it.

She swallowed. "This is all quite grand." She smiled, hard, and hoped she didn't appear overeager.

But his gaze didn't linger long on her face as he turned back to the stairs.

"Yes, it is at that. I didn't have time to write ahead to let them know of our arrival, but I'm sure Mrs. Collins can have a bath drawn immediately."

He started up the stairs, and it was several seconds before she realized she was to follow him. His voice bounced back at her against the harsh surfaces of the stone facade.

"My sister likely has something you can wear, but Mrs. Collins can probably find suitable clothing for you in the interim until you can visit the seamstress in the village."

"Mrs. Collins?" she called after him.

He'd reached the top of the stairs by then and turned. She didn't miss the sheepish look on his face when he realized how far behind him she was, and her chest twisted again.

She swallowed down the hurt and gained the top of the promenade to stand next to him. It was all just the oddity of the situation. It wasn't about her personally.

Now if only she could believe that.

"Yes, the housekeeper. I'll send a messenger to Raeford Court for my sister. She'll be able to assist you..." He gestured vaguely about her person, and reflexively, she drew in a breath to make herself smaller, and it sparked a shower of sadness in her. "With everything," he finished.

They reached the massive front doors then and without

waiting for them to be opened, he marched inside, holding the door open for her to enter.

She was used to ancient Scottish keeps and moldy English castles, so she was not prepared for the glittering grandeur of Ravenwood Park.

The front hall was a confection of white marble and gilt chandeliers. The central staircase was bracketed by smooth banisters of warm, polished wood that drew the eye upward to the balcony above and then farther to the mural-covered ceiling adorned with exquisite plaster medallions.

And this was only the foyer. She couldn't imagine what the rest of the house looked like.

The quiet that surrounded them was interrupted by the efficient sound of clipped footsteps coming from the back of the house. A woman appeared in a crisp uniform of black and stark white, her hair ensconced in an equally brilliant white cap.

"Your Grace." Her tone was firm with a hint of surprise. "We were not made aware of your arrival."

"Mrs. Collins, I offer you an apology. Our return was rather…hasty." He spoke the last word as if it should entail all that had occurred in the last several days.

Della wasn't sure why, but when Andrew had spoken of Mrs. Collins, she'd pictured a plump, pleasant woman with a chatelaine of keys and a smiling disposition.

But Mrs. Collins was none of those things. For one, the woman could not have been more than fifteen years Della's senior, perhaps only a handful of years older than Andrew himself. She was also beautiful with chestnut-colored hair and wide green eyes.

Della drew in another breath, her shoulders hunching as if she could disappear.

It was, of course, at that moment that Andrew introduced her. "May I introduce my wife?" he said with a sweeping hand in her direction. "Della Darby, the Duchess of Ravenwood."

Mrs. Collins curtsied immediately. "Your Grace, it is an honor to meet you." Her face remained pleasantly neutral at the news that surely should have rocked the head of staff of a household such as Ravenwood Park, but Mrs. Collins did nothing more than slightly widen her eyes. "I'm sorry we were not informed of your arrival. I would have had the staff ready to receive their new mistress."

Della thought she might be sick. Not only was she a duchess of a house the size and grandeur of Ravenwood Park, but she also had a staff.

A staff that included the incredibly beautiful Mrs. Collins.

Andrew waved off Mrs. Collins's concern. "Our departure was unexpectedly hasty, and really, the situation at present is highly unusual, and protocol is the least of my concern." He took Della's arm then and drew her forward, and Della wished she might disappear into the floor. "A bath is in order, immediately, and if you could have the duchess's rooms readied for my wife."

Then she felt it. His hand at the small of her back pushing her forward. He was handing her off to Mrs. Collins like a mother would hand off her wailing child to a nanny. She was just another nuisance then, handed off for the servants to deal with.

She couldn't even summon the strength to raise her chin.

"I must send a messenger to Raeford. Can you send a footman to my study? I'll have a letter ready for him."

"Of course, Your Grace." Mrs. Collins bowed her head as Andrew disappeared toward the back of the house.

Della watched him go. He hadn't even acknowledged her since entering the house.

What was she to expect really? It wasn't as though he'd married her for love. She'd never expected to marry for love, but then she hadn't realized she might fall in love with the man who would marry her. It seemed one-sided love was its own special torture.

Someone touched her elbow then, gently, but it was enough to have her start.

"Your Grace." Mrs. Collins's eyes were kind as she peered up at Della.

Up.

The woman was even the proper diminutive size Della knew men found attractive.

"It seems you've ruined your dress. Might you have brought something you can change into after your bath?" Mrs. Collins's eyes drifted to the door as if expecting Della's luggage to appear.

But there was no luggage. Della didn't even have a book now.

She pressed her hands to her stomach. "I haven't any things."

She hated how weak her voice sounded. In all the years and through all the times she'd been handed off to someone, she'd never lost her fortitude. But it seemed she had found the one thing that held enough power to slay her, and it was nothing more than a handsome face.

Mrs. Collins frowned. "We'll find you something, Your Grace. You must be tired. Let's get you upstairs."

She was nice. Andrew's housekeeper was nice and pretty and young.

Never before had Della felt so out of place.

* * *

"You caught a wife in Scotland then?"

Andrew looked up from the estate report his steward had left for him. He had taken refuge in estate business the moment he'd left Della in the care of Mrs. Collins. It was easier to focus on crop yields and drainage than to think of how he was going to keep Della safe.

He hadn't expected the MacKenzie to catch on so quickly that his daughter was missing, and he worried the man was sharper than he appeared. Now Andrew had to hope he'd paid a handsome enough sum to keep the lips shut of the few people who knew Della had passed through Brydekirk with him. If the MacKenzie discovered Andrew's name associated with his daughter's disappearance, he would have a map leading directly to her.

For once, Andrew took comfort in the archaic marriage laws that both made their ramshackle union legal and made Della his property by rights. He couldn't think of her in that way. She was too...well, *much* to think of in terms of owning her, but in this instance, he would. Because it kept her safe from the dishonorable machinations of her father.

Did the MacKenzie really think one of those gentlemen he had summoned to his keep would swear fealty to him in a marriage contract? The practice was barbaric and only served to show how little he thought of his own daughter. Andrew could not allow that to happen to Della.

In the meantime, he had to stay away from her.

The one moment he had lost his resolve, lost himself in her, disaster had struck. It might have been hyperbole, but thinking in such terms kept his wits sharp. This time it was only a mail coachman with the news of a missing daughter, but next time it could be the MacKenzie himself. Andrew had to stay focused and keep Della from danger.

Which meant he had to stay away from her.

He couldn't look into those fathomless blue eyes and not forget the world around them. He couldn't watch the way those same eyes fluttered closed in desire or listen to the small mewling sounds she made when he touched her, caressed her, consumed her.

God, it had not been his best attempt at lovemaking, and yet he was still rattled by it.

For the first time in his life, making love had been about more than physical release. It had been about exploration and discovery, and he had only just started and now he had to stay away from her.

The two days in the carriage had been agony. He wanted nothing more than to hold her in his arms, but then more than ever he had had to stay alert. The MacKenzie could have found them at any turn, and he didn't wish to risk being caught unawares.

He'd already dashed off a letter to his solicitors in London. If he must, he would marry Della again to ensure the legality of their union, but he also wanted to be prepared should the MacKenzie prove another legal point to regain possession of his daughter.

So, when he looked up to find his best friend standing before him, Andrew felt a modicum of relief. Should it come to it, he knew he had an ally in Benedict Carver, the Duke of Raeford.

"I failed to mention I might be in search of a wife, did I?"

Ben came into the study and took a chair in front of Andrew's desk. He wore no coat despite the falling autumn temperatures, and his shirtsleeves were rolled up to show tanned skin. His trousers and waistcoat were serviceable wool, and had he not known better, Andrew would not have known him for the duke he was. Ben Carver looked every inch a farmer, and it made Andrew smile.

"You may have mentioned it in passing, but I made the assumption you might find her in London like the rest of us blokes." He gestured widely. "I apologize for assuming the worst of you."

Andrew tossed down his pen. "I'm appalled you would think so lowly of me, Raeford."

Ben settled back in his chair and crossed an ankle over the opposite knee. "A wife though, Andrew. That's rather more than a stag. Care to tell an old friend how it came about."

Andrew reclined in his seat and told his friend about what had happened over the past three days. By the end of it, Ben was leaning forward in his seat, elbows to knees.

"Do you think the MacKenzie will find her here?"

Andrew shrugged. "I had hoped we would have more time before he realized what happened, but I've learned the man is a great deal more conniving than I had anticipated."

"He really offered his daughter to those men? In exchange for sworn fealty?"

"We were encouraged to sample the goods." Even saying the words now in the safety of his own home left Andrew tasting bile.

Ben made a sound of disgust as he sat back. "You had no choice but to marry her."

Andrew nodded. "And now I must keep her safe. I think we should head to London as soon as possible. I like the feeling of putting more space between us and the MacKenzie."

"It doesn't mean he won't try to follow you," Ben offered.

"I know, but I should think the man will be reluctant to go so far south before the start of the next parliament session."

Ben raised an eyebrow. "Do you think that should keep him in Scotland?"

Andrew leaned both elbows on his desk. "I hope it would give him pause to think through his actions before doing something hasty. Besides, from what Della has told me of her childhood, I can't think her father would be too quick to get her back. Unless he had some idea of where he hoped to marry her off to."

"You mean if he were seeking an alliance of some sort with one of the selected gentlemen?"

Andrew picked up his pen and slid it through his fingers as he thought it over. "He mentioned her dowry as an enticement to the gentlemen he had gathered. I didn't think of it at the time as more than a father attempting to marry off a daughter to a gentleman who would provide a beneficial connection, but I've had time to think now, and I wonder if the MacKenzie didn't have certain alliances in mind."

"You mean he chose those gentlemen on purpose because he thought to gain something specifically from any one of them?"

"Well, Della lived with her maternal grandparents until her father summoned her to Scotland. Why bother with her at all unless the MacKenzie had a bigger plan?"

"Perhaps her grandparents were putting pressure on him to see her wed?"

"Annoying in-laws then?"

Ben's smile was sardonic. "In-laws can be such pests."

"I will let that comment go as I pity you, old friend. I cannot imagine being shackled to my sister."

Ben sat back with a hearty laugh, one filled with such contentment and pleasure it had Andrew's chest squeezing in envy.

"I can assure you I require no pity. All is well in Raeford." His friend's smile suggested things were more than well in his marriage, and Andrew couldn't help but feel a lift at the thought.

His sister's marriage hadn't started in such a beautiful place, and it bolstered Andrew to know they had found happiness.

He wondered briefly if he'd ever find a place in his

marriage like that, but even at just the thought, an unpleasant weight settled in his stomach. He wouldn't have a marriage like Johanna and Ben. He just knew it. His body responded to Della's in a way he'd never experienced before, but it wasn't love that had brought them together.

Despite everything, he'd known Ben and Johanna had a mutual attraction even before the truth of Ben's intentions were revealed. Andrew and Della didn't have such a friendly base from which to work. They were just two souls thrown together in a dire situation.

But did that mean it was hopeless?

"Speaking of Raeford, I had hoped my sister might be able to provide some clothing for Della. I know they aren't of the same size, but we're rather desperate. Della wasn't able to bring any of her things with her, and the one gown she was wearing was the unfortunate victim of a pine tree."

Ben hissed in a breath. "Do I dare ask?"

Andrew nodded sagely. "It's how I was able to get her out the window. There was a convenient tree to provide egress."

"Your wife climbed a tree?" Ben's voice had taken on an air of astonishment.

"Yes. The situation called for it. It wasn't as though she had much choice."

Ben's eyes had widened and stayed that way as Andrew explained.

"What?" Andrew was finally prodded to ask.

But Ben only shook his head. "It's nothing really. It's just…well, nothing." Ben waved it off, but Andrew could tell there was more that his friend wasn't saying. Whatever it was, it left a lingering smile on his friend's face and Andrew wishing to know the jest. "I'm sure Johanna has found something adequate for her to wear. Are you thinking of leaving for London in the next few days?"

Andrew nodded sharply. "I hope to be underway as soon

as I can have some gowns fashioned for Della. I hate to leave Ravenwood Park so soon, but the estate seems to be in order."

"I'm always happy to check on the place for you, you know that. Johanna and I don't plan to return to London until Christmastime, and even then, it will be a struggle to get her to leave."

"You're thinking of spending time in London during the holidays?" This was the first Andrew had heard of it. As far as he knew, the other sisters were plotting how to have the Christmas holidays at Ravenwood Park so they could make excuses to see Johanna.

Ben ran a hand through his hair. "Johanna is concerned about Viv and Eliza traveling."

Viv and Eliza were both pregnant and due at the beginning of the new year. Travel would be difficult in December for both of them, and it would be just like his sister to put their comfort first.

"I'm not going to Margate," Andrew said quickly.

Ben laughed. "You've no wish to spend the holidays at the shore?"

Andrew shuddered. "Do you know what she is like?" he asked, referring to his eldest sister, Viv. "So damn proud of those hops."

Ben laughed again. "You should be proud of her after everything that's happened."

Ben's reminder sent a chill through Andrew, and he rose to his feet. He didn't like remembering what happened to Viv when he had thought he'd managed an excellent match for her. When she'd returned to her childhood home in a fit of rage and tears, crushed and heartbroken, he knew he'd failed her as a brother. He didn't like to be reminded of it, and he knew he would never let it happen again.

To any of the women under his care.

"I'm only glad the situation has resolved itself. I shouldn't have liked to address matters further."

Ben's smile faded. "Address matters further? Do you mean Viv's marriage? I hardly see how she would allow you to meddle in her marriage."

Ben was right. Viv was headstrong to the point of being stubborn.

"Be that as it may, I am her brother, and it's my duty to care for her."

Ben's expression folded in question. "Duty to care? You're sounding rather old and curmudgeonly, old friend. I think all of the Darby sisters are more than capable of taking care of themselves, don't you agree?"

Andrew folded his arms over his chest. "I don't."

Ben let out a bark of laughter and stood. "I am not at all surprised to hear as much. Especially after the show of bravado in the garden when I first came home."

His friend referred to an incident in the Ravenwood garden in London when Andrew heard Johanna had scampered off into the dark with a rake. He didn't regret the show of strength he had demonstrated when discovering the pair. If it had been anyone other than Ben, it would have been warranted. Come to think of it, Ben's intentions at the time hadn't been all that honorable either, but Andrew had only learned of that later.

"With Mother dying so young and Father staying rather apart from us, the job was left to me to care for them."

Ben's brow furrowed. "That might be but they're adults now. Do you not think them strong enough to make decisions on their own?"

Andrew was saved from having to voice a reply by a crash over their heads. It was loud enough to reverberate through the entirety of the room.

Ben sucked in a breath. "I suppose it's not going well."

"What's not going well?" Andrew had felt the scrape of trepidation down the back of his neck even before his friend had spoken.

Ben pointed to the ceiling where the crash had originated. "Johanna brought some gowns for Della to try. She went directly upstairs when we arrived."

"Johanna is upstairs? With Della?"

Ben nodded. "She made me swear not to tell."

"You left Della alone with Johanna?" Andrew seethed, but he didn't wait for a reply. He was already running for the door.

CHAPTER 8

A bath was just the thing.

It was all she needed to feel restored and scrape together the last of her confidence. It would most assuredly be all right. At least, that was what she thought as she brushed out her damp hair while she sat on the window bench in the duchess's rooms overlooking Ravenwood Park sometime later.

The sun was on the cusp of the horizon and just about to sink out of sight. It was that moment when the last burst of light filled the sky, and with it, came a burst of hope.

She was safe. She was clean. And soon she hoped she would eat.

Her stomach growled as if in agreement with this thought.

She ran the brush Mrs. Collins had found for her through her hair lazily as her gaze remained fixed on the line of trees to the west, glowing bright orange and gold with the setting sun.

Tomorrow would be a new day. She would be well rested and clean, and everything would seem better.

Perhaps Ravenwood Park would have a library. Surely, she couldn't be in the way if she kept to the library. But no. She was a duchess. There were things required of a duchess she was sure, but she hadn't an inkling as to what they were.

Her mother had never bothered to teach her much, and her grandmother—well, they might have shared a house, but that didn't mean they had to share their time as her grandmother had always been quick to point out.

Her stomach twisted now.

Would she be up to the task of being a duchess? She just had to be. She had no choice but to succeed. She couldn't let Andrew down.

Perhaps there was a book on being a duchess. Her spirits lifted at the thought. That was just the thing. She'd look in the library for one tomorrow.

Feeling better already, she relaxed into the cushions along the bench and began braiding her hair for the night.

Her fingers stilled on the strands as she caught sight of her nightdress. Mrs. Collins had found that as well. It was a cast off from Ravenwood's cook, and it had certainly been lovely once. It was worn along the edges, and the bodice sported a spray of frills that only served to accentuate her already exorbitant bosom. It was also too short. It ended somewhere in the middle of her calves and was entirely indecent. However, it had no holes and was free of sap, so Della would not complain.

But she would hide in her room until more suitable clothing could be found.

She would not let Andrew see her like this. Not that she thought she was in danger of seeing him.

Her eyes drifted about the room.

The duchess's rooms.

They were beautifully appointed with delicate rosewood furniture and thick, luxurious trappings in a deep navy, accented with sprigs of rose and honey. It was the nicest room she'd ever been in. Her grandmother had made sure Della occupied the smallest guest room in Bewcastle, and she had been fortunate the room had a single window and a bed. The duchess's rooms were sinful luxury in comparison.

She hopped down from the window seat and returned the brush to the dressing table, pausing to skim her fingers over the glossy surface of the fine wood. The slender legs tapered from the base until they spilled into fine arches along the floor, and she traced the line of it down the edge of the table front.

She stopped when her fingers encountered the slightest variation in the wood and bent to examine it. The leg had been repaired. Had she not touched the wood, she never would have known. It was expertly fabricated. She ran her fingers over it again. How sad to think such a gorgeous table had seen such damage at one point. Whoever had fixed it must possess extraordinary skill to hide such a flaw.

She backed up to look at it more closely. No, she wouldn't have been able to tell had she not touched it.

She moved to touch the mended piece again when a sharp knock sounded on the door. Before she could bid the person enter, the door was thrown open.

"I assure you, Your Grace, I was able to find a suitable nightdress for Her Grace, and I've already sent a note down to the seamstress in the village that a fitting will be required first thing tomorrow."

Della had thought Mrs. Collins was beautiful, but the woman who entered with her was far more beautiful, and Della's stomach dropped to her toes.

This woman was of moderate stature, but she held herself with a loftiness Della could only aspire to. Her warm dark hair was swept back to reveal full features, delicate brows, and a warm smile.

A smile just like Andrew's.

Della reached out to the table beside her, forgetting her tin of shortbreads had been lost.

"You must be Della!" the woman said without preamble and swept Della into an embrace that threatened to cut off her air.

It was glorious.

Unshed tears stung the backs of her eyes in an instant. Della had never felt the force of such…what was it? Kinship? Friendship? Neither seemed possible as she'd never met this woman before and yet, there they were.

This was Andrew's *sister*. She knew that without a proper introduction. The word played over and over again in her head. Was this what it was like to have a sibling? This unconditional response of love and acceptance?

The woman backed up enough to study Della's face. Della wanted to shrink under the scrutiny, but she raised her chin and waited.

The woman seemed to come to some kind of conclusion because she shook her head satisfactorily.

"I'm Johanna. I'm sure my brother has failed to mention me, but I've brought gowns." She gestured behind her to a maid whose arms overflowed with gowns.

The maid gave a small smile as if it were every day her mistress barged into the bedchamber of a woman she didn't know, and at nightfall, no less.

Johanna touched Della's arm and leaned in conspiratorially. "I heard you were forced to leave in a hurry. I do hope nothing of value to you was lost."

Della thought of her Melanie Merkett novel but shook her head.

Johanna squeezed her arm. "That's at least something. Come. Let's see if any of these will work."

The maid had laid the gowns atop the bed and was in the process of spreading them out.

Della eyed the pile with mounting doubt. "Lady—er, I'm sorry. I don't know—" Had Andrew said she was a duchess?

"Johanna," the other woman returned with delicate force and a snap of her chin, forgoing any mention of titles.

"Johanna," Della said, even though she didn't feel quite comfortable using the woman's given name considering the brevity of their relationship. "My underthings were all taken to be laundered." Della slid a glance toward Mrs. Collins.

Johanna only waved a hand. "I thought as much. I've brought underthings as well."

A second maid appeared, and Della wondered if she'd been there the entire time.

This maid presented a basket, and setting it atop the small bench at the foot of the bed, slipped the top free to reveal an assortment of underthings. Fine linen chemises, bountiful crinolines, and even two corsets.

Della looked around for a dressing screen, but she knew there wasn't one. When Mrs. Collins had shown her to the rooms earlier, she had left immediately so Della could undress. Johanna seemed to not carry the same notions of propriety.

"I think we should try the peach first." Johanna pointed to a peach day gown the first maid had unearthed from the pile. "I think this corset might fit you best. I had only Andrew's description of you to go off, and you know how obtuse men can be."

Della had only ever truly interacted with her father, grandfather, and Andrew, so she wasn't much of an expert on the subject, but she nodded as if to agree with Johanna.

Johanna held up the corset in question but soon she shook her head.

"No, this won't do at all." She dropped her arms. "I suppose Andrew wasn't flattering you with his description."

The breath caught in her lungs. She swallowed and drew in enough air to say, "Andrew's description?"

Johanna's smile was immediate and full. "Oh yes. Andrew has always been good about details, and I should have trusted him on this one. He compared you to the statue of Hera our father commissioned for our mother that sits in the folly in the garden of Ravenwood's London home."

Della tried to scramble through those words, but only one thing stood out. "Andrew compared me to a…statue?"

Johanna had been puzzling over a set of crinolines but looked up at this, her eyes lit with a secret joy Della couldn't discern.

"Oh yes. It's a gorgeous statue of voluptuous proportions. Our father had it commissioned as my mother's wedding gift. It's striking and beautiful and magnificent, and I can see exactly why Andrew should compare you to it."

Striking.

Beautiful.

Magnificent.

The words fell through her mind like a waterfall, tumbling one over the other so she could make out none at all. She was flooded with a lightness that left her dizzy, and when she finally blinked back to her senses, Johanna had wrapped a corset around her over her nightdress.

"I hardly think this will do, but it will help us get an idea of the right shape for you. I would hate to diminish your natural features." Johanna popped around the side of Della from where she was holding the corset together at Della's back. "I bet you would look stunning in a bodice fitted with a sweetheart neckline."

Stunning?

Perhaps she was overly tired. She hadn't slept in a bed for two days. Maybe it was exhaustion clouding her faculties.

A squeezing sensation that had nothing to do with nerves started around her midsection, and she realized Johanna was attempting to tie the corset.

Della's hands flew to her stomach where her fingers encountered the sharp boning of the corset. She traced the ridges only to find a spot where the stitches had frayed.

"Johanna, I'm not sure—"

She tugged with greater ferocity, and Della had to dig her bare feet into the carpet to keep upright.

"I'm sure with just a little more adjustment we can get it tied."

Johanna gave another tug, and the first sound of a stitch ripping had Della peering down at her torso. Her fingers trailed over the frayed seams, but it seemed to be holding tight.

"Johanna, it really isn't a bother—"

"Your things are not likely to be dry by morning, and I will not have you be forced to attend the seamstress in your nightdress. We will make this work."

The determination in the other woman's voice had Della snapping her lips shut.

Mrs. Collins came around the bed and joined Johanna at Della's back.

"Perhaps if we pulled it tighter through here," Mrs. Collins offered.

The air whooshed from Della's lungs at the next tug, and dark spots clouded her vision. She sucked in a breath, but it was scant and useless. The light around her continued to dim.

"Almost got it now," Johanna sang.

Della knew she was close, but her voice sounded so far

away, as if she were in a tunnel somewhere deep underground.

There was a final tug, and Della stepped back with the force of it.

"Ah ha!" Johanna cried from behind her. "I knew we would get it."

That was the last thing Della heard before she fainted.

* * *

He didn't bother knocking.

The sound of frantic voices coming from within the duchess's rooms was enough to have him charging through the door. The scene he discovered there was enough to send his blood cold.

Della was unconscious on the floor. His sister straddled her, her hands tearing at what appeared to be a corset, but if that was what it was, he couldn't understand why it was so tight. It had turned Della's sinfully voluptuous body into a contorted monstrosity.

But if it were a corset that was cinched that tightly...

"Move." He shoved his sister out of the way and leaned over Della, his hands going to the edge of the corset, but the damned thing didn't budge even when he gave it all he had. "What the hell were you thinking?" He hated the menace in his voice, especially as it was directed at his littlest sister, but something unnatural gripped him, something he'd never felt before.

He had to get the damned corset off. Della wasn't breathing. She wasn't *breathing*. Fear seized him. His hands shook as he scrambled to gain purchase, and he was gripped by the sudden need to see her eyes, those blue, blue eyes that put the sky itself to shame.

"Watch out, mate."

Someone pushed at his shoulder, but he wouldn't have moved if hell itself licked at his boots.

"Andrew."

He stirred at his best friend's firm tone, and somehow, he managed to sit back, allowing Ben access.

In a single fluid motion, his friend knelt swiftly and drew a knife from his boot. Bringing it forward, he sliced neatly through the top of the corset. Ben moved with such deftness only the top of the corset split, leaving Della completely untouched. The tear was enough that the delicate fabric tore apart, the sound of ripping cloth piercing the sudden quiet in the room.

Della's lips parted softly, and he could hear her draw air into her lungs. This was immediately followed by a torrent of coughing, and he lunged forward, pulling her into his arms to help her sit up and breathe.

"Easy, darling. Easy. It's all right now." He brushed the hair from her face, ran his knuckles down the soft skin of her cheek. He had to touch her. He was overwhelmed with the need to do so and yet held himself back, cradling her until he was sure she was breathing properly. "Open your eyes, Della. I need to see your eyes."

She blinked, and he caught sight of that hypnotic blue. She seemed to register his face, and her eyelids slid shut on a groan. He could only sympathize.

He looked up to where his sister knelt on the other side of Della, her fingers speared through her hair as she held her hands pressed to her head.

"What the hell were you thinking?" He prided himself on how well modulated he kept his tone, but then he registered his sister's face. "Do you have a black eye?"

The skin around her left eye was a mottled purple hue outlined in red.

She dropped her hands. "I tried to catch her, and the crown of her head hit me in the eye."

The laugh came immediately, and he tried very hard to suppress it. It came out as not much more than a snort, but Johanna folded her arms defensively across her chest.

She looked to her husband. "Is it truly a laughable matter? Della could have died."

Ben slid his knife back in his boot. "Yes, but you can't see your face. You would be laughing too." He hid his own laugh behind a trembling smile.

"Oh bollocks, I'm so sorry."

They all looked down at the sound of the raspy words to find Della quite awake, her gaze fixated on Johanna's face and likely the blackening eye.

Johanna touched the skin around her eye gingerly. "Is it so very bad? I shall have to write to Viv immediately. It may send her into convulsions." Her grin was entirely mischievous.

Della struggled to sit up, but Andrew tightened his arms around her.

"Hang on now. Just rest and breathe. How do you feel?"

"Embarrassed." The word came out slightly stronger than the last ones, and he felt a flood of relief.

Johanna laughed. "Why should you be embarrassed? I made my new sister faint. How is that for a first impression?"

Della's lips had parted as if she wished to speak again, but her mouth shut abruptly at Johanna's words.

"I think it gives a clear understanding of just what I had warned her about," Andrew said.

Johanna's eyes widened. "Excuse me? Warned her about?" She put fisted hands to her hips. "Just what precisely must you warn her about?"

"The Darby sisters," Ben said dryly from beside them.

"Exactly," Andrew agreed.

Johanna pushed to her feet. "There is no warning required. We are quite lovely people." She cast her gaze down at Della. "Except for the minor near-death occurrences we may cause." She brushed her hands together as if it were every day she caused such a debacle.

Andrew slid his gaze to his best friend. "That's a rather interesting thing to carry in your boot." He raised an eyebrow in question.

Ben cast a glance at his wife. "And it's not the first time I've had to use it in my wife's presence."

"I thought not." Andrew frowned.

Mrs. Collins appeared then, although Andrew had a vague sense she had been in the room when everything occurred. But now she knelt before Della with a cup of tea.

"Drink slowly, Your Grace. This will help set you to rights." She met Andrew's gaze. "We should get her into the bed, Your Grace."

Reflexively his arms tightened around her, unwilling to let her go. He knew it was probably best though and loosened his grip long enough for Mrs. Collins to take Della's elbow. He kept his arms around her as Della gained her feet, and when she swayed, he tucked her under his arm. It was only a couple of feet to the bed, otherwise he would have insisted on carrying her. As it was, he didn't wish to cause her further embarrassment, as unfounded as it was.

Mrs. Collins pushed him out of the way as she and a couple of maids took to tucking Della in and plying her with tea and small biscuits. Johanna flopped on the other side of the bed and set to chattering straight away, asking if she were all right.

"I think it's probably best to allow Della to get some rest. She's had a rather taxing couple of days." Andrew attempted to drill a hole into the back of his sister's head with his glare, and it seemed to work since she pivoted to face him.

"You couldn't expect me to wait when you sent word you brought home a wife. We've waited ages to have another sister. I couldn't possibly have held off my visit until tomorrow."

Andrew looked at Ben, but his friend was carefully avoiding making eye contact.

Andrew supposed the man could not be blamed.

"Besides, I couldn't let her go without clothing, Andrew. Even you can understand what a handicap that would be."

He crossed his arms over his chest. "I can see how that would be difficult."

"If you had given her time to pack a bag…" Johanna let her words trail off.

"There was no time to pack a bag. That's inherent in the means in which we left."

Ben stepped between them and raised a friendly hand in Della's direction.

"Hello, I'm Ben." He leaned over Mrs. Collins's shoulder to allow Della to see him. "I'm married to her." He pointed to Johanna. "And best friends with your husband." He pointed over his shoulder as if Della had never met Andrew. "I'm terribly sorry about all of this, but there's no reason to worry. You have tremendous allies in the lot of us who have the unfortunate ability to say we married into this bunch."

Johanna reached over Della to punch her husband in the shoulder. Ben's smile never faltered.

Della's lips turned up into a tentative smile. "It's very nice to meet you. I look forward to meeting the others."

Ben straightened and looked back at Andrew. "She's a rather brave one, isn't she? The first sister tries to kill her, and yet she's still game for meeting the rest. Well done, Andrew."

"Just ignore them," Johanna said, patting Della's knee. "Everything will be fine. You're a Darby now, and we take care of our own. Just rest, and I'll be back in the morning, and we'll set everything to rights."

Johanna hopped from the bed. Only then did Andrew realize there was a smattering of gowns about the room as well as underthings scattered here and there. He wasn't sure exactly what had transpired, but he felt a pang of guilt for Della.

It had been a trying couple of days, and her world had been upended so completely without her permission. And then he'd accidentally sicced his sister on her. He was turning out to be a terrible husband.

But more than that, he felt the knot in his stomach tighten. He had been so fraught with worry over protecting her from her father, he had never thought to be concerned about what his own family might do to her.

He knew the image of her unconscious on the floor would haunt him forever.

He turned to the door as Johanna and Ben made their way out of the room. They said their goodbyes to Della, and Andrew followed them into the hall, shutting the door softly behind them.

They were several steps down the hall before Johanna turned on him.

"She's wonderful." Her eyes shone with excitement.

"You hardly know her."

Johanna shook her head. "It doesn't matter. I can already tell I like her."

He crossed his arms over his chest. "And how is that exactly?"

She poked him in the shoulder. "Because you like her."

He dropped his arms. "Johanna, I already explained. This wasn't—"

"You of all people should know by now it's not how something starts that matters. It's how it ends."

Andrew cast his gaze between his sister and his best friend, the truth of her words seeping deep into his bones. A curl of doubt found its way into the knot in his stomach, and he couldn't help but wonder.

What if he let himself fall in love with Della?

It wasn't as if it were impossible. He couldn't deny the consuming attraction he felt for her, and he had already admitted he liked her. It was hard not to. Della had an intrinsic ability to see the good in everything when all the evidence suggested she'd lived a neglected life. A person with innate good was irresistible. If only he weren't sworn to protect her.

"I will keep your words under advisement."

Johanna scoffed a laugh and shook her head. "You were always the stubborn one, Andrew."

He wrinkled his brow. "I am not. Viv's the stubborn one."

Johanna reared back. "You think Viv's the stubborn one?"

"Of course she is." He looked to Ben. "Isn't Viv the stubborn one?"

Ben held up both hands. "I'm not getting mixed up in this. It's enough being an innocent victim here."

He walked away in the direction of the stairs. Andrew made to follow, but his sister placed a hand on his arm.

"Andrew. Listen to me. I know I'm just your little sister, but believe it or not, I have something important to say."

He stilled, realizing for perhaps the first time that his little sister had grown up. She was married now and in charge of a household all her own. He knew firsthand the things she'd accomplished at Raeford Court to bring the old estate back to life, and he'd personally witnessed the lengths she would go to, to save the things she loved most.

Right then he felt like one of them, which left an uncomfortable weight on his chest.

"It's all right to let go sometimes and just let yourself be. You don't always need to take care of everyone."

"I don't take care of everyone," he said automatically.

Johanna dropped her hand and shook her head.

"You do, Andrew. You take care of all of us." Her eyes drifted over his shoulder to the door to the duchess's rooms. "But I think you might be surprised to find your wife doesn't require someone to take care of her."

She didn't say anything more. With a final squeeze of his arm, she left him standing there in the corridor, leaving him to wonder at a great many things.

CHAPTER 9

She had given her sister-in-law a black eye.

That was her introduction to Andrew's sisters.

A. Black. Eye.

Della groaned and buried her face in her hands, shaking it back and forth as if by doing so it would undo the events of the last several hours.

To say nothing of the fact that she'd fainted on her.

On her sister-in-law. When the poor woman had done nothing more than help her.

Della groaned again and sank back in the pillows of the bed.

She pressed a hand to her middle, willing her nerves to settle, but her resolve did little to combat her racing mind. Her first introduction as a duchess, and she'd completely flummoxed it. True, it was only a member of the family, but that still mattered to her, and she'd ruined the entire thing.

She was clearly not cut out to be a duchess, and she was going to disgrace Andrew.

The thought had her turning to the plate of biscuits Mrs. Collins had left on the table by the bed, but before she could pick one up, the light of the flickering candle caught her attention as it played over the surface of the wood. Instead of picking up a biscuit, she moved her hand to the side and traced the scar on the surface of the table.

The mark was light and faded, and it was this that drew her attention. Because the scar was wide, suggesting at some point the scratch had been deep, it also showed how lovingly it was repaired. If the candlelight hadn't flickered, and if the stain atop the scar hadn't resulted in a slightly different hue, she might not have noticed it.

She withdrew her hand and studied the table for several minutes.

From the size and quality of Ravenwood Park, as well as Andrew's carriage and dress, she assumed the Darbys were wealthy. Why then had so much furniture been repaired instead of replaced? Her grandmother was forever purchasing new furniture when there was so much as a loose thread in an upholstered chair. But here there were two pieces, in the duchess's rooms no less, that exhibited such evident marks of repair.

She snatched a biscuit and popped it into her mouth whole.

Were the Darbys impoverished?

Had she unwittingly attached herself to a man who could not afford to support her?

She closed her eyes as she chewed.

Oh, Della, why are you like this? Why are you always such a nuisance?

Surely, she must be mistaken.

She washed down her biscuit with the last of the tea Mrs. Collins had left and settled back against the pillows. She had only one clue to suggest Andrew lacked funds, and she wasn't going to let her mind get carried away with it.

After several minutes however, she knew she was nothing

but a liar. She opened her eyes and stared at the plaster medallions in the ceiling. This would never do. If she had her book, she could at least attempt to distract herself and perhaps sleep would come eventually, but at this rate, she was likely to simply lie here, her thoughts churning until she made herself sick.

She threw back the covers and stood, her nightdress falling to hardly below her knees as if to spite her.

It needn't matter. The hour was late, and the house was likely asleep. She hadn't a single notion as to the location of the library, but it was better to attempt to find it rather than lie in bed and worry.

Mrs. Collins had taken all her things to be cleaned, and so Della was barefoot when she stepped out into the corridor moments later, holding the candle from her bedside aloft to get her bearings.

Earlier Mrs. Collins had brought her up the central staircase and turned right to follow the corridor into the west wing of the house. Della would simply retrace her steps. It was likely the library was on the floor below somewhere. It would be a room available to guests, which would suggest it wouldn't be located in the same wing as the family rooms.

The long corridor stretched before her gloomily, and she shut her eyes. Melanie Merkett would never be afraid of shadows in the night. She opened her eyes and pressed ahead.

Her candle flickered with an unseen draft, and she raised a hand to shield it. If she lost her light, she'd likely lose her way and then where would she be? Andrew would find her asleep on the floor wherever it was she had stopped in the dark, unable to find her way and simply gone to sleep where she was.

She found the staircase without trouble and made her way down. The marble was cold against her feet, but she kept going. The quiet began to grate. Where did the servants sleep? Where did Andrew sleep, for that matter?

Her grandmother and grandfather slept in different wings. Was that how all homes of the peerage were constructed? She didn't know.

She made her way around the staircase to the corridor Mrs. Collins must have emerged from earlier to find a similar hallway as the one above. It stretched in opposite directions in a seemingly endless march, and Della swayed with the enormity of it.

She turned right. After all, if the library weren't down this wing, she could simply turn around and go in the other direction.

By rights, she should have been exhausted, both emotionally and physically. The last three days had completely changed her life, and yet this was the way with a nervous disposition. Sometimes the worry was too great, and sleep was just not to be had.

She was nearly to the end of the corridor without finding success. The doorways she had passed had all led into various drawing rooms, a music room differentiated by the presence of a piano, a breakfast room, and what might have been a ladies' salon. It was hard to tell from the meager light of her candle, but that room had been furnished with a good number of settees and embroidery hoop stands.

She took several more steps before a noise at the end of the corridor caused her to freeze.

Someone had opened a door.

She was never in her life more aware of her underdressed state than she was at that moment. She had no wrap and no slippers. She could almost feel the chill of the night air cut through her thin nightdress as if she wore nothing at all, and heavens, her ankles were still hanging out for all to see.

She took a step back.

Should she try to hide? From whom was she hiding? And where would she go?

Footsteps, soft and steady, came from the shadows at the end of the corridor.

She should hide.

But as soon as the thought formed, a man appeared in the dimness ahead.

"Della?"

Relief sang through her at the realization it was only Andrew. And then she realized it was Andrew, and she crossed her free arm over her torso as if that would hide anything.

It needn't matter anyway. He had already seen everything after the debacle earlier. He and that other man, Ben. Was he also a duke? Lud, she was a disaster unto herself.

"I couldn't sleep," she stammered in her haste to get the words out.

Andrew was in front of her within an instant. "Are you hurt? Unwell? Is there something I can get for you?"

She could see his face now that he'd stepped into the ring of candlelight, and his features were drawn with worry.

She smiled as brightly as possible. "No, no. It's nothing like that. All is well. If you could just point me in the direction of the library, I'll be sure to get right out of the way."

She thought he would be relieved to hear she required nothing from him, but instead, his brow furrowed more deeply.

"The library?"

"I lost my book if you recall. I was hoping I might be allowed to select one from your library."

Something passed over his eyes then, and she swallowed, taking a step back.

"Of course I should have asked for your permission. I'm terribly sorry. I shan't overstep again, I promise. So sorry. I'll just go back to my—" She had turned to flee when he caught her arm, turning her back to him.

"Della, of course you may read a book from the library. Read as many as you would like." He slipped her arm through his and took the candle from her. "The library is this way."

She thrilled at the way he so naturally took her arm, the way he pressed it to his side and wove his fingers through hers as if he were afraid of losing her in the dark.

"Are you sure you're not feeling unwell? I can send for a doctor."

"No." She said the word quickly, embarrassment flooding through her at the thought he might go to so much trouble for her. "I'm fine really. It's only sometimes I have difficulty sleeping when my mind is preoccupied."

He squeezed her hand. "I know the past several days have been unexpected, but I promise you are safe now."

She liked the way his voice took on a deeper note when he spoke of caring for her. It was such a novelty to know someone else was thinking of her with such a care, but it also gave her cause for more worrying. She didn't want his care to turn into obligation.

They had returned to the main staircase then and continued along the corridor.

"This is an interesting construction for a house, isn't it? With long corridors such as this."

"The third Duke of Ravenwood enjoyed foot races."

She peered up at him. "I beg your pardon?"

He flashed her a sardonic grin. "He enjoyed foot races, but he didn't like getting his shoes wet. He constructed the house to conduct foot races during house parties no matter the weather."

She stopped and faced him. "Surely you jest."

He raised an eyebrow. "I do no such thing. You would be surprised what men are capable of when they obtain both wealth and leisure. They must find something to occupy their time." His tone changed at the final sentence, almost as though he were reflecting inwardly, and she wondered at that.

He nodded to the door behind her. "The library, Your Grace."

She turned to find an oak-paneled door slightly ajar. She pushed it open without hesitation and stepped through, only to stop in her tracks once more.

Her grandfather had boasted of Bewcastle's library, but it was nothing compared to this. The room in which she found herself was several yards in width and stacked two stories tall. The walls were lined with bookcases, both on the main floor and on the balcony above. Library ladders dotted them, and she could just make out a circular wrought iron staircase in the far corner that intruded onto the balcony above.

A fireplace interrupted the books at one end of the room and at this end there was a long wide table as if inviting one to sample several books at once. Tall windows broke up the bookcases on the opposite wall. She was pleased to see window benches installed in each of them, and she thought of the rainy days she might spend there.

It occurred to her for the first time that this was for the rest of her life. Ravenwood Park, Andrew, and this library. What had that gentleman said earlier? She had married into this bunch, the Darbys. She was one of them now. It hadn't really settled in until she saw those window benches, and finally she could see herself there.

She felt a weight shift along her shoulders. It didn't disappear, but she could carry it better now.

She turned to thank Andrew, only to find him leaning in the doorway, a curious expression on his face. Almost as if she'd caught him in the middle of pondering something. Something about her.

Her momentary lightness fled at the sight of his face, and she raised her chin. "What is it?" she ventured.

He shook his head, and when he spoke her toes curled into the floorboards from just the growly sound of his voice. But his words, his words undid her.

"It's just that you're so beautiful in the moonlight."

* * *

HE HATED how his words could bring that wary look to her face, almost like she didn't trust him. Such behavior was learned, and he hated that she was taught to distrust kindness.

He pushed away from the door and went to her, lifting his hand to cradle her cheek in his palm even as he told himself to leave her be.

But he couldn't resist touching her, feeling her smooth skin against his palm, hearing the way her breath caught when he caressed her. He stroked her plump lower lip with his thumb, thrilling at the way he could light the fire in her eyes with such a simple touch.

"You're always so beautiful, and yet you don't seem to know it," he whispered, tracing the line of her lips now, following the path of her jaw until he slipped his thumb beneath her chin and tilted her face to accept his kiss.

Only he didn't kiss her. He drew his lips close, close enough that he could smell the clean scent of her skin, but he didn't kiss her. He hovered just over her lips, knowing how it must torment her.

"Do you know how beautiful you are, Della? Can you understand?" He whispered the words across her lips, and he felt the flutter of her eyelashes, but she didn't answer him.

He pressed his lips to the corner of her mouth, lightly,

teasingly. He moved to the other corner, and this time pressed just a degree harder.

Still, she didn't move, didn't whimper. But he saw the way her chest rose and fell in rapid breaths, heard the flutter of her eyelashes against her cheeks.

He whispered his lips over the line of her cheekbone to her temple and pressed a kiss against the soft skin there.

"So beautiful," he murmured with his lips still pressed against her skin.

He slipped his arm around her waist carefully, his hand tracing lightly along her back. He could feel every knot of her spine through the thin fabric of her borrowed nightdress, and he knew if he only closed the distance between them, wrapped his arm more tightly around her, he could feel all of her pressed against him.

He wanted it at the same time he was afraid of it. He couldn't let himself lose control again. Every time he let his guard down something happened, and he couldn't afford to do it again. No matter how much he craved her kisses or how beautiful she looked with moonlight spilling over her.

Then why was his hand moving lower and lower still? Why did he press his lips to her forehead, her cheeks, her jaw?

She sighed. The sound was so soft, so wistful, he almost thought it a dream, but then she moved. It was so slight, he might have made it up, but her body curved. Not into him, but into the place where his lips touched her jaw, almost as if her body yearned for more.

It was then his resolve snapped. He could feel it let go entirely like a dam breaking. Desire rushed into all those places he had so resolutely barricaded, and he wondered why he had attempted it at all.

He grabbed her, wrapping his arm fully around her until she pressed against the length of him, and it was just as glorious as he knew it would be. He groaned against the soft place just in front of her ear where his lips were pressed. Groaned with the ecstasy of it and the anticipation. He could feel every curve as she fitted against him, and now he wanted to touch her everywhere.

He pulled away far enough to capture her mouth and steal the kiss with which he had teased them both. He plundered and took, heedless of her desire, but it didn't matter. Her moan told him all he needed to know.

He buried his hand in her hair, holding her against his kiss while he explored her mouth, her lips. His hand at her back traveled farther, daring to cup her buttocks and pull her snuggly against him.

God, he was hard, and the feel of her soft body against his was almost enough to undo him. He knew she could feel the length of him, and she didn't shy away from it. Instead, she put her hands against his back, her fingers digging into his muscles. Fire burned through him, and he found his fingers clawing for the hem of her nightdress.

He shifted, guiding Della backward until they reached the table that sat at the end of the room. Only then did he allow his exploring fingers to gain purchase, pushing her nightdress to her hips.

God, as suspected she wore nothing under it, and she was bared to him. *Finally.* But it wasn't enough. He wanted to see all of her. In the moonlight. Now.

He pressed her back until she was on top of the table. He tried to remember that this was still very new to her, and he pleasured her with the kisses he knew she enjoyed.

"Please let me touch you," he whispered against her ear, but her hands had already found their way to his shoulders, her fingers pressing into his flesh.

"You must touch me. Please," she whispered back, and he couldn't help but smile at her urgency.

He wasn't alone in this. Whatever this was between them it was mutual, and it only served to make him burn hotter.

He ran his open palms along the curves of her thighs, spreading her legs for him. He traced the pale skin to where it ended in the nest of curls at her mound, but he wouldn't let himself go farther.

Instead, he followed the line of her torso up to where a neat line of buttons marched their way down her front. He spent aching seconds undoing each one, knowing that if he ripped the nightdress from her, she would be without clothing entirely. When the last button slipped free, he shoved the nightdress from her shoulders. He pulled her arms from around him and pressed each of her open palms to the table behind her. The loosened fabric of the nightdress spilled down her arms revealing her breasts to him.

He stilled as the moonlight fell over her. Her breasts were full and magnificent, the nipples puckered in the chill night air. He wanted to stroke her breasts, suck each of the nipples into his mouth in turn, but he did none of that. He lifted a solitary finger and traced the curve of her right breast, following the pale skin to the dusty pink of her areole.

"I've never seen anything more beautiful." The words were choked with desire, and finally he bent his head, replacing his finger with his lips.

She arched into him, a cry escaping her lips, and he wrapped his arms around her until she was bending over them, offering her full breasts to him. And he took. He was not strong enough to resist, and when her fingers returned to his shoulders, her grip frantic, he lost what little resolve he had left.

He sucked her nipple, rolling his tongue around it, before moving to the other breast, delivering the same exquisite torture.

He traced the line of her breastbone with his tongue,

traveled up the column of her neck until he captured her mouth once more. She writhed in his arms now, her mound pressing against his hard penis until he was afraid he would come in his trousers. He had to be inside of her, and it had to be fast.

He pulled away, his fingers scrambling to undo the buttons of his trousers.

"Andrew." The sound of his name, weak with her desire, almost undid him.

Finally he was free, and he gripped her hips, pulling her to the edge of the table. He buried himself in her in a single, smooth thrust. He groaned with the ecstasy of it. She spasmed around him, her muscles tightening at his intrusion, and his fingers flexed into the softness at her hips.

"Saints, Della, you feel too good."

Her head was thrown back, but she looked up at this, her eyes half-closed as desire tightened her features.

"Too good?" Her voice was breathless, but he could still hear the uncertainty.

He pulled her against him, her breasts pressed against his chest, and he knew the next time he would have time to undress. He wanted to feel her naked body against his. The way her nipples hardened, the rounded softness of her belly, the supple curve of her thigh over his hip. He wanted all of it.

"Too good," he repeated against her lips, nibbling playfully before sucking her lower lip into his mouth.

He began to move, sliding into her in long, even strokes until she whimpered. Only when he thought she couldn't bare it any longer did he pick up his tempo, moving faster, harder against her. He kneaded the soft skin at her hips as he tightened his grip, holding her even as she squirmed against him.

"Andrew, please," she moaned.

He slipped a hand between them and found her sensitive

nub. He flicked his thumb across it, once, twice, thrice, and she jerked against him as her muscles tightened along his shaft.

"Oh God, Della. Please tell me this feels good. I want it to be so good for you."

"It is," she whispered. "It's so…so…" But her voice faded away as her head fell back, as her fingernails dug into the skin at the back of his neck.

He circled her nub at the same time he withdrew and plunged, moving deeper within her. He could almost feel her tighten, sense the crescendo of her climax as it grew. He resisted the urge to bury himself within her, to pound her into her release and his. He held himself back, torturing her with each deliberate stroke.

"Andrew, please," she moaned again, and this time she lifted her hips, grinding against him even as he tried to hold her at bay.

The sensation was too intense, and he felt himself slip, felt the edge of his release too close.

"Della," he moaned, and his need overtook him.

He pounded into her now. Vaguely he heard the scrape of the table legs against the floor as he buried himself in her over and over again. Her full breasts bounced with the force of his thrusts, and he reveled in it, capturing one to knead against his palm, rolling the nipple between his fingers, unable to resist touching her just a little longer.

But it was too much. She was too wet and too tight.

He flicked his thumb over her nub relentlessly, and he felt the moment her orgasm hit her. She went entirely still around him, and he leaned forward, letting himself go.

The power of his release buckled his legs, and he put his hands against the edge of the table to hold himself up. When a semblance of strength returned, he straightened and gathered her into his arms, holding her against him.

He didn't want to think about how perfectly she fit there, nestled in his arms, her head just under his chin. Slowly his breathing evened out, and the strength slowly returned to his legs, but he didn't let go of her. He held her and wondered why he enjoyed that even more than making love to her.

It felt so good to just hold her.

But she hadn't made a single sound, and she'd grown impossibly still in his arms. Reluctantly he drew back far enough to see her face.

"Della, are you all right?" He placed a single finger beneath her chin to raise her face so he could see her expression.

When her eyes fluttered opened, he thought he saw a dampness there, and fear that he might have hurt her spiraled through him. But then she blinked, and he thought it only a trick of the moonlight.

"I'm quite all right," she said, but her voice was soft.

"You should be in bed." He reached for the nightdress that was still caught along her arms. "I shouldn't have kept you up."

He withdrew from her only when he afforded her the decency of her nightdress. He turned away while he fixed his trousers and when he turned back, she had slipped off the table, the nightdress returned to rights as if nothing had ever happened.

He held out his hand to her. "Come. You'll need your sleep before we leave for London."

She had been reaching for his hand but stopped at his words.

"London?" Her eyes widened, and even in the dimness he could see the very real trepidation in them.

"Yes, London. I want to put as much distance between us and Scotland as possible."

"But aren't there things required of a duchess in London? I haven't any training and—"

"Don't worry," he said, stepping forward to snatch the hand that lay forgotten at her side. "My sisters will be there to help you."

What little color he could see in her face drained away.

"I gave the last sister who tried to help me a black eye."

He laughed. "Yes, but she deserved that. I know you will find Eliza and Louisa to be much more helpful."

CHAPTER 10

She didn't know how long she would have to worry about her next encounter with one of the Darby sisters, and so she worried about that too.

Della would admit she had been somewhat relieved when Johanna appeared the morning after the great corset debacle with the seamstress from the village in tow, along with two patterned gowns that would be adequate to see Della to London where a modiste could have a new wardrobe made up.

While the gowns were a welcomed sight, Della had been more pleased to have the opportunity to make amends with her new sister-in-law, but Johanna only waved her apology off. Apparently, worse had occurred between Johanna and her sisters in their childhood, and it was nothing to sport a black eye now. In fact, according to Johanna, she found it intriguing and enjoyed conjuring stories to tell people of what had happened.

Siblings were strange beings, Della was coming to learn.

As for the new wardrobe, she didn't see the reason for such expenditure when she was sure she could send for the rest of her clothing from her grandparents' home, but Andrew said she needn't bother. A new wardrobe was hardly a consideration.

This news had perplexed her as she continued to ponder over the state of the repaired furniture at Ravenwood Park. It seemed she wasn't quite sure what to make of Ravenwood, both the estate and the man.

For she was certain no one had ever been made love to so thoroughly as Andrew made love to her, and yet outside of the ducal bedchamber, it was as though she didn't exist.

It was hard for her to interpret his actions, and she knew she was prone to believe there was some fault with her. But how could…

Well, she turned pink when she thought of it. The things he did to her…to put it plainly, she hadn't even heard of them in the novels she had read, and she had read a great many novels.

After the interlude in the library, he had escorted her directly back to bed, but instead of returning her to the duchess's rooms, he'd ushered her into his own. She hadn't realized the rooms were connected, and when she entered the ducal chamber, she had a difficult time keeping her eyes from straying to the connecting door.

Had he meant to keep her close all along, or was he simply placing her in the bedroom that her title required?

She just didn't know, and her lack of experience was enough to send her stomach into a tumbling routine that would be the envy of any circus performer.

She'd slept in his arms that night. It was becoming quite a habit, and one she found utterly delightful. She'd fallen immediately to sleep with Andrew's reassuring weight pressed to her back, and the next morning had felt more like herself than she had in days.

A good night's rest coupled with a new, clean gown had

her spirits restored when they set off for London until she discovered Andrew would not be riding in the carriage with her but had insisted on riding horseback out front. He claimed he wanted to be aware of their surroundings as they made their way south, should anyone be following them, but Della couldn't help but feel a pang of guilt that he might find her presence in the carriage suffocating.

She normally would have enjoyed spending the long quiet hours with a good book, but she'd forgotten to retrieve a novel from the Ravenwood library, for which she wholeheartedly blamed Andrew for distracting her, even though she knew her thoughts were too jumbled to concentrate on a text at that moment.

Her mind was ablaze with the memory of the night before, and she touched her torso and chest where Andrew had…well, it still astonished her. The things he'd done. The things he had said. She almost felt…desirable.

When they arrived at the first posting inn that night, she expected Andrew to acquire separate rooms, but he didn't. He ushered her into a small room much like the one they'd shared on their wedding night and shut the door behind them, sending the lock home with resolution.

She slept once more in his arms after another thorough lovemaking session, but the next morning, Andrew was once more atop his horse, and she spoke naught to him except for when they stopped to attend to necessities.

Was this how marriage worked? Was he simply using her to fulfill her duties as his duchess? She just didn't know, and more, she didn't have anyone to ask.

She knew their marriage had been the result of impossible circumstances, and she wasn't one to construct illusions of grandeur. But surely not every husband made love to his wife the way Andrew did to her. Surely not every husband in an arranged marriage said such heartbreakingly kind things to his wife.

Her heart tripped on the memories she captured every night on their journey south. She remembered the name of every posting inn, of every hamlet and village they found themselves in, and she couldn't help but worry that it might all end when they reached London and Andrew discovered how ill-fitted she was to be a duchess.

Would he send her back to Ravenwood Park? Banish her to the depths of Yorkshire where no one would know of her ineptitude?

Her heart squeezed at the idea, and she pressed a hand to her chest. It couldn't possibly happen, but it didn't mean she could stop her wandering thoughts from straying to the most sinister of outcomes.

Of course none of this came to be, and if she ever learned from her own experience, she would worry far less. For when they arrived in London, it was much as it was every other time they arrived at a destination on their journey.

Andrew introduced her to the household servants before taking her immediately upstairs to bed.

Well, it wasn't quite like that. They had arrived well past sunset, and Andrew had ordered a bath and a tray sent up. It had been a long trek on the road, and she was rather dusty, hungry, and tired. The thought of facing both her new staff and another new house was gut-wrenchingly exhausting.

It was as if Andrew knew as much, and he tucked her away in the ducal chambers once more. After lingering in a warm bath, she found him picking at the supper tray in the sitting room.

She joined him but found her appetite was not as ravenous as it should have been. Her nerves were just as tightly wound as ever, and yet the Cornish hen and potatoes held little appeal.

THE DUKE AND THE LASS

Tomorrow would be her first day in London society as the Duchess of Ravenwood, and she wanted nothing more than to sleep.

Again, it was as though Andrew could read her thoughts, and instead of making love to her, he tucked her into bed and in his arms, and she slept.

She was rather grateful for this when the next morning she found another Darby sister at breakfast.

Della had managed to find her way to the breakfast room after Andrew left her early that morning to check in with his solicitors and was feeling rather proud of herself when she stumbled on the threshold, her eyes fixated on the blonde beauty chewing thoughtfully on a piece of toast while perusing the newspapers.

She looked up and smiled, her wide blue eyes extraordinary. "You must be Della." She dropped her toast and, brushing her hands on her napkin, stood.

Della prepared a curtsy as she was sure this sister was another duchess, but before she could move, the woman swept her into an embrace tighter than the one Johanna had given her.

"Oh, I'm so glad you've finally arrived." She pulled back and studied Della's face. "When we received Johanna's letter, we couldn't imagine what Andrew had done, but Johanna had nothing but wonderful things to say about our new sister, and we couldn't wait to meet you."

"We?" Della asked, although she wasn't even sure which sister it was she spoke with.

She vaguely recalled Andrew saying Louisa was the fairer of the two sisters who resided in London, but at the moment, her thoughts had taken to jumbling about her head as she tried her best to act as a duchess would.

And much to her annoyance, she also concentrated overly much on not giving this sister a black eye.

Louisa laughed and pulled Della in for another hug. "Oh, I'm so sorry. There are quite a few of us." She pulled away but captured Della's hand to draw her back to the table. "I'm Louisa. Eliza said I should be the one to take you to the modiste today as Eliza is not enamored of fashion."

Louisa sat Della down in the chair next to the one she had been occupying and oddly enough went to the sideboard and began to fill a fresh plate. She returned within seconds and placed the full plate in front of Della.

Della could only stare. Her grandmother was never one to partake heartily in meals and had regularly scolded Della for eating too much. Yet Louisa had piled the plate with eggs and sausages and tomatoes as though it were no matter.

"You'll want to eat up," Louisa said then, and Della realized she had been staring at her plate for too long. "A trip to the modiste can be taxing, and you'll want your strength."

Della picked up her fork. "I've never had a session with a modiste."

Louisa sat back in her chair with a shake of her head. "Andrew said you might be inexperienced with such things."

Della looked up at this. "Andrew said that?"

What did that mean? Did he already suspect she would fail him as a duchess?

"I caught him just as he was headed out the door this morning. He always seems rather cross when one of us appears at his doorstep." Her grin was playful. "I can't say I blame him. We're rather a troublesome lot."

Della swallowed her eggs. "He indicated as much. His trip to Scotland was rather brief for such a long journey to get there. He seemed to feel the pressure of familiar obligations required his immediate return."

Louisa's brow wrinkled. "Andrew said that?"

Della nodded. "Yes." She worried her lower lip. "Well, he did say that before the necessity of our marriage became

THE DUKE AND THE LASS

apparent. He said he wished to return to London almost immediately."

"How odd. He told Johanna he was planning to take a long holiday."

Doubt speared Della directly through the chest, and she stabbed another bite of sausage. "Oh?"

Louisa shook her head. "I'm almost certain of it. Perhaps something came up that I'm not aware of."

Della.

Della was what had come up. She had ruined Andrew's holiday; she was sure of it. Drat and feathers. She stabbed another sausage. She would make it up to him. She had to. She would request the latest fashions from the modiste that day and show Andrew she could be exactly the duchess he required. The thought helped to push back the guilt that swamped her.

"Perhaps," Della said now with a forced smile.

Louisa clapped her hands together, suddenly changing the subject. "Oh, I am so very glad you're here. We've waited such a long time for Andrew to wed. It was as if he were waiting for the rest of us to get through our eldest sister Viv's quest to see us all married. It will be so lovely having another sister."

Johanna had said that as well, and something uncomfortable wedged itself in Della's chest, almost as if she feared Louisa would discover her for the impostor she was. For surely Della couldn't be a sister. She'd never been one before. She didn't know what it entailed, and if her history were any indication, she would fail at this too.

She set down her fork. "Well then perhaps it would be best if we were to get started. I'm sure it will take some time for the modiste to fashion my new wardrobe, and I should have obligations in town as the Duchess of Ravenwood." It was a statement, but she was hoping it would lead to Louisa revealing more about what would be required of Della. She hadn't had time to find a book in Ravenwood's library about such things, and now she had no other method of discovering what it was she was expected to do.

Louisa pushed up from her chair, her smile bright. "You are absolutely right, Della. There is so much to be done." She helped Della to her feet and squeezed her hand. "We are going to make you the most splendid Duchess of Ravenwood yet."

Della smiled even though Louisa could not know just how important her words were.

* * *

Andrew had only been to Ashbourne House but one time, and that was for his sister's wedding.

His recollection of that time had been a bit of a blur. Viv had only returned to Ravenwood House months before, shattered from finding her husband abed with an opera singer. He had been so sure of the Duke of Margate for a match, and when she had come home, it had shaken his foundation.

He could recall too clearly the moment she had walked into his study, her eyes swollen from crying, her hands twisting the fabric of her skirts as she tried to maintain her composure.

He'd made a mistake, and it had cost his sister so much.

He swore then to never make that mistake again. So, when Dax Kane, the Duke of Ashbourne, had asked for Eliza's hand in marriage, Andrew had taken a different tactic. He'd asked Eliza if she wished for the marriage.

He had learned from Viv that it needn't matter if the match looked good on paper. It didn't matter if everything came back above board from Andrew's discreet poking into a suitor's background. All of that was only preliminary.

He'd done a thorough investigation into Margate when he'd asked for Viv's hand, and Andrew had found the man satisfactory and granted his blessing. But he never asked Viv if she wished for the marriage.

He regretted it still, even though she and Ryder had worked things out between them.

Now it appeared he would be responsible for the future of another woman, and because of that, he found himself knocking on Ashbourne's door.

He was admitted straightway and taken to the duke's study. Andrew glanced around but neither saw nor heard any evidence of Eliza. He wondered if she were still abed at this hour as she was well into her second pregnancy.

The butler announced him and quietly backed out of the room. Dax stood upon seeing Andrew, and it struck him that they had never been acquaintances before the man had married his sister, and he wondered why. Like many other things, when he became responsible for his sisters his focus tended to preclude all else, including friendships.

"I understand congratulations are in order," Dax said by way of greeting. "But I have a feeling if you're standing at my door this early in the morning, there might be more to your hasty marriage than you've let on."

"I'm afraid I've come to ask for your help."

Dax held up a hand and went to the bell pull in the corner. A footman arrived quickly, and Dax dispatched him with a murmured command.

"Coffee?" He asked of Andrew when he turned back from the now closed door.

Andrew eyed the cart that sat beside the duke's desk and nodded. "I think that's probably in order."

Dax poured and handed him the cup before pouring one for himself. Instead of settling at his desk, he indicated for Andrew to take one of the chairs arranged around the fireplace.

He'd hardly taken a sip of his coffee when the door opened again.

"My wife hurried off to Ravenwood House before she had her breakfast. I trust the urgency was a matter of necessity." Sebastian Fielding, the Duke of Waverly, barged into the room.

He barged into any room really, and Andrew did not take this as a sign of aggression.

Dax held up his cup. "Please help yourself to coffee. I think we might need it."

Sebastian paused and slid his gaze to Andrew. "Ravenwood, you look as though hell itself is licking at your boots. Whatever is it, man?"

Andrew held up his cup. "Marriage, I'm afraid."

Sebastian joined them after fetching himself a cup of coffee, reclining in a chair and resting one hand along the arm of it, his fingers tapping gently. "To that I can attest."

"So, what is it you need our help with?" Dax asked.

Andrew took a fortifying sip of his coffee and told them. He relayed what he had discovered at MacKenzie Keep, the night he had barricaded himself in Della's room, and the subsequent rescue. Their journey south in the middle of the night and the resulting marriage. He told them everything.

"I met with my solicitors this morning, and they assure me the union is legal and binding. The MacKenzie has no footing on which to retrieve his daughter."

"But you don't trust him, especially because you denied him the benefits of a marriage contract," Dax supplied.

Andrew shook his head. "I'm afraid he'll try something rash like taking her by brute force."

"Does he know it was you?" Sebastian asked.

Again, Andrew shook his head. "I can't know for certain, but the morning we left the inn at Brydekirk the mail coach had just arrived. The driver said the MacKenzie was looking for his missing daughter in Kettleholm."

"So he knew she was missing fairly quickly, but you said you created the ruse that you had left much earlier in the day."

"I did. I left first thing that morning."

Dax propped an ankle on the opposite knee. "That should be plenty of time to establish an alibi. You shouldn't be a thought in his mind in regards to his daughter's disappearance."

"I shouldn't, but I can't trust that completely." Andrew pressed his fingers against his coffee cup. "Too many people saw us in Brydekirk for me to be certain of our getaway."

"How many people?" Sebastian asked.

"I was forced to use a seamstress to conduct the ceremony. She was clearly a charlatan."

"And you don't think she would be above revealing what she knows in exchange for earning a coin?" Dax asked.

"Precisely." Andrew didn't like the feeling he got in his gut when he thought of Madame Liliberte. "There was also the innkeeper, but he seemed to be more inclined to keep our secret."

"Did you conceal your identities?" Sebastian this time.

Andrew shook his head. "I didn't conceal my name. I was hoping should the MacKenzie make inquiries he would only learn that I had stayed at an inn in Brydekirk that night. I never used Della's full name. It was only on the testimonial of the ceremony and that was all."

Sebastian leaned forward, elbows to knees. "If anyone is going to tell it would be this Madame Liliberte person?"

"Most likely, yes."

Dax set down his cup. "What is it that you require from us?"

"While I know our marriage is legal, I don't trust the MacKenzie not to resort to physical force."

Dax's expression turned grim. "Do you think he might try to hurt her?"

Andrew shook his head. "I think he might try to kidnap her."

"Hell's teeth. He can't do that," Sebastian said in a hissed whisper.

"But he might try it. He assembled those men at MacKenzie Keep for a reason. You know how he's regarded in Parliament. He was looking for an ally, and I've denied him of that."

"The man is a right awful bastard," Sebastian stated calmly.

"Yes, he is, and I think he planned to gain influence by leveraging his daughter."

"What sort of father would do such a thing?"

Andrew recalled the frayed hem of Della's traveling cloak as he'd seen it that first night.

"I have a suspicion Della has been largely ignored by her family. I wouldn't be surprised at all if her father were using her only for the political advantage."

Sebastian sat up, his fingers returning to the arm of his chair with a rapid staccato. "This is madness. Should we go to the Metropolitan police?"

Dax answered, "What would be the point? They couldn't do anything as a crime hasn't been committed, and it's not as if they would attempt to interfere with a member of the peerage."

Andrew knew his brother-in-law was right. While the police force was a step toward orderly justice in London, it was still in its infancy and trod carefully around those who had felt above the law for hundreds of years—namely titled gentlemen.

"Unfortunately, I think you're right. My only other alternative is to ask that—"

"We watch out for her," Dax finished.

Andrew nodded. "Yes, exactly."

He hated asking for help, but his need to protect Della trumped his own pride. He would do anything to keep her safe, and if it meant enlisting the aid of his brothers-in-law, he could take comfort in knowing there was more than just he looking out for her safety.

He knew his own judgment was getting cloudier every day he spent with her. The journey to London had been the longest one of his life. He thought by choosing to ride he would avoid the proximity of a carriage. The idea of a week spent cloistered in a carriage with Della was both heaven and hell. He had to stay objective if he were to keep her safe, and yet...

He couldn't seem to stop touching her, kissing her, making love to her.

He was like a randy youth again in his first blush of lust. He craved Della the way some men craved gold or opium. And yet he continued to push her away.

He was aware he was doing it, and he couldn't stop it. It was only fair that she should demand an explanation for the way he treated her, but he couldn't help but think he continued to treat her the way he did because he knew she would never question it.

He was an absolute bastard for doing it. For taking advantage of her like that. He got to enjoy every piece of her except the one that would hinder his judgment.

Because he knew if he spent even more time with her, he might just lose his heart to her, and that would never work. He couldn't protect her if he fell in love with her. He had already failed to protect his sister whom he loved dearly. He couldn't allow it to happen again.

He had to maintain his distance. He would give her his nights, but he couldn't afford to give her his days.

And he hated himself for it.

It wasn't supposed to have been like this. He had always expected to marry some quiet debutante from an old and weighty title. They would have children, of course, and God willing, an heir to carry on the title. But Andrew had never expected more than that. In fact, he would have preferred it.

But that just wasn't how it was with Della.

She was fire and thunder and rain and wind all at once, and she could never be contained. How could a woman who tried so very hard to remain unnoticed cause such a disruption in his life?

Her life had been completely upended, and she'd been forced to marry a man she hardly knew in order to protect herself, and yet all she asked for was a library.

"You know we will do everything we can to help." Dax turned to Sebastian. "We should ask around at our club to see if anyone has heard of the MacKenzie poking around for favors."

Sebastian nodded. "It could give us an idea of what he might be hoping to accomplish through his daughter's marriage." Sebastian pushed to his feet. "I'll head there now. I would think we would wish to exercise discretion in this matter. We wouldn't want any additional attention brought on the Duchess of Ravenwood, am I correct?"

Andrew stood as well. "Della has spent the whole of her life in her grandparents' castle in Cumbria. I can't imagine how much she will be forced to reckon with in the coming days. I wish very much to spare her undue strain."

Dax stood then. "Of course. We'll keep our inquiries as discreet as possible. In the meantime, I think it's probably best if we were to host a dinner here so you may introduce her to society. We'll be able to control the guests that way."

"Thank you. That is more than I could have asked for." Andrew felt something shift at his brother-in-law's kindness.

"Don't thank me. My wife would have my head if I didn't offer." His smile only too clearly showed his true affection for his wife, and Andrew felt a spark of envy.

They said their goodbyes and left Dax in his study. Andrew planned to head toward Ravenwood House, knowing Della would be occupied with Louisa at the modiste's when Sebastian stopped him with a hand on his arm.

"I think we've come to a point where we can be honest with one another. Don't you agree, Andrew?"

It was the first time Waverly had used his given name, and Andrew felt a moment's unease.

"I suppose it is."

"I think you may have suspected that Louisa and I did not wed of our own volition."

His statement struck bone as Andrew had long suspected something had forced Waverly's hand. He turned to face the man fully now, his fists involuntarily flexing.

"I had a suspicion."

"Louisa wished to keep the details of our marriage private because she said you took your sisters' protection rather personally. I hope you can forgive me for concealing matters from you. I always wish to keep my wife happy."

Andrew couldn't fault the man for that, and as his wife was Andrew's sister, he was almost glad to hear it. Almost.

"What is it you are trying to say?"

Waverly looked about them as if he were suddenly uncomfortable, and Andrew recalled how the man had always been called the Beastly Duke before Louisa had married him. He wondered how uncomfortable this conversation was making him, and Andrew straightened, understanding how important this must be to Waverly.

"Louisa and I did not begin our marriage in love, but we found it along the way. I only hope you will consider as much in your own marriage. I know your sisters would wish to see you happy."

Andrew shifted. "I find the emotion of love can cloud one's judgment. Della deserves—"

"From what I've heard of Her Grace, she deserves to be loved." Waverly spoke the words quietly.

"But someone must protect her."

Waverly's smile was knowing. "You might be surprised at how capable the women we love are of protecting themselves."

He walked away then, leaving Andrew to ponder just how tired he was of such knowing smiles from his sisters' husbands.

CHAPTER 11

She felt like a cream puff.
This was not the worst of it, however.
She also looked like one.

Louisa had taken her to Beauchamp's Boutique on a street chocked full of equally tasteful establishments. Della knew she should have remembered the name of the street. Louisa said it was London's shopping district, but Della had been too overwhelmed by the traffic and people and noise so recalled very little of it. It was all just a blur in her mind.

It must have been for had she been thinking clearly, she never would have agreed to whatever it was she was wearing. But then, she hadn't agreed, had she?

She closed her eyes and tried to picture the shop. Madame Beauchamp was a kind woman, probably a handful of years older than Della, which had been a relief. Della hadn't been sure what to expect, and her mind kept conjuring images of Madame Liliberte, no matter how hard she tried to rid the woman from her thoughts. But Madame Beauchamp was nothing like that. For one, she smelled of roses, and her shop possessed nothing fouler than the lingering aroma of brewed tea.

Della couldn't even have said if she had seen any of the gowns that were displayed about the shop. She had marched up to the proprietress and stated she wanted gowns in all the latest fashions and colors.

Della tried to remember what happened after that. She remembered a good deal of negotiating on the part of Louisa, but Madame Beauchamp had been dutiful in fulfilling Della's requests.

Louisa had been right to try to negotiate with her. It was easily apparent that London's latest fashions were made for women with a healthier complexion and smaller hips.

And a great deal smaller bosom it would seem.

Della adjusted her bodice, but it did no good. Distressingly, she pictured her breasts springing free at any moment, and if her luck continued as it had been of late, they would pop free and into her soup course.

She studied her reflection in the mirror of her dressing table, her eyes focused on the delicate button that held the top of her bodice in place.

One single, solitary, lonely button. It was all that was holding her bosom in, and Della did not like the idea of her modesty resting on so very little.

There was nothing to be done for it. She raised her chin. These were the latest fashions, and she would be the best duchess for Andrew.

"Almost finished here, Your Grace," said Parker, the upstairs maid who had been promoted to Della's lady's maid.

Della thought it was rather unnecessary, but the butler, Mallard, had insisted. Now Parker expertly twisted Della's hair into a perfect chignon with small curls escaping around her forehead to soften the appearance.

If it weren't for the cream puff of a dress, Della might

have felt pretty. But taking in the entirety of her appearance, she couldn't help but feel her hairstyle was nothing more than the embellishment atop a petit four.

She released a breath and closed her eyes, the ever-familiar feeling of failure sending tears to her eyes. Tears she refused to shed.

She blinked and focused on her reflection. There was nothing for it. This was how she would appear at the dinner that would introduce her to London society, and that was that. Perhaps she could woo them with her debonair wit.

Her shoulders slumped, and she let her chin fall.

"Thank you, Parker." She met the maid's eyes in the mirror and forced a smile.

She gathered her wrap and reticule and made her way downstairs. There was no point in dithering. It would be best to get this over with.

Andrew was already in the foyer when she came down the stairs, and he turned as she stepped beside him.

She raised her chin and sucked in a breath, hoping to make herself at least appear smaller, but she knew there was no hiding the way the fabric strained across her bosom.

Andrew's smile faded as he took her in. "You look…lovely."

It hurt. It hurt so very much, and she fell back on the years of pretending everything was all right to keep her smile in place just then.

"Madame Beauchamp says it's all the rage this season. The color is daffodil sunrise."

"Daffodil and sunrise? That's quite a lot of yellow," Andrew muttered.

Her smile wobbled, but she caught it and spread her lips farther. "Yes, it is rather. Would you help me with my wrap?"

She was afraid if she attempted it herself, the buttons on her bodice would give up entirely.

He took the length of silk and draped it delicately over her shoulders. It was impossible to miss how careful he was not to touch her.

Since they had arrived in London, they had taken on a routine of sorts. He left in the early morning hours to attend to business matters or some such thing, he never did tell her what, and she busied herself with acquainting herself with the staff and the running of the household. Or at least, she pretended to do so. In reality, she hadn't any clearer idea of what was expected of her than before she'd become a duchess.

There was an uneasy silence in the carriage for most of the ride to Ashbourne House. She had yet to meet Eliza, and Della's stomach twisted with nerves.

"Eliza is the second oldest sister, correct?" Her voice was overly loud in the quiet of the carriage, and it was almost as though she startled Andrew from his perusal of the passing London landscape.

"Yes, Eliza is second eldest. I had hoped you would meet Viv before the Christmas holidays, but it seems they've had a good harvest in Margate, and they are staying to see things through." He returned his attention to the window.

She relaxed her face. There was no point in smiling if he didn't see it.

The carriage came to a halt faster than she'd expected, and suddenly her stomach tumbled until she was sure she would lose what very little she had eaten that day. She wasn't sure exactly why, but the sweets that had given her comfort no longer proved useful, and she'd taken to noticing how her appetite remained small.

It was a curious thing, but she figured perhaps she'd obtained a heroic level of strain, and her body simply could no longer tolerate it. That sounded very much like her.

Andrew handed her down, and soon they were standing in the foyer of Ashbourne House.

The space was crowded with guests shedding their outer garments as uniformed servants took hats and wraps and cloaks. She was suddenly gripped with a desire to keep her wrap. Perhaps she could say it was part of her ensemble, but Andrew slipped it from her shoulders before she could say otherwise.

She felt exposed and vulnerable, and she drew in a breath, rolling her shoulders as if it might help her to disappear. Andrew took her arm and led her into a drawing room off the vestibule. She tried to remind herself it was only Andrew's sister, but that somehow made it worse.

It was crowded where they stood by the door, and she scanned the room, wondering why Andrew didn't shift them to a different spot. But then her eyes fell on Louisa in the opposite corner, and she smiled her glorious friendly smile in Della's direction, and Della felt the pull and safety of familiarity like a magnet.

"Oh, there's Louisa," she said to Andrew and slipped her arm from his to go over to the woman.

Louisa's smile slipped a little as Della stepped away from Andrew, and she hesitated, wondering what she had done wrong. It was only when she was halfway across the room that she realized they had been standing in some sort of receiving line as guests entered and greeted a couple who must have been their hosts.

Great bloody bollocks.

She'd already ruined it.

She froze, paralyzed at the thought of making things worse, and so she stood in the middle of the drawing room, and she could feel the weight of the stares of all the gathered guests like an anvil about her neck.

She had never been more aware of her cream puff dress

and the straining button on which her entire reputation rested.

Her heart shattered.

Her first foray into London society, and she'd already made a mess of things. Andrew no doubt regretted saving her from her father. It was obvious she could never be the duchess he deserved.

And so, he could never love her.

The thought came out of the darkness with the quickness and severity of lightning. She tamped it back, but it refused to go away. Standing in the middle of the drawing room with all eyes of society bearing down on her, she could only think of one thing.

She wanted Andrew to love her.

The realization ran deep, shaking her to her bones, and she stood suspended in the middle of the drawing room, comprehending fully the futility of what she had tried to do.

She could never be Andrew's duchess, and he would never love her.

It was so obvious to her now.

But then the strangest thing happened.

The tall gentleman who had been standing next to Louisa separated himself and came to stand beside her.

"It is rather masterfully done, don't you think?" he asked without preamble. "I heard it was rendered by Chauvin himself." The man looked up, his expression serious.

Not knowing what else to do or exactly what was happening, she followed the man's gaze.

A mural was painted into the plaster of the ceiling. It was a pastoral landscape of muted design, delicately rendered and inspiring. It was rather lovely really.

"I can see how you would be arrested by its beauty. You must have an eye for art."

She snapped her attention to the man beside her.

He was saving her.

This stranger whom she had never met was saving her from societal suicide.

She blinked, unable to move her gaze from his face. "Yes, it is. Quite beautiful that is. You say it was rendered by Chauvin?"

Who the hell was Chauvin?

The man was prevented from answering by the arrival of a second gentleman.

"Ah, I see you've noticed our murals. Ashbourne House has forty-seven in total. There's no record of who painted them, but you can tell by the brush strokes and use of the muted palette that speculation would suggest it's by Chauvin himself." The man shrugged. "If only there were a way to prove it."

"Yes, if only," she muttered, unable to pry her eyes from the second gentleman.

He was so gorgeous it must have been a sin. For a moment, Della feared she had dropped into the middle of a Melanie Merkett novel. Who were these men, and why were they coming to her rescue?

"I'm so pleased you enjoy them. I hope you'll take the time to explore the rest of the house after dinner. My wife would be happy to accompany you." He gestured behind him to the front of the receiving line she had unwittingly abandoned at the woman who stood there, trying desperately to hide a smile as she cradled her rounded stomach.

Eliza.

It had to be.

Della felt something shift inside of her like a row of dominoes spilling over on one another.

These gentlemen were Andrew's brothers-in-law. They had to be. And they had stepped in to save her from what would have been a disastrous introduction.

Her gaze traveled the length of the receiving line, desperate to find Andrew, but she stopped as she noted the expressions on the faces of those who still waited to greet their host and hostess. There were quiet whispers and curious glances, soft smiles and knowing nods.

But no one looked at her in judgment.

Not a single frown, wrinkled brow, or dismissive nod.

They were curious about her. That was all.

She raised her chin. "I should like that very much. Thank you, Your Grace."

Finally, her eyes found Andrew. He stood toward the back of the line, his arms crossed over his chest.

He was trying to hold back a laugh, and the sight of it had her hopes falling.

Was that all she was to him? A source of mockery?

Perhaps he was right.

After all, her brothers-in-law would not always be there to save her.

* * *

She was perfect.

When she had slipped from his arm at the receiving line at the first glimpse of Louisa, it hit him how important it was that she like his sisters. He hadn't realized until then just how much it meant to him that she get along with them.

He was well aware that he had earned the title of the Unwanted Duke thanks to the same sisters. Apparently, the infamous Darby sisters were too much for a prospective bride to comprehend, but watching Della's face transform at the sight of one of them had something stirring in his chest.

Not for the first time did he think he had done the right thing in marrying her. To protect her had certainly been a consideration, but he wasn't fool enough to deny there hadn't been an ulterior reason to marry her.

Every night he found himself in her arms he knew the real reason he had been so quick to marry her.

But while the physical attraction was undeniable, it was her performance that evening at dinner that solidified what he already knew.

She was just so damn likable.

She made mistakes and still held her chin high. She laughed at unbearable circumstances that would drive others to disagreeable natures.

When he thought of marriage, he saw what others in society had and knew it would be far more bearable if he found a partner instead of a wife. Someone who was more than just filling the role society had determined for her. Someone…like Della.

He shifted uncomfortably at the thought, knowing how close he tread to a dangerous line. He couldn't let himself get caught up in the wonder of his new wife should he let his guard down. They were not out of danger, and he couldn't yet relax.

He was reminded of this as Dax approached him with a glass of port after dinner. They had adjourned to the drawing room where brandy and port were being served. It was customary for the gentlemen to remain at the table and smoke their pipes and drink while the ladies retired, but this dinner was rather informal as it was out of season, and Eliza had suggested they all retire to the drawing room after the meal for more conversation.

It was a perfectly calculated move, Andrew knew. It would give more of the guests at dinner an opportunity to speak with Della and solidify her place in society as the Duchess of Ravenwood.

He couldn't have underestimated how important that was

until Dax leaned in close on the presumption of handing him the glass of port.

"We uncovered some rumors at our club."

Andrew gave no outward sign that he'd heard him.

"It seems the MacKenzie is making his way south."

"Does he know who his intended target may be?"

Dax shook his head, sipping his own port. "From what I've gathered, the man has made his way to Bewcastle. I was hoping you may know why."

Andrew turned the glass of port in his hands, careful not to squeeze it too tightly as a surge of something so primal it was almost frightening shot through him. So, the MacKenzie was on the hunt. It didn't scare him. It only served to ignite his focus on his wife.

"Della's grandparents reside in Bewcastle. She's lived with them the better part of her life. I should think the MacKenzie might believe she tried to return."

Dax shifted, a smile coming softly to his lips that did not match his words but would suggest to anyone watching that the two men were doing little more than swapping stories of horseflesh or cards.

"That is possible, but what will happen when he finds she is not there?"

Andrew's eyes zeroed in on Della as she sat perched between Eliza and Louisa on the sofa while she spoke with two of the other ladies who had been invited that evening.

"I can only hope he may give up the hunt."

Dax swirled the port in his glass. "I should think that unlikely, don't you?"

Andrew was saved from answering by Sebastian's approach.

"Did you tell him of the news from the north?"

Dax nodded. "Della's grandparents are in Bewcastle."

Sebastian glanced in Della's direction. "He thinks she might have run away then. That's promising, is it not?"

Andrew saw Sebastian in a different light since their conversation on the pavement in front of Ashbourne House. He had always seen the man as reserved, and at times, Andrew had wondered if he lacked all social decorum. But it wasn't that at all. Sebastian simply had a way of homing in on what mattered and blocking out the rest. Andrew envied him such focus.

"It is rather," Andrew replied.

He was hit with a sudden urge to see his wife home. The night, by his standards, had been a smashing success. Della was well and thoroughly introduced to society as his wife, and she had done it in such a way as no one could possibly forget. For how she had shone standing there in the middle of the drawing room staring up at the ceiling. How she was flanked by two powerful, well-respected dukes as she considered the mural there.

He knew the truth of it. He should have realized Della would not have had any sort of tutoring in what was expected of one in society. She likely hadn't realized they were to greet their hosts first, but none of it mattered. For now, she was unforgettable. He had seen the way the other guests were enchanted by her.

To say nothing of Eliza's brilliant strategy as a host. She'd invited a marquess and a marchioness who were distant cousins of Queen Victoria herself, an earl who had the ear of the prime minister, and a viscountess who it was rumored could end a lady's reputation in society with the single refusal of an invitation. The viscountess was now seated adjacent to the sofa on which Della perched, and she leaned so far forward to hear Della speaking she may fall from the chair.

Yes, it was by all accounts an absolute success.

And now he wanted nothing more than to take her home.

That primal surge roared up in him again as he mulled over the new information of her father's whereabouts. Andrew knew they couldn't escape notice forever, but he was surprised to learn the MacKenzie was already on the move. He would have bet a guinea the man would have not been inclined to travel before spring, not wishing to subject himself to the cold discomfort of winter travel.

Which reminded him of another matter.

"Were you able to learn anything of the man's doings in Parliament?"

Sebastian shook his head. "From what I've gathered, he is a sailboat without wind."

Dax frowned. "The MacKenzie is so ineffective in the political sphere, I imagine he viewed his daughter's marriage as the last attempt to gain footing there."

Andrew felt the weight of this new element. "He may be even more desperate to retrieve her as I denied him the opportunity to negotiate a marriage contract."

"Which means he was robbed of the opportunity to contractually win your fealty. A weighty thing in any political decision," Sebastian said.

Andrew nodded gravely.

Neither Dax nor Sebastian answered and instead exchanged watchful glances.

"Then I think it's best that we close ranks on this and keep an ear to any rumors that might come to town," Dax said.

Andrew thanked his brothers-in-law for the information and bid them farewell before moving to the seating area to collect Della. But before he could interrupt, Louisa stood and pulled him aside.

"Andrew, you must do something," she whispered.

He blinked. "Do what?"

THE DUKE AND THE LASS

Louisa moved only her chin in the direction of his wife.

"Your poor wife. She insisted on that monstrosity because the cut and fabric are the rage this season, but they do nothing for her. Can't you see that?"

He could admit that it was difficult to see things clearly when it came to Della. Her personality and charm often distracted him from her physical appearance. She had worn nothing more than a tattered and sap-riddled gown for the better part of two days when first they'd met, and it hadn't mattered at all to him. When she had appeared earlier in the evening, he'd been put off slightly by the vibrant yellow of the gown, but he knew he understood very little of fashion.

But he bent a critical eye to Della's ensemble now and realized of what his sister spoke.

"What is that?" he whispered.

"It doesn't matter what it is. It only matters that you must say something to her. I tried to get her to try something else, but she insisted on only what was in fashion this season. Not even considering what might display her attributes to an advantage."

"You mean what she's wearing is hideous."

Louisa did nothing more than frown, clearly not willing to call her sister-in-law anything unpleasant.

Andrew sighed. "Are all of her gowns like that?"

Louisa nodded, her lips melding into a thin line.

The gesture was like a punch to his gut. In his mind he saw Della as she had entered the great hall of MacKenzie Keep, the worn hem of her traveling cloak and the washed-out grays of the gown beneath, the way she'd unconsciously tried to hide the toes of her worn slippers beneath the flounces of crinolines.

He no longer saw the yellow contraption in which she was ensconced. Now he saw only armor.

He squeezed Louisa's hand and moved forward to interrupt the conversation at hand. The viscountess was reluctant to let Della leave, and only acquiesced when it was determined Della should come for tea soon.

Several long minutes later they were finally in the carriage.

He sank into the bench opposite his wife, his head throbbing with the weight of his thoughts. He absently rubbed at his aching temples as the carriage rocked forward.

"I'm so terribly sorry."

He blinked, his gaze flying to Della's face at the watery sound of her voice. In the weeks he had known her, he had never heard her sound so defeated.

"Whatever for?" He had been caught up in thinking how quickly he might get a letter to Ben to warn him of the MacKenzie's journey south, that Della's sudden interjection startled him, scattering his thoughts.

She crushed the edges of her cloak between her hands. "I'm so terribly sorry, Andrew. I promise it shan't ever happen again. I'll find a book. I swear it. I'll—"

He raised a hand, the only thing he could think of to stop her incessant chattering. He couldn't bear to hear her so remorseful.

"Della, whatever are you speaking of? Find a book? Find a book about what?"

She withdrew, sinking back into the bench as she hunched her shoulders as if to appear smaller. He hated it when she did that. Her chin remained firm, but she didn't speak.

"Is this about the book you lost? I'm sure Louisa would be happy to take you to a bookshop—"

"It's not about that. I'm sorry. I shouldn't have bothered you with it."

He stared, unable to comprehend what sort of conversation they were having. He had to figure out how to tactfully acquire new gowns for her and get the letter off to Ben. Would it reach Ben in time? Would he be able to inquire about the MacKenzie's travels in the village? Surely a belligerent Scotsman would be noticed by someone.

She watched out the window now, her gaze resolutely not meeting his.

He crossed his arms. "Della, do you like the gowns you purchased from the modiste?"

Her eyes were wide as though he'd startled her. "I was assured this is the height of fashion this year."

"You didn't answer my question. Do you like them?"

Her lips parted, but she didn't say anything right away. "Do you think it unsuitable?" She plucked at her skirts like one would pick up a soiled handkerchief.

He leaned forward, elbows to his knees. "Della, do you like the gowns?"

Her brow wrinkled. "Why would it matter if I liked them?"

"Because you're wearing them." Before they had reached London, conversations with her had not been this trying. He worried what might have changed.

She dropped her hands in her lap. "That hardly matters. They're fashionable. I want to present the title of Ravenwood in a favorable light."

"The title of Ravenwood?" He pictured her that first night in her bedchamber, her hand plucking fingers of shortbread from a tin. He thought that Della wouldn't care a fig about how she appeared in society. Why would she suddenly care now?

He didn't know for sure, but he thought it had something to do with the neglect he had discovered in so many parts of her life.

Her chin remained firm. "Yes, it's important that I perform my duties as the duchess appropriately. That's why it was so—" She stopped abruptly, her eyes widening ever so slightly as if she remembered something. "Oh, never mind." She turned her attention back out the window.

He leaned forward farther and snatched her hands from her lap, pressing them between his. "Della, what in God's name are you talking about? Why are you wearing such a hideous gown and what are you sorry about?" His tone had turned sterner than he would have liked, but he was suddenly gripped with the sense he was losing control. And he couldn't lose control. It was too dangerous.

She blinked, and for the first time, her chin fell. "You think my gown hideous?" Her voice was so soft and vulnerable, almost like that of a child.

"Della, that's not—"

The carriage stopped, and he shot a glance out the window only to find they had arrived so quickly at Ravenwood House.

"Della, I—" He tried again, but the tiger had already thrown open the door and stood waiting for them to exit.

Della didn't wait for him to hand her down. She slipped from the bench and calmly and quietly made her way into the house.

CHAPTER 12

The hour was late before she worked up the nerve to knock on the connecting door.

She had spent several hours replaying his words repeatedly in her mind. He thought her hideous.

Hideous.

In fairness, he had said her gown was hideous, but that was only one degree removed from what she knew to be the truth.

That he found *her* to be hideous.

He must. She was too big and far too graceless. She had proven that tonight by publicly embarrassing him.

So why had he told her she was beautiful in the moonlight?

She scoffed at the memory. That had been before they returned to London. Before he could be reminded of what he *should* have had.

She had seen the women society deemed acceptable. Beauchamp's Boutique had been filled with them. Tonight at dinner, she'd seen even more of the slender, diminutive beauties who exhaled grace effortlessly. Della had no hope of comparison.

She was so utterly unprepared to be a duchess, and it was enough to crush her heart. There was so much against her. How could she possibly believe she could be enough for Andrew? How could she possibly believe that she wouldn't yet again be a burden to someone?

And now, after seeing her in the cream puff of a dress, she knew he found her absolutely repulsive.

This thought rendered the most pain.

He hadn't come after her when she'd left him in the carriage and for that she was grateful. It had taken what little strength she'd had left to maintain her composure until she'd reached her rooms.

She'd dismissed Parker immediately. It wouldn't take much to get her out of that horrid gown, and she didn't want to give the servants anything over which to gossip.

As soon as the door had closed behind the maid, Della sat down at her dressing table and let the tears come. They weren't tears of pity. She was never so maudlin. It was more a welling up of frustration and despair.

Was this what she was destined to be? How could it be that time and time again she would be nothing more than a nuisance? Would she ever find her place?

By the time she knocked on the connecting door, she had mentally prepared herself for a return to Bewcastle, the shunned Duchess of Ravenwood, so inept at her duties that her husband should send her to the far reaches of Cumbria.

This carried with it too many echoes of her mother's own journey, and instead of hauling out her gowns, all of which she was now convinced should be burned immediately, she had chosen to confront Andrew instead.

If he should think her gowns hideous, she would ask that he select what he might find pleasing. If he thought her behavior abhorrent, she would ask that he instruct her as to what he would wish to see from her. She could mold herself to his liking. Whatever it took, she could do it. She must.

The idea of spending the rest of her life neglected and despised in her grandparents' moldering home was one thing, but to think of a future without Andrew was unbearable.

She rapped again, but after several minutes of silence, she realized he might not be in his rooms.

A new wave of doubt assailed her.

She hadn't turned around to see if he left the carriage after her. Had he instructed the driver to take him somewhere after she exited?

Once more she wondered if he had a lover. She recalled the night at Ravenwood Park when she had found him lurking in the dark. Did he keep a mistress in London as well? It would be rather convenient for him. The thought sent her stomach churning, and she backed away from the door.

She wasn't looking where she was going and knocked into the stool of her dressing table. She reached out a hand to catch herself, but in her haste, she became unbalanced and crashed into the stool with both of her knees as she caught herself against the table.

It would have been enough for the stool to simply fall over, but her knees had bent at the last moment, and it sent the delicate piece of furniture wheeling end over end on the rug until it crashed against the hard planks of the bare floor. She closed her eyes against the splintering sound.

She kept her eyes shut, letting the room go silent around her once more. The servants were surely too far away to have heard her, and yet she worried she may have awoken someone. That a knock on her door didn't immediately come only served to tell her what she already feared.

Andrew was not in his rooms.

A new pain flashed through her, but she threw open her eyes and marched over to the chair, limping slightly against a twinge in her knee. She rubbed it absently as she bent to pick up the stool. One delicate rosewood leg had snapped at the base and hung lopsided against the cushion.

Gingerly, she picked it up, her heart thudding until she realized the leg had been repaired once before. She examined the wooden appendage and noticed a column of lighter colored wood, a patch that had been inserted to secure the leg to the stool after the piece must have previously broken. She felt somewhat relieved that she had not been the one to break it initially, but she still felt guilty for the work that must be done to repair it again.

For surely it would be repaired. She was coming to understand the Dukes of Ravenwood did not buy new furniture when the old could be mended.

She set the stool aside and as she straightened, her stomach gave a low rumble. She put her hand to it. Now was not the time for her nerves to get the better of her. She turned and faced the connecting door once more, but it did no good. She snapped up her dressing gown and took a taper from the table by the bed.

She had been in Ravenwood House for a week now and felt no fear in wandering the corridors at night. She would find her way down to the kitchens and fetch herself some bread and cheese. Surely that would be easy enough. She refused to bother the servants again when her nerves were simply being unreasonable.

She made her way down the central staircase before weaving her way to the back of the house where the servants' stairs would lead her to the kitchen. She knew she would find something suitable to calm her nerves as she had developed what she hoped was a pleasant relationship with Cook.

When she'd first arrived, Mallard, the butler, had presented Della with the week's menu with instructions from Cook to let her know of any changes she wished to make. Instead of passing a message through Mallard, Della had requested Mallard's assistance in finding the kitchen so she could speak with Cook directly. She learned very quickly that this was not the typical behavior of a duchess as the kitchen collapsed into a state of paralysis at the mere sight of her.

However, when Della expressed honest interest in what Cook was preparing at that moment, a sort of kindred relationship had formed.

Since then, Cook had been sure there was a platter of cheeses and breads for Della whenever she should require it. It was a long way from shortbread, but she supposed Cook would have prepared that for her as well should she ask.

Tonight, she would satisfy herself with bread and cheese while her thoughts ran amok. She didn't wish to examine too closely why it was that the thought of Andrew having a mistress upset her. She had heard gentlemen often kept mistresses. Perhaps it was just the way of things, and Della had to be the one to learn to accept it.

Even more, a mistress might keep the pressure off Della in terms of Andrew's physical needs.

This thought had her stopping entirely, her hand going out to the wall to steady herself.

She hadn't considered that. Was Andrew going to his mistress to fulfill his sexual desires? She had only her relations with Andrew from which to judge what was required from a wife, and now she worried she wasn't adequate in that role either. If Andrew found her hideous, then perhaps she was failing there as well.

But then why did he come to her every night? Why did he whisper such sweet words to her? Was it all a charade? Was he simply telling her what he thought she wanted to hear so he could find some kind of sexual release until he could arrange to meet with his mistress again?

She couldn't breathe. Her lungs burned, and her heart stampeded. Was there nothing about her marriage that was real? She knew Andrew had been forced into it. She would not deny that, but did that mean there was no possibility it could turn into something real?

Once more despair gripped her, and she saw her future yawning before her like an empty void. Was this what her mother had felt? Is that what had driven her back to her parents' moldering home? What had forced her to endure her own mother's cruel nature?

As Della stood immobilized in the corridor in the middle of the night, she understood only too well why her mother had fled. Anything was more bearable than this consuming power of hopelessness.

A noise at the end of the corridor startled her enough that she nearly dropped her candle. As it was the flame spluttered, and she willed her hand to stop shaking. If the light went out, she would be plunged into darkness.

The door at the end of the hall opened, and for some strange reason, Della held her breath. It was probably just a servant finishing a task that had taken longer than expected. Perhaps it was Mallard himself checking on the house before retiring for the evening. There were any number of explanations that should not have had her frozen to the carpet.

But it wasn't any of those things.

It was Andrew.

He emerged from the servants' stairs as if it were the most natural thing for him to have been below stairs at this hour. He closed the door softly behind him, and she knew he hadn't registered that she was there yet. He must have seen the light from her candle, but she could tell by the bent angle of his head, he was lost in thought.

Was he still heady from the throes of desire he'd experienced in the arms of his lover?

She was going to be sick. The candle began to shake in earnest now as both her insecurities and her imagination ran away from her.

Andrew must have noticed the vacillating light because he looked up, his gaze instantly finding hers.

"Della." His voice was oddly breathless as if she'd startled him, and he closed the distance between them in three brisk strides.

He took the candle from her, holding it aloft as he drew her against him with an arm around her back. Her body tensed, not wishing to feel his strength, not wishing to remember what this was like, but it was too late. He was all muscle, true, but it had always been more than that when it came to Andrew. For he was the only person in the world to make her feel like a lady.

She closed her eyes, wishing it all away.

"Della, what's wrong? What's happened? Is it your father?"

Her eyes flew open at the mention of her father, and she studied his face so close to hers in the flickering light of the candle.

It wasn't the afterglow of lust that preoccupied him. It was something else. Something darker. He was worried.

She couldn't stop herself from reaching up and touching his cheek as if she could banish the haunted look from his eyes. But then she snatched back her hand as she pushed against him.

"What about my father?"

* * *

He hadn't meant to tell her anything. He didn't wish for her to worry. They couldn't know for sure that her father even knew of her whereabouts or even of their marriage.

But when he'd seen her, standing in the corridor in the middle of the night, her hand pressed to the wall as if it were the only thing which held her upright, fear had seized him.

He had only stepped away for a few hours, and it wasn't as though he'd gone far. It was just that after the events of the dinner, his sister's revelations to him, Della's own success, and the subsequent odd conversation in the carriage ride home, his head had been stuffed, and he'd needed time to process it all. And there was nothing better to help him process troubling information than good, clean physical exercise.

Others may not have viewed it as such, but that was how he saw it.

He had returned only when he'd felt the claws of the issues that plagued him loosen their grip on him, and he thought he might be able to sleep. He'd still been muddling through what he'd left behind when he closed the door to the servants' stairs behind him. That was why he didn't realize she was there at first, but when he did, his heart had thudded in his chest so loudly he thought she could have heard it.

He hadn't hesitated, hadn't taken a moment to think it through. He'd simply moved, eating up the distance between them with long strides so he could pull her into his arms. He had to touch her, feel her body pressed against his to know she was all right.

He had assumed it was her father, but too late he realized what haunted him might not be what haunted her. She had confirmed it in short time, and now he'd given her another reason to look so stricken except—

She no longer appeared frightened. Her chin had firmed,

and she met his gaze directly when only seconds before he had thought she might drop the candle from her hand.

He didn't wish to have this conversation in the hallway. Not only because a servant might overhear but because the night had grown cold, and Della wore only a nightdress and robe. She had appeared not much more than a ghost when he'd first spotted her, and now he worried she might grow chill.

"Not here," he said and took her hand, leading her to the central staircase.

He could be sure to find a fire in his bedchamber, and he planned to set her before it while he told her of what he'd learned. He wondered at how natural it felt to hold her hand, but then this was not the first time he had done it. He could almost say he'd come to anticipate it, the feel of her soft skin against the rough planes of his palm.

The stairs creaked as they mounted them, and it was the only sound in the vast house. It struck him suddenly how quiet the house had become. For the first time since he could remember, the house was not filled with the cacophony of children racing down its halls, running up the stairs, or filling the rooms with musical lessons.

He wondered if he and Della would have children. It was entirely possible. While he had tried to remain objective, his strength to resist his wife had never lingered into the night. There was something about the closeness of darkness that had made him think it was safe to let his guard down then. Almost as if nothing bad could happen while they were safely tucked into bed.

He knew this for the excuse it was because every time he thought of Della, his heart raced a little faster. He knew what that feeling meant, and he would not name it.

He felt the heat of the fire as soon as they entered his bedchamber, and he shut the door against the drafty night when Della slipped inside. She did not progress into the room he noticed, but instead, kept her back to the door.

He wandered over to the fire and added more coal even though the bright flames needed no more fuel. It was at least something to do with his hands while he gathered his thoughts.

Still, she did not move.

"I learned today that your father has traveled to Bewcastle. I can only assume he's looking for you."

He didn't miss the small intake of breath from behind him, but he couldn't turn to look at her. If he did, he would find himself in her arms again.

"How do you know this?"

Her voice was strong, and he chided himself for thinking it wouldn't be. Finally, he turned to face her.

"I asked my brothers-in-law to assist me in keeping track of your father's whereabouts. I wanted to be forewarned should he be heading for London."

"Your brothers-in-law." It wasn't a question, and oddly, her expression clouded somewhat at the mention of Dax and Sebastian.

"Yes, they are both well-respected gentlemen in society with connections of their own. I thought they may hear something before my own solicitors or other connections did. In this instance, it proved useful."

"Does he know of our marriage?" She spoke as though their marriage were something that did not involve them, and it unsettled him.

He took a step forward. "I don't know. I can only assume he might believe you went back to your grandparents."

"Of course." She looked down, blinking furiously as if to avoid his gaze.

He was in front of her in two strides, pushing her chin up with a bent finger.

"Della, what is going on?"

She startled him by jerking her chin free and stepping back, putting a distance between them.

"Isn't it obvious?" Her voice was strong even as her eyes were wild with an emotion he couldn't discern. "I've trapped you into this marriage, and I've failed at every turn to be the duchess you require, and now my father will come to London to cause further trouble for you."

He blinked, struggling to process her words. "What are you talking about? How have you failed? Della, you've been nothing but a success."

She laughed, the sound harsh and grating. "How can you say such things? If it weren't for your brothers-in-law, tonight would have been a complete disaster. I could have ruined everything for you, and not to mention—" She stopped speaking so abruptly she choked on her own words.

"Not to mention what, Della?" he pressed when she'd sucked in a gulping breath.

She shook her head. "I'm very tired. I should like to retire for the evening if there's nothing more."

She turned toward the connecting door of their rooms, and something in him snapped. When faced with the possibility of being bartered to her father's cronies, she had not balked. When he'd all but kidnapped her in the dead of night, she had risen to the challenge.

But now she ran from him, and he wouldn't stand for it.

He caught her arm before she'd taken two steps, swinging her about to face him.

"Della, stop." He said the words as softly as his rising frustration would allow. "You must tell me what's gotten into you. I don't understand why you're upset. Please. You must explain to me."

He pushed a lock of hair that had fallen loose from her

braid behind her ear, letting his fingers trail over her soft skin.

She tried to shake her head again, but he caught her chin.

"Della, I don't know what's happened, but I can't help but feel that I lost you somewhere between Brydekirk and London."

Finally his words seemed to penetrate whatever fog had taken hold of her, and for the first time that night, he looked into her eyes and saw her. Della. The wild Scottish lass who had not hesitated to tumble out a window and into his arms while a band of drunken men threatened to break down her door.

"Andrew, I'm not good enough." She licked her lips. "I can't do it."

He forgot himself entirely at the pleading, desperate tone of her voice, and he slipped his arms around her, holding her tightly to him even as her hands flattened against his chest in weak protest at his touch.

"I don't understand. You need to explain it to me." He spoke carefully, as he would to a child, but she only shook her head.

"Della." He touched his lips to hers. It was not more than a brush of his lips against hers, but he hoped it would be enough to remind her that she could trust him, help her to remember what it was that existed between them.

He felt her eyelashes flutter closed, and her fingers dug into the front of his shirt.

"Andrew," she whispered against his lips, and then she tilted her head, offering her lips to him.

He shouldn't do this. He still didn't understand why she was upset. She hadn't explained anything, and now the tendrils of desire had begun to fog his brain. She let go of his shirt front as she slipped her arms around him, her hands flattening against his back as she pulled him nearer.

Maybe this was what she needed. She needed him, physically, to set right what had upended in her mind.

"Della," he murmured against her lips.

Her hands slid down his back, cupping his buttocks as she pressed herself into him. Lust spiked through him, and he felt himself harden as she ground against him.

"Della," he moaned now, pulling free from her hypnotizing kiss to set his forehead against hers. "Della, I don't want to do this. Not when you're upset. I want you to talk to me."

She shook her head the smallest of degrees. "But I don't want to talk. I only ruin everything when I talk."

"Della—"

She captured his mouth again with a fierceness he couldn't deny. Her arms came up and wrapped around his neck, and now her body hung against his. He could feel every curve of her. Her full, weighty breasts, the swell of her stomach, the mesmerizing curve of her hips.

His hands reached for the tie of her robe before he could think better of it. He shed her of the garment within seconds and soon her nightdress followed. He carried her to the bed, and after carefully laying her atop it, went to work on his own clothes. He was naked within seconds and stretched out across her, tracing the way the firelight licked across her body with the tips of his fingers.

She arched into him, a whimper escaping her lips. She'd grown bolder in their lovemaking, and now she caught his hand and pressed it fully against her. Her eyes opened, and she captured his gaze, refusing to let it go as she directed his hand across her body.

First, she drew it up her hip and across her body to the valley between her breasts, coming achingly close to first one nipple and then the other. He swallowed, trying to hold her gaze, and yet he couldn't help but watch what she did with his hand.

She tugged it lower, over her belly and down, across the flat plane of her pelvis and over to the gentle curve of her thigh. He swallowed as she pressed his palm between her legs. She arched, lifting her breasts and moving his hand higher. His penis throbbed as he watched her draw his hand so painfully close to her hot center before pulling it away. She did it again, coming closer this time, and he swore he could feel how wet she grew as she teased her own body.

"Della." Her name was a raspy groan, and with one last stroke, she lifted herself against his fingers and released his hand.

He plunged a single finger inside of her, and she cried out, her hips coming off the bed as she gripped his wrist to hold him there. She was so very wet, and he wanted nothing more than to be inside of her, but not yet. He shifted and replaced his hand with his mouth.

"Andrew." He felt more than saw her sit up, her hands grasping his head in obvious surprise. "Andrew, you can't—"

He licked her, and she collapsed against the mattress. He drew his tongue across her sensitive nub in a single, slow swipe, making her groan and writhe.

"Andrew, please."

He did it again, holding her hips in place as she squirmed. He touched just the tip of his tongue to her. Once. Twice. And again. He slipped a finger into her once more as he stroked her nub with his tongue, and he felt her muscles convulse around his finger. One more stroke, and he sent her over the edge.

He entered her even as the last of her climax echoed through her body. He could feel it in the tightness of her wet sheath, the way it grabbed at him, pulling against him until he thought he wouldn't be able to hold back.

He bent his head and sucked first one nipple into his mouth and then the other. He sucked and nibbled and tortured her until he could feel her body coiling once more. Only then did he trail kisses up her chest, along the column of her throat, until his lips pressed to her ear.

"Della, you are not a failure. To me you are perfect in every way just by being yourself. Don't ever forget that. Don't ever forget how perfect you are when you are just yourself."

"Andrew." Her voice was weak and unsteady, and he wondered if it were from his words or from what he was doing to her body, but he didn't have time to think on it.

With a final thrust, his world exploded around him, and he came, hot and hard, the strength leaving his body until he collapsed. He moved just enough so he wouldn't crush her and then he wrapped his arms around her, holding her tight and hoping it was enough to vanquish whatever doubts still lingered in her mind.

CHAPTER 13

Out of all the trying things she had encountered in the last several weeks, this was by far the one that frightened her the most.

Della was to have tea with a viscountess.

The invitation had come the day following that disastrous dinner, and according to her sister-in-law Eliza, this was not a viscountess to ignore. The lady was held in high regard by members of the *ton*, and she came from a family with an old and weighty legacy. Not at all someone to be trifled with.

Andrew received the news of her invitation with gusto while Della wanted nothing more than to consume an entire batch of shortbread. She tried to listen to Andrew. This invitation would go further to solidify her place as the Duchess of Ravenwood and present a greater challenge should her father appear to refute her marriage.

She had hoped her father would never reappear, but after Andrew told her of what he'd learned, she now feared her father lurked at every corner in London, waiting to jump out at her and snatch her away from this life she had stumbled into. A life so full of wonder she could hardly believe it.

A life that was too good for her as her continued failings served to remind her. But she had hoped she would be worthy of it. With enough practice perhaps she could.

But every time she attempted to bolster her courage, she could only remember the faces of those who stared at her when she'd unknowingly stepped out of the receiving line that night. They knew her for the fraud she was, and she was doomed to fail as the Duchess of Ravenwood. She was going to let Andrew down. *Had* let him down in fact.

And then how could he ever love her?

She shoved the thought away. She hadn't even been able to talk to him of her fears, and now she wished for him to love her. Preposterous. Love intimated a level of relationship of which she would never be capable if she continued to let her insecurities get the better of her.

She hadn't even been able to tell Andrew what it was that had plagued her that night. When faced with the incredible confidence that her husband seemed to carry so naturally, the words to mark her insecurities had simply stuck in her throat. How could she explain to him how swiftly she compared herself to every other woman in a room? How could she tell him how easy it was to find fault with everything she did?

He wouldn't understand. He *couldn't*.

And this had stopped her from speaking.

She slumped against the bench as the Ravenwood carriage carried her to tea with the viscountess. She was beginning to suspect that being the best duchess possible would not be enough to win Andrew's affections if she couldn't even speak to him.

The viscountess lived in a stately home fashioned in the Federal style along a small square in Mayfair. It was an appallingly short distance from Ravenwood House, and she could have very easily walked, but Andrew did not want her traveling on the streets without him. The coachman, St. John, was attentive and alert, she had come to find, and she did feel better having him with her, she could admit.

But still. Andrew was being rather overprotective she thought. What did Andrew expect her father to do after all?

Her earlier thoughts of him jumping out at her from around a street corner returned, and she swallowed, slumping farther into her seat.

But the tiger soon threw open the door and offered her the step down. It was best to get this over with. Perhaps this time she could prove herself up to the task of being the Duchess of Ravenwood.

The interior of the viscountess's home was just as finely appointed as the exterior, and Della followed a footman to the drawing room where she was to take tea. The viscountess was already seated at the table by the window, her finger skimming the page of a book open on her lap when Della entered.

Della could admit her heart sped up at the sight of the book and wondered perhaps if they may speak of novels they had in common. That would make this entire thing far more palatable.

The viscountess set aside the book and rose at Della's entrance.

"Della, I'm so glad you could come," she said, striding toward her.

The viscountess was older, and several gray hairs perforated her dark hair and fine lines spread out from the corners of her eyes. The woman was slender and several inches shorter than Della. She also wore a plain muslin gown of the palest blue that highlighted her warm eyes. In all, the woman was remarkably beautiful, and Della sucked in a breath and hunched her shoulders.

"Lady—"

The viscountess waved her off before taking her hands. "Please. You must call me V. I shan't have us standing on titles. It's rather clunky." She squeezed Della's hands and smiled. "You look lovely today. I trust you're settling in well."

Della wore another of Madame Beauchamp's creations. This gown was of the brightest pink Della had ever seen outside the confines of a candy shop, and the bodice sported lines of small bows marching up her front as if they were signposts pointing to the location of her breasts.

She'd never felt more ridiculous in her life.

The gown, while sized properly, was not constructed for a woman of her height, and she had to remember not to lift her arms too far or she would surely split the thing down the back.

She forced a tremulous smile. "I'm quite well. Thank you, my...V," she said, the smile faltering as she tried to affect casualness when addressing the revered woman by what seemed a familiar nickname.

"Oh, I do hope you're not finding society matrons to be too vexing. I should think arriving here outside of the season has helped." She squeezed Della's hands a final time before releasing them and indicating she should take a seat at the small table in the alcove.

Holding her breath, Della sat, and miraculously, her bodice did not split in two. She eyed the tea settings as V poured and felt a loosening of the trepidation that gripped her. She had taken tea formally with her grandmother and her matronly friends several times at Bewcastle. Della had only to keep from upending the entire teapot on herself now. Surely, she could manage that.

She had to. This tea was far too important to mess up.

"I'm finding London to be rather a big change from what I am used to," Della ventured.

V dropped a cube of sugar into her cup and looked up. "I

can imagine. You're from Cumbria if I recall. That's quite a journey. I'm sure you miss your family."

Della pictured her grandmother's pinched face and forced a smile around the rim of her teacup. She took a small sip to give herself time to swallow the sudden unpleasantness in her throat and finally said, "Yes, it's been a challenge."

She wasn't sure of what she spoke, but she thought her words covered all manner of tribulations.

V offered her a plate of small sandwiches, and Della was careful to select the ones she thought wouldn't completely fall apart in her hands. They were so delicate and filled with even more delicate things like watercress, which was sure to just fall everywhere the moment she took a bite. Shortbread would never betray her like that.

"That is to be expected. And how are you finding the Darby sisters? I can assure you the *ton* was quite surprised to hear His Grace had taken a wife. After all, he had not earned the name the Unwanted Duke without reason."

Della dropped the sandwich to her plate, her eyes flying up to meet V's.

V's smile was knowing. "I had thought no one told you of your husband's epitaph. I should think it a remarkable woman who has married the only Darby brother."

Della straightened, forgetting entirely about the delicacy of her attire. "The Unwanted Duke?"

She couldn't possibly be speaking of Andrew. He was... well, he was everything she had ever hoped a husband might be and never dreamed actually existed. He had his faults. Of that, she was not blind. He was rather overprotective, and he enjoyed kippers with his breakfast, which she was still attempting to come to terms with, but in all, he was more than she could have ever hoped for.

V nodded. "Oh yes. Hadn't you wondered why he was still unattached? The Ravenwood title is old and respectable. Any father with a daughter to marry off would have pounced on him years ago." V leaned in conspiratorially. "I heard a rumor you have Scottish ancestors. Perhaps that is where you've acquired your bravery." She winked and her smile was slightly humorous.

It was then that Della burst into tears.

She wasn't sure who was more surprised by the sudden display of emotion, but without hesitation and heedless of the tea service, V reached across the table and took Della's hand, squeezing it comfortingly.

"Oh Della, I had a suspicion all was not as it seemed. I know only too well what it's like to have one's life scrutinized with such lethal exactness as the *ton* is capable of. Please, dear, know that you can tell me anything. That is, after all, why I invited you here today. I thought you may be in need of a friend. One who is not related to your husband." There it was again. That friendly, humorous smile that suggested warmth and camaraderie.

Della had never really understood how alone she was until she saw that smile. Sure, she had Andrew, but as she had proven the night after her introductory dinner, she couldn't even speak to him about things of a delicate nature.

She squeezed V's hand in return. "I've made a mess of everything."

"Surely not everything. You've only been here for a few weeks."

Della laughed through her tears, the tightness in her chest easing when she thought it never could.

"Give me time then. I'm sure I will get to the rest of it."

V laughed now. "I'm sure you will. You seem like a capable girl." She squeezed her hand a final time and released it. "Did you know I was once a confirmed spinster?"

Della blinked. "I'm sorry?"

The night of the dinner everyone had asked after V's

several children, and while her husband had not been in attendance, Della had assumed V was happily wed.

V nodded and took a sip of her tea. "I was quite on the shelf when his lordship appeared and swept me off my feet. But do you wish to know the worst of it?"

Della could only blink.

V set down her cup and leaned forward. "I was not the one to put myself on that shelf. The *ton* did that for me. So trust me when I say I know only too well what they can be like."

Della shook her head. "But you're so…beautiful," she blurted out.

V laughed, and Della realized for the first time how beautiful the sound was. Of course it was. A beautiful laugh to match a beautiful woman.

"Thank you. But looks hardly matter when one's reputation is the cause for such banishment."

"Reputation?" Della sat up at this, but V suddenly tilted her head as if studying Della more closely.

"Would you like to know a secret?"

Della could only nod.

"I think I only captured his lordship's attention when I started being myself and stopped being the woman the *ton* had made me out to be."

"And who were you?"

V's smile was secretive, and a strange glint came to her eye. "That, my dear, is a story for another day." She reached across the table again and patted Della's hand before moving to pick up the plate of petit fours still on the teacart next to the table. She offered it to Della. "First we must speak of that horrid gown you're wearing. Do you know I've seen several debutantes in similar ensembles this year, and they all appeared just as atrocious? Do you ever wonder if those who deem things fashionable have any sense at all?"

Della laughed for the first time in what seemed like forever. "I would rather wear a gown that doesn't showcase so much of my private bits."

V laughed and took several petit fours for herself. "Then we must do something about it, shan't we?"

Della wrapped both of her hands around her teacup. "You make it sound so easy."

V's eyes flashed to Della's face. "Oh, but it is. That's what no one tells you." She picked up a petit four and used it to gesture at Della. "You're told you must live up to certain standards. You must perform the duties required of your title. But such a notion has several flaws."

"It does?"

V nodded. "First, who is it that created these rules? I am never one to follow standards set by those from whom I would not accept advice, and so I eye such standards with a critical bent. And second, I refuse to follow standards that would require me to be less than myself. That's what put me on the shelf, and I will never make that mistake again."

Della blinked. "Are you saying I should...rebel?"

V laughed. "Hardly. You don't deserve the criticism that such a thing would entail. What I am saying is you should be more yourself. I suspect His Grace didn't marry you because you were like every other debutante, did he?"

Della picked up a petit four and took a very large bite.

It was more than an hour later when Della emerged from V's townhouse, and when she entered the carriage, she instructed St. John not to return to Ravenwood House. She directed him to Beauchamp's Boutique instead.

* * *

She drew a full breath simply because she could.

She was not in danger of losing a button or splitting her bodice completely down the back.

When she had stepped into Madame Beauchamp's, the modiste had turned from where she was helping a very young woman select fabrics, a knowing smile coming to her lips.

Apparently the talented seamstress had known Della would be back and had taken it upon herself to fashion a couple of gowns in preparation. Della wore one of them now, only Madame Beauchamp had been forced to add a couple of darts to the design.

"You have lost weight, ma cherie," the modiste had mumbled around a mouthful of pins. "Is London not to your liking?"

Della had been unable to remove her gaze from her reflection in the mirror. Madame Beauchamp had been pulling in the waist of the gown, and for the first time in nearly her entire life, Della had a silhouetted waist. And hips. Gorgeous hips over which the sapphire skirts of her gown fell like a waterfall.

It wouldn't take very much for Della to believe herself to be pretty.

To me you are perfect in every way just by being yourself.

Andrew's words came back to her. She had wanted to dismiss them as nothing more than heated words spoken in a moment of passion. But standing there before Madame Beauchamp's looking glass, Della might have begun to believe them.

She had turned gently from side to side as Madame Beauchamp had finished pinning up the hem. Della *had* lost weight. She could see that now that she wore a properly fitted gown. She wasn't thin by any stretch of the imagination. It was more that a burden she hadn't known she had been carrying had been lifted from her person.

She was lighter now. That was it. And it spread through her with the beauty and promise of sunshine after a rainstorm.

She couldn't be sure what it was, likely a culmination of things, but when she returned to Ravenwood House hours later, she felt different. While V had instructed her to be herself, Della couldn't help but think that was easier in theory rather than in practice, but there was some truth to the matter.

Andrew had married her, hadn't he? And that was when she was simply the neglected, sheltered daughter of a mad Scotsman and a selfish mother.

She stopped in the foyer of Ravenwood House as a footman took her cloak and gloves.

When had she begun to think of her mother as selfish?

She had very few memories of her mother. Della had always been left at Bewcastle while her mother claimed to be attending to duties required by her title. Even at a young age, Della had known this meant her mother was attending house parties where Della would not be wanted.

Funny how now she would think of it for what it really was. Her mother abandoning her to pursue her own pleasure.

Della pressed a hand to her stomach, one thought tumbling over another in her mind. She would never neglect her child like that, should she be blessed to have children.

Her eyes traveled up the central staircase before her as she wondered where Andrew was. It was time she told him of her misgivings. Perhaps if she spoke of them, they wouldn't seem so daunting.

But when she inquired of Mallard where His Grace might be, she was informed he was not at home. This gave her pause as the hour was late, considerably later than she had expected to be, and mistakenly, she had believed he would be home from the day's business and worrying over her whereabouts.

She asked Mallard to let her know when His Grace should return and asked that Parker be sent up to the duchess's rooms. The maid arrived as Della pulled the gowns she had ordered from Madame Beauchamp from her dressing room and piled them on the bed.

In short order, they had sorted the gowns and those with fabric that would not cause fresh cut blooms to shiver in comparison were sent below stairs for Parker to determine if she might fashion something useful from them.

Della informed Parker to expect a new order of gowns in the next week, and that they would make do with the two gowns Madame Beauchamp had sent home that day with Della and two of the gowns in the original order that were not entirely repulsive.

It would be enough to see her through until the new gowns arrived. She was only grateful they were outside the season. Otherwise, four gowns would not at all do for the societal engagements she would be required to complete as the Duchess of Ravenwood.

The thought had her pausing as she bundled up the ribbons she had been sorting at her dressing table. A new stool had been acquired by Parker, but Della couldn't help but wonder if the old stool would return at some point, freshly repaired.

Della suspected Ravenwood House might have a library to rival that of Ravenwood Park, and she had yet to find a book that might instruct her on the duties of a duchess. She rose, putting away the ribbons, with the intention of summoning Mallard to ask for his help in locating the library when a different thought struck her.

She changed direction and instead settled at the rosewood desk by the window. She dashed off two identical notes and pulled the bell pull to summon a footman.

"Please have these delivered as quickly as possible," she instructed the young man.

He gave a quick nod and was off to find a messenger boy to deliver her letters.

Still Andrew had not returned, and she found herself staring out the window of her bedchamber expectantly. Her window faced the street, and she thought she might be able to see him arrive. But then she had taken the carriage that day and the coachman. Had he taken a hackney then?

Something didn't seem quite right, and she left her perch on the window seat and ventured out into the corridor.

Ravenwood House was a spectacular example of old English wealth built in the latter part of the previous century. It had been updated after the Napoleonic War, but in all, much of the original Federalist style had been maintained. This was fortunate as it made it easier for her to follow the corridors without getting lost in twisted passageways and cramped Jacobean chambers littered with tapestries and opulent carpets.

In the weeks she had been there, she had learned the location of the formal dining room, the breakfast room, and Andrew's study and had learned the names of the seven different drawing rooms. And those were just the ones for guests. There were also the four family drawing rooms. What a family required four drawing rooms for was beyond Della's comprehension.

She had no idea where she might wander to until she found herself making her way down the servants' stairs in the direction of the kitchen. Perhaps she would see if Cook had made any of her sticky toffee pudding. She hadn't eaten much at tea with V, and it was still hours until dinner. A bit of pudding would be just the thing.

She had thought her presence in the kitchens would not be so unusual now, but when she turned the corner, all activity ceased as though her appearance there were more shocking than a bolt of lightning striking in the middle of the room.

She tried a smile. "Hello," she said to Cook and the scullery maids who were filling their scrub pails at the water pump. "I was wondering if…" Her voice trailed away.

They weren't looking at her.

Their eyes had drifted to the left of Della. She turned and spotted a corridor off the kitchens. She had never been down there, and she wondered where it might lead. Perhaps there was a commotion she couldn't see from where she stood at the bottom of the stairs.

She tried again. "I was just wondering if…"

Their eyes darted to her and back down the corridor, and it was then that realization dawned on her with a sickening tightness around her throat. The air was sucked from her lungs, and her stomach heaved.

Andrew.

Andrew emerging from the servants' staircase. In the dead of night.

Andrew.

She didn't bother speaking again. Instead, she picked up her skirts and marched across the kitchen and down the opposite corridor.

"Your Grace!" Cook shouted after her, but she ignored the woman.

Halfway down the corridor she suddenly wondered what she was going to do. What was she looking for? Was she hoping to find the room in which Andrew met his lover? Had she been thinking, she would have realized how odd it would be. To have a room below stairs in which to carry out clandestine assignations with one's mistress.

THE DUKE AND THE LASS

But she wasn't familiar with how such things worked. Perhaps Andrew preferred it this way. He could very well think it kept matters discreet and in his control. Della knew only too well how much Andrew liked to stay in control.

She passed two empty rooms, one appeared to be an office of some kind and the other was a washroom. It struck her then that she hardly had any right to confront Andrew. If he should have a mistress then so be it. There was nothing she could do about it. Pain spiked through her, so intense she stopped and pressed a hand to her chest.

But she couldn't stop now. So much had changed in the last several hours, and if she stopped now, if she allowed Andrew to continue to lie to her, to keep secrets from her, then she was choosing to remain the neglected and unwanted Della she had been.

While she may have been neglected and unwanted, she didn't have to accept it. She could like herself even if no one else did.

She plunged ahead. There was a door ahead of her, closed tight against the corridor, and as she approached, she heard noises coming from within. At first, they didn't make sense to her, but then a soft thumping noise became distinct. Bile rose in her throat. She knew only too well what that noise could be.

She took the last several strides across the corridor and without hesitating threw open the door.

She had underestimated the strength of her anger, and the door bounced against the wall behind it. She caught it as it swung back to her, her hand closing around the wooden panel in confusion.

Andrew stood before her as she had suspected. He wore only his trousers, boots, and his shirt, the sleeves rolled up to his elbows. He held a large wooden mallet in one hand and in the other...

"That's my dressing table stool," she whispered, unable to comprehend the sight before her.

Andrew's lips were parted in surprise, his eyes riveted to hers.

"It is," he said, his voice equally as quiet.

She stood there, her hand still wrapped about the door, suddenly unsure of herself. The room was larger than she had anticipated for a room below stairs, and several windows were set high in the walls opposite and adjacent to the wall with the door. A work bench ran underneath one set of windows while bins of what appeared to be various pieces, sizes, and colors of wood ran under the other set.

Andrew stood in the middle at a worktable on which the dressing table stool rested. The table's surface was scarred with knicks and blemishes and bits of paint and stain. In fact, the entire room carried an air of repeated and intentional use as though Andrew came here often.

"You repair furniture." She spoke the words even as the idea formed in her mind.

He didn't have a lover. He had a hobby. A hobby which he apparently wished to keep secret.

She stepped fully into the room and shut the door behind her. She held the doorknob between both of her hands behind her back as she continued to study her husband.

"I do," he said, setting down the wooden mallet he had been using to pound a slim dowel of wood into the base of the stool where the leg had snapped off.

She realized now what the soft pounding sound was and felt foolish.

"And you do not wish for people to know of this?" she asked, keeping her tone neutral.

She couldn't understand what might be untoward about the repair of furniture, but then Andrew picked up a rag on which he wiped his hands, averting his gaze.

"Dukes are not expected to engage in such manual labor."

She thought of the dressing table at Ravenwood Park and the bedside table.

"It's not manual labor. It's art." She didn't know where those words came from, but she realized it was the truth. She let go of the doorknob to step forward, placing her hands softly on the edge of the worn worktable. "Besides, who would dishonor manual labor with such rubbish? I have it on good authority that one must not accept standards set by those from whom one would not accept advice." She smiled as she repeated V's words from earlier.

Andrew's expression was almost sheepish. "Is that so?" He set aside the rag, and placing both palms on the worktable, leaned toward her. "And just where did you hear this?"

"From someone of authority. Trust me." She smiled and straightened so she could meander about the room.

It was neat, surprisingly so, but then it shouldn't have been a surprise. Andrew had proven time and again that he liked things to be a certain way. His workshop should prove no different.

She stopped at the bins of various wood. "You've repaired a great many pieces. I'm particularly impressed with the dressing table in the duchess's rooms at Ravenwood Park."

She heard the sharp intake of breath behind her.

"You knew that was repaired?"

She nodded and turned. "You have a room like this at Ravenwood Park, don't you?"

His eyes narrowed. "How do you know that?"

She smiled mischievously. "Because I discovered you lurking in the corridors there in the middle of the night as well."

He smiled and rubbed the back of his neck with one hand. "I suppose I have been discovered. Will you tell my sisters now?"

She wrinkled her brow. "Is that your greatest fear? That your sisters should find out you have a hobby?"

"They will torment me endlessly with the knowledge."

Her frown deepened. "The viscountess told me at tea that you've earned the name the Unwanted Duke thanks to your sisters."

His smile turned chagrinned. "Is that so? I think you discovered a great deal at this tea. What else did the viscountess say?"

Della shrugged. "Not much."

"Oh?" Andrew turned away as he made his way to the opposite side of the worktable and around to the door. He reached over and flicked the bolt home, the sound echoing in the room.

Della swallowed, a sudden anticipation building inside her.

"And did the viscountess tell you to get this gown?" He approached her the way she imagined a cat would stalk its prey through the grass. She backed up but the workbench was just behind her, and there was nowhere to retreat.

He stopped in front of her and raised a single finger. She watched it as he lowered his hand to the edge of her bodice, tracing the delicate skin there. Suddenly she realized why his hands were so callused, and she arched into his touch, wanting to feel his rough hands on her.

"Because you weren't wearing this gown when you left this morning."

She closed her eyes, and while she wanted to say it was in embarrassment for the pink monstrosity she had worn earlier, she knew it was because of the sensual onslaught he was now waging against her. And he'd only touched her with a single finger.

"I wasn't," she managed, but any more words were beyond her.

His finger trailed up to her shoulder where the cap sleeve left much of her exposed. The finger kept going until it caught under her chin and lifted her face to his. She readied herself for his kiss, her toes curling in her slippers as she prepared herself for the slow, consuming burn of it.

But it never came. Instead, his lips pressed to her ear, "And what do you suggest should be your punishment for discovering my secrets?"

Her body clenched in her most private place. "Punishment?"

He flicked out his tongue to lick her ear. "Yes, punishment."

She tried to find words, but she couldn't even draw a breath.

And then suddenly he was gone, and her eyes flew open.

"I think I shall have your dessert at dinner tonight." He rolled his sleeves back down as he took his jacket from where he'd hung it on a hook behind the door. "I think that will be punishment enough. I do believe Cook has made her famous sticky toffee pudding."

"You wouldn't?"

His grin was devilish. "Of course I would."

He went to open the door, and she stopped him with a hand on his arm.

"Andrew, do you only repair broken furniture?"

He looked at her quizzically. "Yes. Why?"

She shrugged. "It's only...well, you're obviously talented. It seems like a loss that you shouldn't make any of your own."

He let go of the bolt he'd been about to open and turned to her fully. "I have a feeling you may be able to understand this better than most, Della. A duke is not expected to engage in things such as commerce and manufacturing. It is often seen as beneath a member of the peerage." He shrugged. "Besides that, I haven't the time for more than tinkering." He moved to open the door again, and she stalled him.

"So, you keep it a secret? This hobby of yours. Because you don't wish for others to know the Duke of Ravenwood would engage in such an unseemly activity?"

"Yes, there's that." He cast his gaze around the workshop. "But it's more that this is mine." He brought his attention back to her. "While I was growing up, there were always sisters underfoot. The only place I could get away from them was in this workshop. My father employed a gardener at the time who enjoyed working with wood. He taught me what he knew, and I took over when he left to be closer to his wife's family in Surrey."

It was something so simple, and yet, having met most of the Darby sisters, Della could understand why it would be so important to him to have a place to call his own.

"And building your own furniture?" she asked.

He shook his head. "Designing a piece of furniture would take the focus and time that I do not have to give it."

"Why?" she probed, but he was already shaking his head.

"I must take care of my family as you know. I can't let my attention stray."

She recognized the determined look in his eye and asked nothing further as he opened the door.

CHAPTER 14

He was growing accustomed to waking with her in his arms.

He lay there, holding as still as possible so as not to wake her. He wanted to enjoy the feel of her for just a little longer. Much like everything Della did, she woke with an enthusiasm that could not be stopped, but he wanted to linger in bed with her.

He had never told anyone of his love for repairing furniture. He had been telling Della the truth. It had largely happened by accident and all because he had been trying to escape his sisters. It had started with the usual things. Rosewood and walnut, although he preferred the sturdier grains of oak. He'd sanded and finished the things that Manford, his father's gardener, repaired, and he'd watched while he worked, learning the precision it required to do such tasks.

It had been thrilling, and more, he discovered that when he bent his mind to the wood, it freed him of the pressures he had as the Duke of Ravenwood and the caretaker to so many sisters. When he worked with wood, it was his only opportunity to relieve some of the burden he carried.

But he was always careful never to lose himself in the making of furniture. He knew Della would ask the question, and she had. But he had been firm in his resolutions. He could not make his own furniture for it would require too much from him, and he couldn't risk losing focus. Not ever again.

But now Della had him wondering.

She had noticed the work he had completed on the dressing table in the duchess's rooms at Ravenwood Park. No one had recognized his work before, and for some reason, receiving her praise had shifted something inside of him. It was as though he suddenly wished for recognition for his work, but that wasn't quite it. It was as though she had shown him there was more to be done. There was more he hadn't considered.

He had thought he would continue to tinker with furniture, enjoying the cathartic nature of it, but now he wanted more. If he were being truthful, he could admit he had been feeling that way for some time. It was as though he were holding himself back when he knew he was capable of doing more, and he didn't like that feeling. It was as though he were leaving things undone.

But then Della stirred against him, and he remembered how much weighed on him. The responsibility and the severe nature of what might happen should he let down his guard. He pulled her closer against him and tried to memorize how it felt to hold her.

Something had changed for her yesterday, but she had yet to tell him what. Part of that was likely his fault. He had distracted her terribly after dinner the previous evening, and she had hinted that tea with the viscountess had been enlightening in some respect. But the best evidence he had that something was different was that damn blue gown she had been wearing.

It was the color of a slumbering sea, and it turned her blue, blue eyes to gemstones. Gone were the hideous frocks that made her look like a deformed and overstuffed pillow. The sapphire gown had put her on display like the crown jewel she was. But no, it wasn't that at all. Because somehow Della managed to make the gown appear inferior. It was just a base on which she showcased her best features.

To him that was all her features, but it was more than the physical. Her attitude had changed when she'd donned that gown. Back was the lass he had encountered at MacKenzie Keep in Kettleholm, practical and strong and determined. He knew it had to have been more than the clothes, but he wondered what it was that had made her disappear in the first place. He worried it was something he had done, and he hoped she would find the courage to tell him.

He knew he was falling in love with her. He had been for weeks, and for so many reasons, he continued to deny it. But when she had charged into that workshop in that sapphire gown, he could no longer deny it. He could only work harder to protect himself against it. For if he let himself love her, it would put them all in danger.

She stirred all too soon, but before she could fully awaken, he slipped his hand beneath the hem of her nightdress and proceeded to distract her for several more hours.

It was late in the afternoon when Mallard interrupted him in his study as he went over estate reports from his steward to inform him he had a visitor. Andrew was somewhat surprised to find the Duke of Raeford's card on the silver tray with which he was presented.

He stood as his oldest and dearest friend swept into his study. It was evident from the mud on his boots and the wrinkles in his jacket that Ben had only just arrived from the north.

"I trust you bring news," Andrew said without preamble.

Ben had not relinquished his hat in the hall and now drew it from his head. "The MacKenzie has been to Ravenwood Park."

This news was not unexpected, but it still rocked Andrew enough that he sat down, indicating for Ben to do the same. He scrubbed his face with his hand before meeting his friend's gaze.

"When?"

"Little more than a week ago. We left Raeford as soon as we could to get here. I would have sent word by messenger, but the message was too important to leave to a service."

Andrew studied the man who was now his brother-in-law and who at one time had caught newts with him along the stream that separated their properties in Yorkshire.

"I don't deserve a friend like you," Andrew said now.

Ben laughed. "I beg to differ, mate. I think the universe had something greater in store for both of us, and we've nothing left but to let fate have its way."

Andrew laughed now. "I suppose you're right. I take it my sister accompanied you."

Ben understood the unasked question. "She's at Raeford House having it opened and aired. She thought it best to give you fair warning that she had returned to town, and that she had no intentions of causing further harm to your wife."

Andrew raised an eyebrow. "I find that difficult to believe."

"I will refrain from commenting," Ben said with an obvious smirk on his face.

Andrew leaned his head back against his chair. "The MacKenzie has found his way to my door. What do you make of it?"

Ben settled back in his chair. "He either knows that you've absconded with his daughter, or he is merely pursuing every gentleman who attended the stalking party to see which one may be housing her."

Andrew eyed his friend. "Which do you think it is?"

"I should not like to underestimate the cunning of a man who is dastardly enough to sell off his daughter so I would assume the first."

Andrew's hands curled into fists. "I have ascertained the legality of our marriage, and while I do not doubt its validity, I worry the MacKenzie may try to cause trouble. I will die before I allow him to hurt Della."

"I hope it does not come to that." Ben's smile was lopsided.

"You're right. I shouldn't wish to leave you with sole responsibility for my sister. That's a fate crueler than most."

Ben's expression folded into a look of concern. "Do you really believe your sisters to be so much trouble?"

Andrew raised an eyebrow.

Ben swallowed. "I'll admit they're not the easiest of companions, but I daresay you make them sound a great deal worse than they actually are. All of them have made incredible matches." He pressed a hand to his chest. "Some better than others." His smile was cocky. "But yet you continue to assert they require your protection. Why is that?"

Andrew straightened. "Because they do. I'm their brother. I must look out for them."

"But they have husbands now. Good ones. Shouldn't you leave it up to them to see to the care and comfort of their wives?"

Andrew shook his head. "The last time I did that—" He stopped and shook his head once more. "Needless to say, I don't feel comfortable leaving them to their own decisions."

Ben gripped his hat in both hands. "As one of those husbands, I must disagree. Your sister is more than capable of making good decisions. She saved Raeford Court, did she not?"

Andrew remembered how only months earlier Johanna had stormed into his study at Ravenwood Park demanding Louisa's unused dowry to save Raeford Court from devastation.

"She's made a couple of good decisions, but she also married a fortune hunter."

Ben had the decency to look guilty. "Be that as it may, she trusted her instincts, and it worked out in the end. Why must you continue to think you know better?"

"Because I do."

Ben shook his head. "That's something one of our fathers would have said, Andrew."

His friend had the power to unsettle him with a single statement like no other could. Well, perhaps Della could now as well, but he clung to his conviction.

"It may seem draconian and archaic, but I just can't let anything happen to them. I'm the only one left to protect them."

"No, you're not," Ben said softly, and Andrew realized he was right.

He held his friend's gaze even as something shifted around him. Andrew thought of the way Dax and Sebastian had stepped in that night to save Della from a social faux pas, but then he remembered what Sebastian had said to him that day on the pavement. He and Louisa had not married of their own free will. Andrew had suspected but then...

Louisa was now the Duchess of Waverly, well respected and admired for her design work. She had a beautiful son and from what he could tell a loving marriage.

And Ben had only just reminded him of what Johanna had achieved.

Both sisters had obtained their current situations through

THE DUKE AND THE LASS

their own instincts and cunning. He could take credit for very little of it, but he held on to the fact that he had played a role in it no matter how minor. He wanted to tell Ben as much, but he knew he would never tell another soul.

He wouldn't be able to protect his sisters if they knew just how much he continued to meddle in their lives. But it was for their own good. He had to remind himself of that.

Andrew stood and rubbed at the back of his neck as he paced away from his friend and to the windows that overlooked the gardens.

"Do you think the MacKenzie will come here next?"

He heard Ben get to his feet behind him.

"He might. I made inquiries at the inns in the village before we left. Discreetly, of course. The MacKenzie still had a room at the Bull and Anvil when we left."

Andrew turned. "He'll be at least a day or two behind you then if he's headed here."

Ben nodded. "It could be argued he won't be here before the end of the week. The road is growing firmer though as the temperature gets colder. Travel was relatively easy for us."

Andrew nodded. "I'll keep that in mind."

Ben fingered the brim of his hat. "Andrew, what will you do if the MacKenzie does come for Della?"

"Nothing," Andrew said, his smile slow. "I won't need to. She's my wife. The law is on my side."

"And what if the MacKenzie doesn't care about the law?"

Andrew's gut churned at the thought. "Then I will teach him to respect it."

* * *

DELLA RETURNED HOME from luncheon just as the clock in the vestibule of Ravenwood House chimed the hour. She wasn't sure how it had gotten to be so late. When she had sent notes to Eliza and Louisa requesting their help, she hadn't expected such a clamorous response.

Eliza had invited her and Louisa to luncheon, and the rest had rather escalated from there. While Della had hoped to merely bend their ears on duchess matters, the sisters had plunged in with a full curriculum on duchess schooling.

Della had thought she would feel somehow lacking or ill prepared when she left for Eliza's, but she found the truth to be rather the opposite. Eliza and Louisa strategized as if this were a military coup and Della the prize.

They analyzed every angle, unearthed every topic, and uncovered every possible snare Della may encounter as the Duchess of Ravenwood, and it was all far more entertaining than a book would have been.

She hadn't really thought to ask her new sisters for help until the day she'd taken tea with the viscountess. Della had grown used to having only herself on which to rely, and she was glad now that she'd written the letters to Eliza and Louisa in the fit of enthusiasm she'd developed after leaving V's and Madame Beauchamp's.

Della shed her cloak and warm gloves and pressed her fingers to her cold cheeks. November had descended on London with a bitter cold she was told was unusual for this time of the year. She welcomed the cold and only wished she'd be allowed to take some exercise in it. However, Andrew was still adamant about her leaving the house with an escort and a carriage.

She handed her things to the footman by the door and stepped farther into the house, only to stop. She had no further plans for that afternoon, nor did she know where her husband was.

She turned back to the footman who was busy hanging her things.

"Excuse me," she said, still unsure how she should address the servants. That was another topic for her to go over with Eliza and Louisa. "Would you mind telling me where I might find the library?"

The footman gave her clear directions and within moments she found herself standing in a room that rivaled the library at Ravenwood Park. She went about the room lighting lamps in the fading afternoon light to better see the towering shelves of books. Unlike the library in Yorkshire, this room contained a great deal more seating arrangements and a small desk pushed under one window. She was disappointed to find there were no window benches, but this was made up for with the plethora of overstuffed chairs.

She rang for a maid, but Mallard himself appeared.

"Your Grace." He gave a small bow.

She smiled. "I was only hoping to get some tea and biscuits, but would you also happen to know where His Grace might be?"

She was somewhat wary of having to always ask about the whereabouts of her husband, but Mallard straightened, giving no sign that she should already know where he was.

"His Grace has stepped out. He instructed me to tell you he truly has gone out this time, and he is not hiding below stairs." Mallard raised a single eyebrow, and she realized this was the only sign he would give to indicate he understood the joke. "He said he would return in time for dinner."

"Oh, that's very good," Della said. "If you please, just the tea and biscuits then."

Mallard gave another bow and left.

While she waited, Della scanned the various shelves haphazardly. There were the usual classics she'd expected as well as some plays, books of poetry, and even some treatises on farming. She was delighted, however, to find an entire shelf devoted to novels. While none of them were her beloved Melanie Merkett novels, they would do.

She selected one at random and chose a chair by the window. It had been weeks since she'd last been able to sit and read a book, and it felt glorious to sink into the chair, the fading afternoon light spilling over the pages of the book in her lap. A maid appeared with her tea and biscuits, and Della settled in for the afternoon.

The novel was rather dry, but the tea and biscuits made up for it, and in all, she was pleased to spend a couple of hours there. She wasn't sure how long she'd been there, but the tea had grown cold, and the plate of biscuits was nothing more than a scattering of crumbs.

She contemplated summoning a maid for replenishment, but she found she was not very hungry. She hadn't eaten much at Eliza's. She'd been too busy talking with her sisters, the subject at hand too engrossing to have bothered with the cold chicken and salad. And now she found herself rather distracted as the novel had finally grown interesting.

She closed the pages of the book and stood, taking herself over to the desk in the corner. She rummaged about in its drawers until she located a scrap of paper. She was unable to find a pen or ink, but she was successful in unearthing a length of pencil. She sat down at the desk and tapped the pencil against the sheet of paper.

It was always best to have a plan, she thought, and if she were to make the most of her time with Eliza and Louisa, she wished to ensure they covered all the topics over which she was concerned.

She held the pencil poised above the paper for several seconds without writing, and then she set the pencil down.

Who was she fooling? There was too much she didn't know. She let her attention drift out the window as she pondered her status as the Duchess of Ravenwood.

She couldn't help but to recall what Andrew had said when she'd discovered him in his workshop the other day. Such manual artistry was not expected of a duke, and so he had kept this woodworking a secret. It seemed entirely rubbish to her. Why couldn't he repair furniture? He was a duke after all.

She realized the double standard in her thoughts. Why was she so quick to find herself lacking and yet was adamant in bolstering Andrew in his endeavors?

She picked up the pencil again and thumped it against the surface of the desk. How was she to ever overcome the voice of doubt in her head? It had been there for so long, it was hard to believe anything else as the truth.

But she must overcome it. It was one thing to acquire nice dresses and another to learn the social protocols required of a duchess, but if Della didn't conquer the thing inside of her, the echo left from so much neglect and scolding would all be meaningless.

That much had become clear to her.

For why would Andrew love someone who didn't love herself?

The thought cut through her with the precision of a knife. She wasn't sure when it was that she'd fallen in love with him, but she'd suspected it all along. And somewhere in the past few weeks she had realized being the perfect duchess wasn't it at all. When she got to the heart of it, she knew what she wanted.

She wanted to be loved.

As soon as she thought it, she felt immense guilt. Who was she to think someone like Andrew could love her?

And wasn't that the very problem.

The pencil stilled against the surface of the desk, and she watched it settle against the wooden top.

To be loved.

It seemed like something so simple, and yet it was something that had been denied her for the entirety of her life. If things were to change now, she had to start with herself.

She picked up the pencil again, ready now to formulate a plan, when a sharp knock came at the door.

A footman entered and bowed, but before he could speak a man blustered through the door, nearly knocking the poor footman off his feet.

Della stood, the muscles of her fingers going lax until she dropped the pencil at her feet.

"Ye think ye could hide from me, lassie." Her father's laugh was raw and crass, and suddenly the walls of the library were too close as her father's harshness seemed to echo back at her.

She froze in place, her hand curling reflexively around the back of the chair she had occupied.

The MacKenzie's red beard was wild about his face, his eyes almost manic. She could smell whiskey on him even as he stood several paces away, and she willed herself not to wretch.

"I understand ye think yerself wed. Well, I'll be having none of that." The bit of his cheeks she could see through his straggly beard were ruddy, and she wondered if it were from the cold or from drink. He advanced, his footsteps heavy and menacing, and vaguely, she was aware of the footman slipping out the door. "I dinnae care what that Englishman thinks he's done. I'll find a way to break this union." He was atop her now, and he gripped her arm in one meaty hand. Pain shot through her arm, but she was too frightened to cry out. "I will have what I want from ye, lassie. And what I want is an ally. Ye won't be takin' it from me."

He dragged her toward the door.

She hadn't spoken a word. She hadn't called for help. She hadn't told him no. She'd said *nothing*.

What a coward she was. What a—

She stopped the litany of self-recriminations because it would do no good. She had to think. What could she do? Her arm ached from where her father kept her pinned in his vise-like grip, and she knew she was no match for him physically. She didn't know where in the house a servant was to whom she could call for help, but even then, what was he to do? A servant was no match for the MacKenzie either.

This was her fate. She had come all this way. She had pushed herself so far beyond where she found comfort, and this was how it would all end.

Her father would take her back to Scotland, and she would not utter a single word in protest.

Of course she wouldn't.

She never had. She had never told her grandmother how awful she was to treat her granddaughter with such disdain. And Della's mother? Ha, there was a joke if Della ever saw one. The woman was more enamored of fancy dress than of her own daughter.

And yet Della never said a word.

She simply went along.

Just as she went along now, letting her life be dictated by others.

She dug her heels in. "Wait." The sound of her voice was shrill in the quiet room, and the MacKenzie stopped so suddenly he nearly pulled her over.

He stared at her, but her mind was a scrambled mess.

Think, Della. You must do something.

"I must...I must..." She licked her lips, her eyes casting about the room. They fell on the desk and the book she had left there. Her eyes snapped back to her father. "I must return the book I've borrowed from a friend."

The Mackenzie sneered. "Ye have no friends, lassie, Yer nothing but a—"

"I am sure the end of that sentence is stunningly poetic, but I believe you are in a hurry, are you not?"

Her father blinked.

"I'll take that for the affirmative. If you do not mind, I'll just gather the book and ring for a footman to see it returned."

"We've no time for ye to be bothering with niceties, lassie. I want to be far out of London before that bastard of a husband of yers returns."

He knew Andrew was gone. Had he been watching the house?

A shiver passed through her, and she used the opportunity to pull her arm free.

"There is always time to show respect," she said coolly, and without waiting for permission, she marched back to the desk.

Her back was to the MacKenzie, and it shielded her movements from him. Quickly, she snatched up the pencil from where she'd dropped it and scribbled on the still blank sheet of paper. She tucked it into the book even as she turned.

She didn't bother to ring for a servant. She marched in front of her father in the direction of the front door. He followed, nearly catching the hem of her gown in his thunderous footsteps.

She found the footman at the door, pretending to look anywhere but at her and her glowering father.

She presented the book to him. "Please see that this is returned to Her Grace, the Duchess of Ashbourne. It's most urgent. Can you see that it gets to her within the hour? I had promised to return it to her today, and it slipped my mind. I shan't wish for her to go another moment without it." She forced the footman to meet her gaze and all but shoved the book against his chest.

"Yes, Your Grace."

"The Duchess of Ashbourne. Return it to her within the hour. Do you understand?"

The footman nodded, his gaze sliding warily to the MacKenzie.

She could feel her father behind her, almost as if his brooding gave off a foul stench.

He didn't allow her to gather a cloak or gloves and simply took her by the arm and forced her out into the cold. A carriage was waiting on the street, and he shoved her into it.

Only as it pulled away and Ravenwood House grew smaller and smaller in the distance did she think for the first time that she may never see Andrew again.

She closed her eyes and prayed for she knew she could not let that happen. She simply couldn't live without him. Not anymore. She opened her eyes and looked at her father to find him wrestling with the stopper of a glass bottle half-filled with an amber liquid.

She returned her gaze to the window as the carriage rocked on and prayed Eliza would get her message.

CHAPTER 15

He did not know what he was doing there.

He stood outside of Grimsby and Sons on Shoreditch High Street and wondered if he'd completely lost his mind.

Shoreditch was not Whitechapel, but he looked around uneasily. This part of London was a working man's place, and Andrew felt wholly inadequate to be here. He watched the tradesmen filter into the mill buildings surrounding him, their tools carried in bulky wooden crates or strapped to them in the pockets of their leather aprons.

Andrew didn't deserve to be here. He wasn't like these men who had spent years honing their craft.

But more, he shouldn't have left Della.

He wasn't sure why he had done it. Perhaps it was Ben's news from Yorkshire that had quelled the urgency in him. If the MacKenzie were still in Yorkshire when Ben and Johanna had left, it wasn't possible for him to be in London before the end of the week, and something Della had said had been bothering him like a sore tooth.

Why didn't he *make* furniture? Why did he only repair it?

He had told her the truth. A true craftsman must dedicate himself to his art, and Andrew had never had such luxury. He had his sisters to protect and now his wife.

He shouldn't be standing outside of one of the finest manufacturers of furniture in London.

But he couldn't get his wife's voice out of his head.

He wanted to make her proud.

The thought came out of the void, but he knew it had been lingering there for some time. Probably for as long as he had suspected he'd fallen in love with Della.

It was a terrible thing to fall in love with one's wife, but he'd watched her grow and change over the past several weeks, and he had never admired anyone quite so damn much in all his life. She'd faced challenge after challenge head on, and not only survived, but flourished.

She made him laugh with her spirited ways and her child-like innocence. She made him burn with desire, and he hadn't slept so well in the course of his lifetime than he did when she was safely tucked into his arms.

He rubbed the back of his neck now and scraped his booted foot impatiently against the pavement. This was absurd. He should have St. John drive him back to Mayfair at once. He was only an impostor here.

He peered up at the white letters painted across the dusky red bricks of the building, declaring it the home of the foremost makers of fine furniture, and Andrew thought his chest might twist until he could no longer breathe. It was a falsehood. He wasn't a furniture maker. He merely tinkered with the stuff. He couldn't think to…

But Della believed he could.

The thought had all others quieting, and now when he looked up at the building, he felt nothing. There were no voices in his head telling him he couldn't do this. That he shouldn't do this. There was only the solid assurance of his wife echoing in his head.

He climbed the stairs two at a time and entered the building before he could change his mind again.

* * *

Never in her life had Della been so grateful for chamber pots.

A cart carrying a load of chamber pots had overturned on its way into London on the Great North Road. The cart had spilled its contents clean across the road. Crates had split open, spewing pottery everywhere. Traffic was being diverted as the men transporting the pots scrambled to clean up the mess.

As it was, it couldn't have been less than an hour before they managed to free their carriage from the melee and get turned around to bypass the wreckage of pottery and wood.

The sun was beginning to set by the time they gained the Great North Road once more. Her father was well into his bottle of liquor by the time London began to fade away, its tall buildings and structures replaced with farmland and the occasional posting inn.

Della closed her eyes and leaned her head against the side of the carriage.

It was too late.

Either Eliza had not received her message, or she'd been unable to locate Andrew or anyone else who could stop her father.

It was hopeless now.

"Do ye know why I married yer mum?"

She opened her eyes and took in her father. His nose was pulsing red, and she knew it was not from the cold that had seeped into the carriage. She tightened her arms about herself, refusing to shiver if only to keep him from knowing how cold she was.

"I think I do not care why you married her," she said flatly.

Her impudence startled him and his eyes widened, but then he let out a raucous laugh.

"I say, lassie. Yer more like yer ol' da than ye realize."

This thought had her closing her eyes again.

But they opened in seconds when the carriage suddenly careened toward the side of the road. Shouts came from outside, and her father lost his grip on his bottle. The thing dropped, shattering against the floor of the carriage as liquor erupted into the shaking conveyance. Della's hands shot out as she tried to steady herself. The smell of alcohol was making her sick, and she strained to hear what was happening outside.

Had Andrew come to save her? Was it one of his brothers-in-law?

But then through the commotion, she heard a crisp, clear voice call out. A decidedly female voice.

"Stand and deliver!"

Della reached for the door the second the carriage jostled to a stop, but her father's hand shot out, knocking her backward and away from the door. He stumbled out first, and she heard rather than saw him hit the gravel of the road.

"Wha's the meaning of this?" He was slurring now and coupled with his thick accent, his words were likely meaningless to someone who wasn't used to his speech.

Finally Della made her way to the door only to freeze at the sight that greeted her.

Johanna Carver, the Duchess of Raeford, wore trousers.

This was the first thing Della registered. She rode on horseback, her hair loose around her shoulders, a hat forgotten at her back. Something primal soared inside of

Della at the sight of another woman so brazenly defying customs that restricted the female sex, but she hadn't time to linger on the thought.

A carriage had rolled to a stop opposite them, and before the horses had thrown back their heads in a settling shake, the door flew open, and Louisa Fielding, the Duchess of Waverly alighted.

"Give us back our sister," she cried even as her feet hit the gravel of the road.

Della watched her father sway on his feet.

"See 'ere!" He held up a finger, and the assembled women waited for surely there must have been more to Della's father's speech than that. But there wasn't. Her father dropped his hand and stared at it as if he'd forgotten he had such an appendage.

Della shook her head and stepped down from the carriage.

"Louisa," she said, catching her sister-in-law's attention.

Louisa's face relaxed the moment she caught sight of Della. Picking up her skirts, Della picked her way across the gravel, the hard stones biting through her thin slippers.

Her father's hand shot out and grabbed hold of her upper arm. He had been swaying on his feet so much, she hadn't expected the sudden movement, and it startled her. She tripped, knocking into her father so she ended up in his arms. They wrapped around her like steel bands, and the air shot from her lungs. She coughed, black dots filling her vision.

How careless.

He might have been drunk, but he was still bigger and stronger than she was. And now he held her captive. While her sisters had been smart to run the carriage from the road, they were no match for the sheer brutal strength of an irate Scotsman.

Unless...

Della let go. She released all the tension from her muscles, sagging against her father. He hadn't been expecting it, and he fell backward, struggling to hold up her weight.

"Bloody feckin' Christ, ye son of a—"

Della smiled. Right there on the road to Scotland, captured in her father's embrace as he tried to haul her away, she smiled. For once in her life, her size had been a boon in her favor.

He scrambled, both to regain his grip on her and to maintain his footing. But something else happened then. Just as Della was sure he would find his grip once more before she had a chance to break free, he let out a gut-wrenching scream of agony. His arms disappeared from around her, and she fell to the ground hard. She heard a ripping and knew the gravel of the road had pierced her new gown. She felt a moment's pity for the darling dress, but then her instincts screamed at her to run.

She tried to gain her feet, but the gravel tore through the paltry fabric of her slippers, and she fell again.

But then hands were on her. Gentle ones. Strong ones. Lifting her to her feet at the same time they tossed a warm, thick blanket about her shoulders.

Eliza.

She must have been in the carriage too. She pulled Della away from her father as he continued to scream and splutter in the middle of the road, his arms flaying in Louisa's direction even as the woman had deftly sprinted out of his reach.

Della tried to make sense of what was happening. Her father clutched the meaty part of his upper arm, and even from where she stood, she could see red oozing between his fingers.

"Ye bitch!" he cried. "Ye would stab a man with a knife like that."

Louisa's smile was nearly feral as she held up the long, slender implement in her right hand, its shape unmistakable. "It's a hatpin actually. Quite handy, isn't it?"

The MacKenzie spluttered and gaped. "Does yer husband know what yer about with that thing? He'd 'ave a mind ta—"

"Who do you think gave it to me?" she interrupted, one eyebrow raised in challenge.

The MacKenzie's mouth opened without sound emerging, spit raining from his pudgy lips to catch in the matted hair at his chin.

"Come," Eliza spoke softly behind her, easing Della into the waiting carriage.

Louisa wasn't far behind, and just before she shut the carriage door behind her, Della caught sight of Johanna. She moved her horse as if the animal were a part of her, neatly side stepping the beast into the Scotsman's path, forcing him to jump out of the way. He threw himself against the carriage in his haste and crumpled to the ground, curses flying from his lips until the last moment.

The carriage the Darby sisters had arrived in had already sprung into motion, and Della heard Johanna's cry as she spurred her horse into a gallop to lead the carriage away from the MacKenzie.

Louisa shook her head as she cleaned her hatpin with a handkerchief. "Four husbands among us, and we can't find a single one when they're needed."

Eliza smiled, her hands cupping her rounded belly where her cloak failed to meet across it. "Who needs a husband when you have sisters?"

Della couldn't agree more. She pulled the blanket Eliza had given her more tightly about her and returned her sister's smile.

CHAPTER 16

*D*ella was not smiling when Andrew discovered what had happened.

It wasn't until the sisters had safely delivered her to Ravenwood House that Della realized the very real challenge she still faced.

Namely telling Andrew her father had abducted her from Ravenwood House.

She hadn't had time to question the servants about how her father had gained entry, but she was certain it was likely something simple. He was her father after all. He had probably said as much and the footman at the door had allowed him in. It was all terribly easy.

But as she paced in front of the fire in her rooms, wrapped in her warmest nightdress and dressing robe, her feet ensconced in slippers and thick woolen stockings, she knew it was going to be much harder to explain.

Because she had endangered his sisters.

To be fair, the note she had sent Eliza had instructed her to find Andrew and tell him what had happened. She had not expected the sisters to take it upon themselves to track her down. Della was beginning to understand why Andrew was so protective of them. It appeared they had a tendency for danger. And that was just the three youngest. Della couldn't imagine what the eldest was like.

She hadn't been gone for more than a couple of hours, but Mallard had treated her as though she had been held captive for years, decades likely. He'd had a teacart overflowing with Cook's toffee biscuits and puddings sent up. There was even a platter of shortbread, bless his heart.

She hadn't touched a single morsel except to consume two very hot, very sweet cups of tea.

It was after six when Andrew finally arrived. She didn't need to listen for the door or his footsteps on the stairs. Instead, he burst into her rooms through the connecting door.

And he was smiling.

He was smiling like she'd never seen him smile before. He appeared almost boyish, and her heart broke in two.

"Della, you will not believe where I've been." He kissed her soundly before moving to the teacart and snatching up a raspberry tart. He popped the whole thing in his mouth in one go and brushed his hands free of crumbs. "I went to see a furniture maker in Shoreditch."

She didn't know where Shoreditch was, but she smiled, hard. "That's splendid."

His eyes narrowed, and his chewing slowed. "Why are you dressed for bed?" He took two strides toward her. "Della, what's happened?"

She didn't want to tell him. Not now. He looked so happy coming through that door. He had almost been elated. He had gone to see a furniture maker. Did that mean he would try to make pieces of his own? She couldn't do it. She couldn't crush him like that. She couldn't give him more reason to worry.

But then he took her by the shoulders and squeezed gently, his gaze steady and warm on her face.

"My father kidnapped me," she blurted.

She hadn't meant to do it like that. She truly hadn't, and as soon as the words left her lips, she regretted them.

He blinked, his fingers flexing in the soft skin at her shoulders. "I beg your pardon."

"My father. He was here. He made me go with him. And I—"

His fingers pinched her skin, and she blinked against the sudden sharpness. "Were you hurt? Della, Christ! What happened? You must tell me."

She pushed against his chest until he released her, and she rubbed at the bruised skin of her arms.

"I will if you would just give me a moment."

But he was already headed for the door.

"Andrew," she called after him. "What are you doing?"

He pulled open the connecting door so hard it bounced against the wall. "I'm going to find him. That bastard thinks—"

"Andrew, he's gone. We ran him out of town when—"

He turned, his face suddenly blank and cold, and it was so much worse than moments before when he was angry.

"We?" he asked.

Never before had a single word frightened her quite so much.

She told him. She told him everything about her father appearing at Ravenwood House that afternoon, about what he had said about how he wished to use her to make an ally, about how he had taken her away but not before she had secreted the note to Eliza in the book, and then the chamber pots.

"Chamber pots? Hell's teeth, Della, why are you going on about chamber pots?"

She stomped her foot like a child. "If you would but shut up for a minute, I would tell you!"

He did, in fact, shut up, and she finished her story as quickly as possible.

He stared at her for several long moments once she had finished, and she wanted nothing more than to step into his arms and take away the pain that was so visible on his features.

"You are never to leave this house again." His voice was so low she almost missed his words.

She straightened, her chin going up. "I'm sorry?" she asked. "That sounded an awful lot like you are trying to make me a prisoner here."

"It's for your own good. You're not to leave this house. Is that understood?"

She opened her mouth, her rebuke ready on her lips, but the words died before she could speak them. Realization crept over her like a mounting fog, slithering through her pores and under her skin.

"Oh God," she whispered instead and took a step back. She shook her head. "That's all I am to you, aren't I?" she asked.

Confusion was clear in his eyes, but she could only shake her head and turn away from him.

"How could I have been so stupid?" She laughed but the sound hurt, and she pressed a hand to her chest. "I've been trying so hard to be the perfect duchess for you. I bought the gowns—twice because I got the wrong ones the first time—and I even asked your sisters for help, but it doesn't matter." She shook her head again. She stood in front of the fire now and even though she studied its flames she saw nothing. Hurt filled her. Like water in a rain barrel, it filled her until there was no room left for anything else, including air. "I just wanted you to love me," she whispered to the flames.

She could feel him behind her, and at her words, she heard him shift.

"Della—" She heard the strain in his voice and turned before he could say anything more.

"You mustn't say anything, Andrew. You mustn't say anything because it doesn't matter. It doesn't matter if what I've done to make you love me has worked, because I know it hasn't." She shook her head as if to confirm her words. "It can't. It can't ever work because you can't love me. You'll never love me. Do you know why?"

Her words had struck something inside of him. She could tell by the way his lips parted and his eyes widened.

"Della, I care about you—"

"Don't give me your excuses, Andrew. I don't need them. I know the truth. You can't ever love me as long as you see me as a responsibility." She shrugged, a strange, strangled noise coming from her lips that might have been a laugh. "I should have known. All of the clues were there." She took a hasty step forward as if propelled by her words. "Louisa said you had planned a long holiday in Scotland, but you told me you had to get to London for familial obligations. Which one is the truth, Andrew?"

He didn't answer.

She took another step forward. "I think the truth is you never planned to be away long because it would leave your sisters exposed. Your sisters have all married good men, and yet you think you're still responsible for them." She laughed, and again, the sound was strangled. "Forget the men they've married. Your sisters are good, strong, brave people. They don't need your protection. They need your love, but you continue to treat them like wards. They're not yours to manage, Andrew. What will it take for you to see that?"

She'd pushed him too far. She saw it the moment it was too late as his eyes narrowed, and his lips thinned.

He closed the distance between them. "They are my responsibility. They will always be my responsibility just as you are, because the second you let your guard down something happens. Isn't that what you've proven today?"

"Don't make this my fault," she shot back.

He scoffed and paced away from her. "Do you know what I went through when the Duke of Margate asked for Viv's hand? I vetted him thoroughly, and do you know what happened?"

Della swallowed. She had heard the story from Eliza and Louisa. "As I recall, it's had a happy ending."

He leered toward her. "But it didn't then. It didn't then, Della, and I was forced to watch my sister return with a broken heart and eyes full of tears. I watched her fall apart, Della, and it was my fault."

She sucked in a breath. "That wasn't your fault, Andrew," she said quietly. "That wasn't your—"

"Yes, it was," he cut her off. "It was my fault. That's why I worked so damned hard to convince them it was Viv's idea to find them all suitable matches. I knew they wouldn't listen to me after what I had done, but they would listen to her."

The air had frozen in her lungs, and she couldn't breathe. Her heart thudded like the hoofs of a galloping horse, and she feared at any moment her heart might leap directly from her chest.

"It was you," she whispered, unable to meet his gaze. "You made certain they all obtained suitable matches. You made sure they were all wed appropriately. But…" she didn't know how to finish the sentence.

"It was easy to convince Viv of it. She was lost in her own heartbreak, and I took advantage of her scorn to press her into service." He took a hard step forward, pointing at the floor with a single finger as if to emphasize his point. "I made her see the importance of the thing. I made her see what had to be done."

"You manipulated her." Her voice cut through the air between them as if she'd thrown a dagger at him.

He stepped back as if her words had found their target.

But she didn't let him retreat. "You took advantage of your sister's heartbreak to see your own needs were met. You pressed your case when she was most vulnerable, and she believed you because she trusted you. She's your sister, Andrew." She shook her head. "You should have been comforting her. Not convincing her to carry out your dirty work."

"It wasn't dirty work. I protected my sisters—"

"You treated them like objects."

Silence rang in the room as her words extinguished further argument. She returned to the fire as she struggled to regain her breath, calm her racing heart.

After several moments, she heard him approach her, could feel him standing so close and yet not touching her. She didn't want him to touch her. For the first time since she'd met him, she was repulsed by the very idea.

"I love my sisters, Della," he said. "I would do anything to protect them."

She turned and faced him, her chin held high. "That's not loving them, Andrew. That's controlling them."

He shook his head and stepped away from her, and although his back was to her, she heard his words clearly.

"You wouldn't know anything about it, Della. You don't have any family."

She didn't know how the pain didn't kill her as his words cut through her, extinguishing the last of her hope.

"Get out," she said, proud at how steady her voice was.

He didn't say anything. He left the room, closing the connecting door behind him.

As soon as she heard his footsteps fade away, she strode over to the door and locked it.

Then she walked to the window bench and curled up on it, laying her head against the cold pane of the glass. She was too tired to even cry.

* * *

When he could no longer bear the heavy silence of the house the next day, he went for a ride.

Or at least, he attempted it.

But the weather had other things in mind. November rain was unlike any other, and it was really more like ice pelting him as he navigated the clogged streets on his way to the park.

What he wanted was a gallop across the fields of Ravenwood Park, but he would settle for a canter through the park. If he could even find the park.

The sleet had frozen his eyelashes, and he knew if he didn't return indoors, he would risk losing parts of his face to frostbite. For some devilish reason, he pressed on.

Rotten Row was deserted. All sensible people having likely fled for cover or not emerged in the first instance. He spurred his horse on at the sight of the empty stretch of pathway and was nearly halfway down it when another rider overtook him. Andrew was startled by his presence, but then the man pivoted, cutting in front of Andrew so he was forced to stop abruptly.

He pushed back the dripping brim of his hat to give the man a stern set down for his recklessness when the rider pulled to a stop and raised his own hat so Andrew could see his face.

He frowned. "I suppose Johanna thinks I'll die of cold."

Ben rubbed the sleet from his face. "*I* think you'll die of cold. Can you not sink into your cups like a normal brooding man?"

Andrew wanted to protest, but his friend was right. He allowed Ben to lead him to a public house on the other side of the park on Marylebone High Street. The Goose Neck was a refined establishment for a public house. The tables weren't even sticky with the wares of previous guests, and the serving maids were all modestly dressed. If Andrew were going to have a thorough sulk, he thought he could at least do it in a hovel like a proper gentleman.

Ben even had the audacity to order tea.

Andrew sent him a look, but Ben only blew on his hands and rubbed them together as if to warm them.

"You may imbibe, but I, for one, would like to thaw." He unraveled the scarf about his neck and hung it over the back of his chair along with his greatcoat. Both dripped water to the floor below.

Andrew had shed his own coat, but he hadn't bothered to remove anything else, and water now dripped steadily along his shoulders. He felt the cold at the same time he didn't. He was oddly hollow and numb.

He had been since he'd heard Della lock the door between them the previous night.

Since then, the sound of the lock had been an interesting accessory to the litany of recriminations he had looping in his head.

He still couldn't understand why he had said what he had. He owed Della an apology. Why in the heat of the moment had he selected the one thing he knew would cut her? Why had he so carefully chosen to attack her where she was most vulnerable?

He was a bastard. More than that, he was a terrible husband, and this hurt more than any names he could conjure.

He'd hurt her.

He'd *hurt* Della.

What was worse was that he'd done it on purpose. He had wanted to strike where it would cause the most damage, and he had succeeded.

He would never forget the calmness in her voice as she'd told him to get out. He knew he had inflicted the hurt he'd wanted to cause, and now he hated himself for it.

And when he truly thought about it, he knew exactly why he had done it.

Because he loved Della, and the thought that he'd let her down, that he'd let her get *kidnapped*, had nearly ended him. At the very least, he knew he had failed as a husband. He had failed to protect her, and in that was his greatest fault.

The serving maid brought them their drinks, Ben's tea and a tankard for Andrew. He took a sip, but he couldn't have said what was in it. It didn't matter. He hadn't eaten that day, and the alcohol did little more than swish around in his stomach, making him slightly ill.

"How did you know what happened?" Andrew asked after several moments of silence.

Ben had settled into his seat across from him and appeared not to be in a hurry to have it out with him. Andrew found it vexing.

Ben raised an eyebrow. "Something about duchess lessons. Eliza, Louisa, and Della showed up at the house around luncheon today."

Della had left the house? He curled his hands around his tankard, and he was grateful he didn't crush the thing.

She'd disobeyed him. Of course she had. His chest constricted with the thought, but then he never should have demanded she stay in the house. It had been a reaction to thinking she may have been hurt. That the MacKenzie could have done something more than carry her away in a drunken rage.

Andrew took a long drink of his ale.

"Duchess lessons?" He recalled Della mentioning as much, but he had given her so little opportunity to voice her perspective. He had been too busy trying to control her.

Isn't that what she had accused him of? Controlling the people he loved?

Loved.

God, he'd been an idiot.

But it didn't change things. Della was still vulnerable, and he was still charged with protecting her. She might see it as controlling, but he saw it as a necessity.

Ben leaned forward, putting his elbows on the table. "Della also said it was your idea to get Viv to find the sisters husbands." Ben's gaze was direct, and Andrew daren't look away. "I don't think I must tell you this didn't settle well with the sisters."

Andrew rubbed at the back of his neck. "It needed to be done."

Ben's laugh was not more than a scoff. "It needed to be done. You sound like my father, and you know I don't mean that as a compliment." Ben's expression turned questioning. "Do you really not see what your sisters are capable of, Andrew? It's nice that you show such concern for them, but they really don't require your influence in their lives. They have it rather figured out for themselves." He took a sip of his tea.

"I thought Viv had it figured out as well. The Duke of Margate—"

"Was a stupid young man. We've all been in his shoes." Ben screwed up his mouth. "Well, perhaps not quite like that, but we've all made mistakes." Ben gestured with his teacup at Andrew. "You're making your mistakes right now."

"I'm not making a mistake."

Ben leaned forward. "You're racing your horse through a muddy path in the middle of a sleeting storm, and you swear you're not making a mistake."

Andrew ignored him.

"Johanna married a fortune hunter, and her life turned out just fine."

Andrew looked up at this and met Ben's smirk.

"The fortune hunter is lucky my sister stopped me from killing him."

Ben wiggled his eyebrows. "I could have taken you."

"You could not have—"

Ben held up a hand to stop him, and Andrew felt the beginnings of a smile, which seemed impossible.

"All I am trying to say is you need to give your sisters more credit. They're remarkable women. I know you feel some kind of responsibility because your mother died so young, and your father was left without a clue as to what to do with you lot. But you can't be responsible for them forever. At some point, everyone grows up and becomes responsible for their own actions."

Andrew was already shaking his head. "No. Not when it comes to them and not now. There are too many things—"

"There are too many things that can hurt all of us. Are you going to protect everyone?"

This silenced him. Ben was right. Andrew could spend the whole of his life protecting others, and at the end, what would he have to show for it?

"If you hadn't allowed Johanna to make a critical mistake, I wouldn't be married to the woman I love now." Ben's smile grew sheepish. "Have you ever thought of the good that can come of making mistakes? Of making unwise choices?"

Andrew closed his hands around his tankard. "Nothing good can come of an unwise choice."

Ben laughed. "I can safely say you're wrong, old friend. I wake up every day thanking God for what I have, and I only have it because Johanna married a fortune hunter. How can you not say there can be no good that comes from committing an error?"

"But Viv—"

"Is happily ensconced in hops with her husband." Ben shook his head, his lips slightly parted. "When are you going to see that?"

"I can't forgive him for what he did to her."

"No one is asking you to," Ben said quietly. "But can you not see how happy he makes her now? Are you so quick to assume that the fault for what happened between them lies squarely at Margate's feet? Surely Viv is not innocent."

Andrew thought of his eldest sister and her hot-headed, stubborn nature and realized Ben might be right. He still didn't like it.

"Even if it were partly her fault, shouldn't it be argued that I should protect them where I can?"

"And prevent them from achieving what they might? Being who they are?" Ben shook his head. "It sounds like you're caging wild animals, Andrew."

Andrew blinked, his jaw tightening. Had Della told his sisters that he'd demanded she stay in Ravenwood House? He suddenly hoped she didn't, for now in the clarity of the moment he could understand what a brute he had sounded. Ordering her to remain under lock and key was barbaric, and he knew that now.

Only…

"But then how do I keep Della safe?" The words were soft and tense with emotion, and he looked up, capturing his friends gaze. "How do I keep her safe, Ben?"

Ben's expression folded into one of miserable understanding. He placed a hand on his friend's arm.

"You have to trust her, Andrew," he said. "That's all any of us can do. We must trust the ones we love to make the right choice when faced with a decision. Didn't she do the right thing yesterday?"

Andrew closed his eyes. "I assume Johanna is rather proud to have played the highwayman."

Ben leaned back in his chair, his face aggrieved. "She won't shut up about it."

They shared a laugh before growing silent. Andrew pushed his tankard about the table.

"I love her, Ben," he said after some time. "I love her, and it scares the hell out of me."

"I know, mate." Ben nodded. "Love is the scariest thing of all. But what are you going to do about it?"

Andrew's gaze drifted to the rain-streaked windows as he shook his head.

"I don't know," he muttered. "I just don't know."

CHAPTER 17

"I'm going to kill him."

Della could understand the sentiment from Andrew's oldest sister, but she hardly thought murder was worth it.

She leaned forward and patted the woman's arm.

"I can relate, but don't you think murder is rather too messy?"

Della liked Viv. She could admit she had been the most skeptical about meeting the eldest Darby sister. The stories from Eliza, Louisa, and Johanna had suggested a formidable force, especially considering the woman's determination to see her sisters wed, and Della wasn't sure if she could stand up to her.

But it turned out standing up to her wasn't required because Viv only used her powers for good. She supported her sisters and defended the weak. Della still wasn't sure which category she landed in, but she hoped it was the first one.

Viv had returned from Margate with her husband in tow after apparently receiving a scathing letter from Johanna.

Della was beginning to understand that the youngest of the Darby sisters served as the principal communicator in the group. It would do well to remember this.

They were gathered in Eliza's drawing room. The topic of today's duchess lesson was invitations, but they'd done little more than discuss the type of paper that was acceptable. They were required to ensure Viv was up to speed on all that occurred, and this took precedence over invitations. Of course it did.

"Not for Andrew," Viv said now. "It would be worth it." She twisted her hands in her lap. "I hate the idea that I was manipulated like that." She pushed to her feet and paced away. "I really thought I was best suited to ensuring you all obtained advantageous matches." She stopped at the window that overlooked the street.

"Well, did Andrew agree with you or did he suggest it?" Louisa asked.

Viv shook her head, never moving her gaze from the window.

"I couldn't say now. It was so long ago, and in my mind, I was always so sure it had been my idea. But now I don't know."

Eliza's son, George, played on the floor with Johanna, and he clapped his hands together as he successfully knocked over a block tower Johanna had constructed for him.

"Again," he cried, hands clapping furiously.

Johanna only smiled and went back to stacking blocks. The sight was so terribly domesticated, Della felt a pinch in her chest in response. She suddenly wondered if she and Andrew would have children or would their marriage be the tense, silent arrangement that they had entered after the day her father had tried to abduct her.

Eliza reclined in her seat, propping her feet up on an ottoman as she pressed her hands to her back with a slight squeeze of her eyes as if she were exhausted. Her belly was large, and the rest of her was quite thin, and Della could only imagine how exhausted the poor woman must be.

"I for one do not care whose idea it was," Eliza said. "It got me this after all." She spread her hands encompassing the room, the house, her life, and Della couldn't help but smile.

"I agree," Louisa said from where she stood behind them, swaying on her feet as wee Simon slept against her shoulder. "Do you think Sebastian would have married me otherwise?"

Viv turned from the window. "I suppose you're right," she said, running her hands over her own expanding stomach. "But would you suggest we let him off the hook for lying to us?"

Johanna wrinkled her nose. "Is it really lying? Or did he mislead us?"

Eliza picked up her head from the back of the chair. "What is the difference?"

"Misleading someone is far more calculating," Johanna said as she placed the last block on top of the tower and indicated for George to knock it over. He did, his laughter filling the room. Johanna looked up to meet Eliza's gaze. "Misleading someone suggests a level of forethought that I do not care for. What else should Andrew think he has the right to meddle in?"

"She's right," Viv said before making her way back to the seating area where Della and the sisters had taken up residence. She lowered herself to one of the sofas. "I suppose we could be angry with him or just be glad everything seems to have worked out in the end. Her gaze traveled around the room, her hands moving absently over her belly until she landed on Della. "But I do think he's been an idiot."

"Oh, of that, we can agree," Johanna said from her place on the floor.

"He owes you an apology, Della," Louisa said softly from behind her, never breaking her swaying motion.

"An apology?" Eliza said. "An apology is far too tame. I'm casting my vote for Viv's idea."

"Murder?" Della asked.

Eliza nodded. "It's the only thing that will do for what he said to you. He should be grateful you married him at all."

Della had thought Eliza had said the words flippantly, but then the other sisters murmured their words of agreement.

Della shook her head. "It's I who am grateful that Andrew married me. If it weren't for him—"

"You would have married someone more deserving," Louisa said matter-of-factly.

"A prince," Johanna said from the floor. "Oh, wouldn't Della make a beautiful princess?"

Eliza smiled. "Especially with a name like that. Princess Catriona Cordelia. And the most dignified of aristocrats would call you Princess CeCe."

The sisters erupted into laughter at this, and Della couldn't help but be swept up in it. She gazed about the room, wondering when it was that her life had become so full. But even as she thought it, her heart stuttered a little.

It wouldn't be complete without Andrew, and she knew now that he would never love her. Her laughter faded, and she plucked at her skirts.

Viv shifted along the sofa and put her arm around Della.

"I know it doesn't seem like it now, but it will be all right. Trust me." Her smile spoke of history Della couldn't fathom. "I should know." She laughed then.

"You should know?" Louisa spoke from behind them. "What about me? I married the Beastly Duke. If that doesn't take a spot of fortitude, I'm not sure what would."

"I married a fortune hunter," Johanna said as George knocked down yet another block tower. "But I was madly in love with him, so I'm not sure that counts," she said with a wrinkled nose.

"I can best all of you," Eliza spoke softly.

Her dog, Henry, had uncurled himself from his spot by the door where Della wasn't entirely certain he hadn't taken up as a means of guarding the women inside the room and now sat perched under his mistress's arm.

"How do you figure?" Viv asked.

Eliza's smile was purely devilish. "My dog tried to eat my husband when he even suggested the idea of marriage."

This drew forth another round of laughter, and for the first time in days, Della felt marginally better.

Viv squeezed her again. "See? When you married Andrew, no one was under duress of being the next meal of a surly canine."

Henry whined.

"I'm sorry, Henry," Viv said. "There is nothing surly about you."

His tail thumped against the floor as if he accepted her apology.

Louisa took a chair, careful to keep Simon steady against her shoulder as he apparently had fallen truly, deeply asleep and the poor woman could finally get off her feet.

"I know just the thing," she said, lowering herself into the chair. "You should host a dinner, Della."

Della shook her head immediately. "I think it's already been made clear how inadequate I am at engaging in dinner parties."

Eliza laughed. "Hardly inadequate. The Countess of Bannerbridge will not stop badgering me about when you might be accepting further invitations. She cannot wait to host you and Andrew."

"The Countess of Bannerbridge?" Della tried to recall the

woman, but that night at the Ashbourne dinner seemed so long ago.

Louisa smiled. "The countess is a lovely woman. You should absolutely accept an invitation from her."

Della's head swam with this new information. "But I made a complete ninny of myself that night."

Eliza laughed. "Not at all. You were like a breath of fresh air. Do you know how many dinners one attends during a season? It was so delightful to have you there to offer a different perspective. I think Louisa's right. You should host a dinner. It will be family and just a few select invitations. It will be a great way for you to try out your duchess lessons on a sympathetic audience."

Viv squeezed her shoulder again. "I think it's a marvelous idea. It will give you a wonderful place to start before the pressure of the season next year. You will be expected to host a ball then after all."

Della shook her head. "I couldn't possibly host a ball."

Johanna waved this off. "Balls are easy. They're always such a crush that none of it really matters."

George made a triumphant sweep of his blocks then, sending them scattering over the carpet. This was met with much glee and hand clapping.

"You make it sound easy," Della murmured, not feeling so sure.

"It's all quite easy when you have sisters," Louisa said, her smile sure and bright even as her eyes were so very tired while she patted wee Simon's back as he slept against her.

Della had never felt more alone in that moment, sitting in Eliza's drawing room, surrounded by the Darby sisters and knowing she'd never be a part of them no matter what they said or did. Andrew's words echoed through her mind with too much force.

Della didn't have family, and she never would. But she

could understand now why Andrew felt such a compulsion to protect these women because Della felt the same. She would do anything to keep these women safe, just as they had come to save her.

She raised her chin.

"I think Ravenwood shall host a dinner. It would be an excellent opportunity to try out my duchess lessons as you said, Eliza." She smiled at the woman.

Johanna clapped with George from the floor. "Auntie Della is going to host a party, George. What do you think of that?"

The little boy threw up his arms and cried, "Again!"

Even though he knew not of the conversation around him, his answer couldn't have been more perfect, and all of them laughed.

* * *

HE TUGGED at his cravat and jacket, but he knew the tightness in his chest had nothing to do with the clothing he wore.

This dinner was a very bad idea.

Andrew didn't like the idea of people coming into Ravenwood House. There was too much opportunity for the MacKenzie to slip in unnoticed.

Even though Della had limited the guest list, it still left the house vulnerable. No matter how he, Dax, Sebastian, and even Ben had tried to find word of the MacKenzie's whereabouts, all had been silent for nearly a fortnight since the man had tried to abduct Della straight out of her home.

Andrew paced across the length of the drawing room now, his frustration driving him to move. He'd only taken a couple of steps when movement at the door drew his eye. He looked up and stopped, seized by the vision that stood there.

Della.

Only it wasn't a Della he had ever seen. She wore a gown of sinful red silk that spilled from her shoulders in wide sweeping sleeves that only served to accentuate the trimness of the waist that spread into a waterfall of skirts. Her pale hair was swept up in a neat twist that showed off the column of her neck and the arches of her cheekbones.

She was no longer the woman he had met that night in the cold, drafty room of a Scottish castle, and he knew it was more than just a change of clothes.

He knew she had lost some weight. He could tell mostly by how slim her face had become, but she was still voluptuous and curvy, and more than ever, he wanted to trace her body with his hands. Preferably while they were both naked.

The thought had his throat constricting. They'd done little more than speak tersely to one another for the better part of two weeks, and most of all, he hated going to bed alone every night.

But as he looked at her now, he realized she held herself differently than she had when he'd first met her. The nervousness that had seemed to vibrate around her was gone, and she held herself with a confidence he suspected she didn't recognize.

She wasn't smiling, but he took a step toward her and said, "You look beautiful tonight, Della." He swallowed as his throat became suddenly dry. "But you've always been beautiful to me."

It was not the apology she deserved from him, and she watched him warily now as though she didn't trust his words, and this more than anything cut deep.

"Della, I—"

He was cut off by the entrance of Mallard. The butler gave a small bow.

"Your Grace, guests have begun to arrive."

"Please show them in, Mallard. We're ready to begin receiving them," Della answered, stepping into place at what would be the head of the receiving line.

"Very good, Your Grace," the butler intoned and backed out of the room.

Andrew took his place beside his wife and watched the door, expecting the first of their guests. But he thought of the interminable hours that lay ahead, acting the dutiful host next to his beautiful wife with so much standing between them.

"I'm sorry," he said quickly, his voice low. "I shouldn't have said those things to you. I shouldn't have treated you that way. This is hardly an appropriate or adequate apology, but I must tell you. I can't stand this silence between us, and I miss you." The words tumbled out of him in a rush.

Her lips parted, but she gave no other sign that she'd heard him as her eyes remained on the door of the drawing room as if waiting for the first guests to arrive. She didn't even look at him, and whatever hope he had mustered that she may forgive him vanished.

There was no time to say anything further. Their first guests arrived, the Earl and Countess of Bannerbridge. Della's smile was bright enough to light an underground cave, and he wondered what the countess held that he did not.

Della vibrated with glowing energy for the remainder of the guests. With each one, she gave special acknowledgment, thanking them for coming. It was as though she had been doing this all her life. When the viscountess she had taken tea with stepped up to greet them, he thought Della might split in two with happiness.

"V!" she proclaimed. "I'm so happy you were able to make it."

The viscountess curtsied and squeezed Della's outstretched hands.

"I'd like you to meet my husband," the viscountess said, drawing forth the tall gentleman behind her.

Andrew knew the man well, but he was distracted by the look of pure awe on Della's face. A part of him he didn't know existed coiled in jealousy at Della's obvious appreciation of the man, and when he walked away, Andrew swore she said, "Well done, V."

He didn't have time to dwell on his feelings as more guests entered.

Louisa and Sebastian, Eliza and Dax, and Johanna and Ben were there, of course. But it was Viv and Ryder that he had not expected.

"Johanna wrote you," he said when Viv stepped up to him.

She smiled and punched him in the shoulder.

"Brother," she said before turning to greet Della with a kiss to her cheek.

Ryder only shook his head, his lips thin in commiseration.

The drawing room was filled with guests within the half hour.

"You've a full house tonight, Your Grace," he whispered to Della. "That's quite a triumph for your first dinner."

"I have your sisters to thank," she said, and he couldn't help but notice an odd tone to her voice, almost as if she were detached from the whole thing, and it made him wince.

Della left his side to mingle with her guests while they waited to be called into dinner, but he remained where he was, watching her, brooding.

"Have you apologized yet?"

Andrew was surprised to find Dax standing next to him, Sebastian behind him.

"I have, but there wasn't time to talk it over."

Sebastian gave a disgruntled noise. "Apologies are one thing. Have you told her you love her? For whatever reason, they seem to like that even more."

Andrew blinked at his brother-in-law. This was by far the least expected conversation he had ever had with the man.

"I have not as such."

"You should tell her." Andrew turned to find Ryder had joined them, followed by Ben.

"You should," Ben agreed. "Sebastian is right. They like that."

Sebastian gave a nod as if to suggest how obvious it was that he was right, but Andrew was distracted by the arrival of Mallard announcing dinner.

Andrew made to move toward the drawing room door as custom would dictate he lead the guests into the dining room, but he was stopped by a commotion at the door leading from the hallway. He didn't need to look up to know who it was. The Scottish brogue was clear enough.

"I've come for my daughter, and I'll nae leave without her." The man barreled into the room, silencing the low murmur of conversation until only a few gasps of surprise punctuated the air.

Andrew curled his hands into fists and made to step forward, but the sound of Della's voice stopped him.

"Of all the bleeding codswallop," she said and then there she was, standing directly in front of her father.

Her height meant she matched the man inch for inch, and in her fiery gown, she appeared the far more threatening of the two. The MacKenzie looked like a man who had been drunk for the better part of a week with soiled and wrinkled jacket and trousers and a beard gone oily and clumped.

Andrew felt as though he were standing on a precipice. He could step forward, shield his wife from her belligerent father. Or he could step back. He could give her the choice to handle it herself. He had only to trust her, and nothing had ever seemed so scary or so simple.

This was the moment that would decide his future. This was the moment in which he knew if he made the wrong decision, he would lose Della forever. Everything became clear in an instant then, and he took a step back.

The MacKenzie pointed a shaking finger at his daughter. "I'll be the one who—"

"You'll be the one who what? If ye think I don't know yer blootered, yer baum's out the windae."

Andrew blinked as Ben sucked in a breath beside him. "There's the lassie you married," he whispered as he elbowed Andrew in the side.

Andrew was man enough to admit he found the sudden brogue in Della's voice rather appealing.

But she wasn't done.

"I'll nae be going anywhere with ye, Da. Yer nothing but a wee bully, and yer rank with drink." She flung out a hand as if to encompass the room. "Dae ye really think to take me awa' from this? Yer eggs are double-yoakit, and ye know it."

The MacKenzie blinked, but Andrew didn't miss how the man had taken a step back toward the door.

Della must have seen it too for she dropped her arms, the fight seeming to drain out of her even as her chin remained firm.

"I'm married, Da. There's naught to be done for it. At the least, I'll nae be a burden to ye no more." She gestured to Andrew then. "Yer attached to the Ravenwood title. Is it nae enough?"

The MacKenzie seemed to shrink before Andrew's eyes, but it wasn't what held his attention. It was Della's words that had his heart thundering and twisting.

I'll nae be a burden to ye no more.

She had it all wrong. She wasn't a burden. She wasn't a

responsibility. She was a beautiful, strong woman that he wanted more than anything to love.

He just wanted to love her.

If she let him.

The MacKenzie was nearly to the door now.

He waved a hand weakly. "It is, lass. It is. I'll get tae now." He scraped and bowed, leaving Andrew to wonder how Della had known that her father was all bluff.

"Da," Della called after him. "Why nae stay and have some scran?"

The MacKenzie hesitated in the doorway.

Andrew didn't know what scran was, but he assumed Della had just invited her father to dinner. He looked about them, at the impeccable guest list Della had constructed for her first society dinner.

And then he looked at the MacKenzie, a drunken old man in dirty clothes.

The Scotsman seemed to understand that he wasn't appropriately dressed, and he ran his hands down his jacket.

"There's a lassie," he said. "But no, girl. I'm nae fit for it." He turned to leave but something stopped him. He looked over his shoulder at his daughter. "Ye've surprised me, lassie," he said. "And nae many people do. I dinnae think yer either me or yer mother. Ye might just be something else." And with that he left.

But Andrew wasn't watching the MacKenzie. He couldn't take his eyes from Della's face as her father's words hit her. He watched the subtle transformation that passed over her features. The way her eyes widened ever so slightly, the way her bottom lip parted from the top one as she absorbed what she'd likely already suspected.

The woman without country or name was now without roots, and he knew she was left wondering where she belonged.

He made to step toward her, the need to pull her into his arms so great he didn't care who was there to witness it, but before he could move, something happened.

His sisters separated themselves from the gathered crowd and one by one took their places beside Della with Louisa stepping the closest, looping her arm through his wife's.

"It isn't any wonder that he doesn't know who you are," Louisa said.

Viv shook her head. "How could he?"

"It wasn't as if he could know," Johanna said.

"Know what?" Della asked, looking amongst the sisters.

Eliza's smile was peaceful and knowing, which was entirely like her. "He couldn't possibly know that you were meant to be a Darby sister."

CHAPTER 18

It was the dead of night when the knock sounded at the door.

She paused in brushing her hair and looked away from the dressing table mirror. She sat on the stool Andrew had mended with his own two hands, but she chose not to think of it.

But she knew who was knocking, and it made all of it seem too bright and real.

She set down her brush.

"Come in," she said calmly and clearly.

It had been a long evening, and while she thought her mind would be plagued by her father's words, it strangely wasn't. She was now bolstered by the true understanding of what it meant to be a part of the Darby sisters, and she thought it likely cushioned the blow of her father's declaration.

Instead, she couldn't stop thinking about what Andrew had said.

I miss you.

Something so little that meant so much. She'd never

known anyone to miss her, and to think he might have been suffering from their estrangement...well, she couldn't quite grasp it. Did he truly miss her? And what did it mean if he did?

She didn't wish to speak to him now. Not with the confrontation with her father still fresh in her mind, not with the strain of the evening still so present.

Her first society dinner, and her drunken father had bumbled right into it.

Andrew had probably regretted his words to her in that very instant. He was likely here to tell her to pack her trunks; he was sending her to Bewcastle.

But suddenly that didn't matter anymore.

Because she knew without anyone telling her that tonight had been a success despite her father's appearance. She *knew* she had done everything perfectly, and what hadn't been so perfect didn't matter. Her father's words had unknowingly released her from some kind of prison she had built around herself. It was as though she had stepped free of a weight that had worn her down over the years. She didn't know what it meant, but she suddenly felt clearer about her future.

She pivoted on the stool to face the door and prepared herself for a scolding.

But that wasn't what happened.

Instead, her husband came through the door and set a small table in front of her.

A small table.

It was of beautiful solid oak with powerful grains that marched across its surface. It was fashioned with four tapering legs that melted from the tabletop in elegant lines. The whole thing was finished with a warm stain and glowed with lacquer.

"It's...it's..." She looked up at her husband. "What is this?"

Andrew gave a sheepish smile. "It's a table."

"I see that," she said. "But what's it for?"

"It's for you." He rubbed nervously at the back of his neck. "I...made it."

She stood straight up, her eyes riveted to the table before her. "You made this?"

"I did." He dropped his hand to hang at his side. "I...I wanted you to have a place to set your book."

She blinked at the sudden rush of tears that came to her eyes at his words.

"Andrew." She had meant to say more, but the single word came out watery, and she bit her lower lip.

"Here." He was still dressed in his formal attire, and he reached inside his jacket. He withdrew a book and placed it on top of the table.

She stared, the tears running unimpeded down her cheeks.

It was a copy of the Melanie Merkett novel she had lost.

She touched a single finger to the book before slipping it over the edge of the cloth cover to the smooth surface of the table.

"Andrew, I don't—"

"I love you, Della," he interrupted, and she couldn't stop her gaze from finding his. "I know you've had a difficult evening, but I've wanted to tell you for some time now, and I didn't know how. I thought...I thought that after what I had said..." He licked his lips nervously. "Well, I thought you wouldn't wish to hear it, but I honestly don't care how you feel about it because I had to tell you. I had to tell you that I love you." He took a step toward her but seemed to think better of it. "I was wrong, Della. I was wrong about so much, but you were wrong too. You're not a responsibility to me." He laughed, almost as if he couldn't believe the words either. "You're so much more, and I don't want you to continue to think that way. It stops you from being so much. From being you, and I always want you to just be you. I hope you know that."

She blinked and felt the tears drying against her cheeks, but her mind remained blank, his words somersaulting in her head.

"Well, that's all I wanted to say. Good night, Della." He pressed a chaste kiss to her forehead and backed out the connecting door, closing it softly behind him.

She was left standing alone in the center of her rooms, her fingers idly tracing the edge of the table he had made for her. The first piece of furniture he had made himself, and he had made it for her. For her books to rest on.

She turned and stamped through the connecting door.

She froze at what she found. Andrew was seated in a chair by the fire, his face in his hands. It was the very picture of despair, and it stopped her heart in her chest.

"Andrew." His name was round with the emotion she poured into it, and he looked up, his eyes startled, his gaze disbelieving.

She was in his arms within seconds, her hands finding the muscles of his back, and her fingers dug in, held on. His lips were on hers, and she gave herself to him, fully and completely.

She hadn't known there was something standing between them, but Andrew had been right. She had just as much to let go of as he did, and anticipation for their future spiked through her.

Andrew pulled away far enough to murmur against her lips. "I love you, Della. I plan to say it enough for you to believe it."

"I do believe it," she said. "And I love you, Andrew. I've loved you almost since that first night when you tried to sleep on the floor of my room."

He pulled back farther, a devilish glint coming to his eye. "Since then?"

She watched him warily. "Well, almost since then."

He pulled away from her even though she held on to him for as long as she could. She watched as he went to the bed, tugging the bedclothes from it before carrying them to the place before the fire. He bent and spread them out until a soft nest had formed.

He then proceeded to remove his boots.

"Andrew," she said, a note of warning in her voice.

"Yes, lass?" he said, tugging the other boot from his foot.

"I thought I told you not to sleep on the floor."

He stretched out on the nest he had made and bent one arm behind his head as he gazed up at her. Memories of the first time she had seen him came rushing back to her, and when something akin to pain blossomed in her chest, she knew it for what it was.

Love.

Complete, overwhelming love.

"I believe you suggested I wasn't to sleep on the floor alone." His voice held a note of desire that was unmistakable.

She raised her chin. "I think you may be correct, Your Grace. An astonishing fact considering you're an Englishman."

She watched him try to hide his smile as she stepped out of her slippers and made her way over to him. She sank down on the nest he had made, careful not to touch him.

"I believe I had said I would join you if you attempted such a thing, did I not?"

"You did," he confirmed and rolled onto his side to face her.

He reached out to snag the belt of her dressing gown, and she swatted his hand away.

"Your Grace!" she said with mock indignation. "What kind of lady do you take me for?"

He ignored her feeble attempts at protest.

"A saucy lass if I'm not being too bold."

Her dressing robe parted under his attentions, and he dipped his hand beneath it, cupping her hip as he turned her body to fit against his.

"Of all the impertinent—" But he silenced her with a kiss, and she forgot anything else she might have said.

It was several seconds later as he nibbled her neck before he spoke again.

"I know I said you were beautiful tonight, Della, but I must make a confession."

Her hands had found their way under his shirt, and her fingers curled into his warm muscles.

"Oh?"

He lifted his head, a wicked smile on his lips. "I was really only thinking how much I wanted to get that gown off of you so I could do this." He tugged the hem of her nightdress up, and his hand traced along her bare skin, molding itself to her every curve.

Heat flared inside of her, low in her belly and spreading outward to the places where he touched.

He groaned as she lifted her hips into him, grinding her body against his.

"Do you have any idea what you do to me, Della?"

She smiled against his lips. "I have some idea," she murmured and proceeded to prove it.

She woke sometime in the night, her skin chilled where it had come out from under the quilts he had brought from the bed. But when she turned, she found him gone from their nest, and she sat up, panicked.

But he was there within moments.

"Shh, darling. I was only seeing to the fire," he whispered.

As sleep clawed at her, she let this pass and her eyes slid shut even as he drew her into his arms and curled her body into the warmth of his.

He pressed a kiss to her ear. "Go to sleep, lass. I'll always be right here."

She fell asleep, knowing without a doubt that he spoke the truth.

CHAPTER 19

It was snowing.

While such a thing was not uncommon in Cumbria, she was rather surprised to see the white flakes falling in London as Andrew pulled her out into the gardens of Ravenwood House. She was glad he had given her time to retrieve her cloak. He had been in such a hurry to see her out the door since he'd arrived home minutes before.

She couldn't be sure what he was about but thought the glee so evident on his face suggested he'd been to see Grimsby in Shoreditch again, but when she'd questioned him about it, he'd brushed it off.

He insisted he had something to show her in the gardens.

It was December, and she hadn't taken to venturing into the gardens as they had been put to bed for the winter, but she couldn't help but get caught up in Andrew's playfulness.

She had been right to retrieve her cloak however.

She flexed her cold fingers in Andrew's grasp, wishing she had grabbed gloves as well, but he'd been too insistent on getting her outside she hadn't wanted to take the time.

They wove their way through the gardens, dipping in and

out of walled sections, hedgerows, and beds black with turned earth.

Finally they spilled out into an area that was more open, and she paused as Andrew stopped suddenly beside her.

They were in a folly.

The perimeter was dotted with stone columns, their tops empty and reaching for the sky. A stone walkway circled them that led onto a stone dais set in the center of the folly. Della's eyes traveled the pathway of the stones, her gaze reaching up until—

The air caught in her throat, and she was unable to stop the gasp that came to her lips.

It was Hera.

The statue stood on the dais in the center of the folly, the snow falling softly around her. She was rendered in a delicate stone, light in color with veins of a darker material passing through it. She was carved with staff and crown, and she was positioned with one foot in front of the other as if she were stepping into battle. The affect was stunning, and the statue came to life with sudden movement.

"It's beautiful," Della whispered, not realizing she meant to say anything at all. She was just so captured by the beauty of the thing before her.

"My father had it commissioned as a wedding present for our mother," Andrew said from beside her, and Della recalled what Johanna had said so long ago.

Della's fingers flexed in Andrew's palm. "I couldn't think of something more fitting."

"I can," Andrew said, and she turned, surprised.

She looked down as he pulled something from his pocket, and her heart gave a thud in her chest.

It was a small jeweler's box.

He didn't open it. Instead, he picked up her left hand and slipped the signet ring from her third finger, the ring he had placed there in the middle of the night in Brydekirk. She felt a pang for its loss, her fingers curling as if to keep it there, but then he spoke.

"A signet ring is not worthy of the bride of Ravenwood," he said as he slipped the signet ring back on his own finger.

Only then did he open the jeweler's box.

The band was of a soft gold, warm in the dim light, and in the center were set three identical sapphires.

"Oh Andrew," she breathed.

He took the ring from the box and slipped it onto her finger, but he didn't let go of her hand.

"I give you this ring, Catriona Cordelia Darby." He pointed to the first sapphire. "A woman with a name." The next sapphire. "A country." And the next. "And roots."

She had no words that could convey what she felt inside of her, except for the most important words of all.

"I love you, Andrew Darby."

And when she kissed him, she couldn't help but know she was exactly where she was meant to be.

ABOUT THE AUTHOR

Jessie decided to be a writer because there were too many lives she wanted to live to just pick one.

Taking her history degree dangerously, Jessie tells the stories of courageous heroines, the men who dared to love them, and the world that tried to defeat them.

Jessie makes her home in New Hampshire where she lives with her husband and two very opinionated Basset hounds. For more, visit her website at jessieclever.com.

Printed in Great Britain
by Amazon